Chasing Freedom
Book 3

Against All Enemies Series, The Prequel

H.L. WEGLEY

Political Thriller with Romance

Publisher's Note: This is a work of fiction, set in a real location. Any reference to historical figures, places, or events, whether fictional or actual, is a fictional representation. Names, characters, and incidents are the product of the author's imagination or are used fictitiously, and any resemblance to actual persons, living or dead, or to events is entirely coincidental.

Cover Design: Samantha Fury
http://www.furycoverdesign.com/

Back Cover Design: Trinity Press International
http://trinitywebworks.com/

Interior Formatting: Trinity Press International
http://trinitywebworks.com/

ISBN-13: 978-0996493741
ISBN-10: 0996493743

Also available in eBook publication

DEDICATION

This book is dedicated to my editor for books 1 and 2 of the *Against All Enemies* series, Dr. Caroline Savage. Along with her husband Shawn, she continues to fulfill the great commission in Panama City, Panama by discipling others despite battling cancer. I am praying for a full recovery for Caroline, knowing that she is in the Lord's hands to use as He will for His purposes.

ENDORSEMENTS

Voice in the Wilderness, **Book 1**

A terrifyingly real political thriller!
How much power does one voice have? H.L Wegley has
written an action-packed, politically terrifying, hair-raising
thriller about the need to guard our freedoms--lest they be
snatched away. An edge-of-your seat race to keep one man
from taking over the United States--don't miss it!
RITA and Christy Award-Winning Author, Best-Selling
Novelist, Susan May Warren

There are several avenues authors take in writing about
the disintegration of the political systems, especially the
government as it functions in the U.S. Each has an
audience but few other authors are as successful as
Wegley in finding that fine line of terror and intrigue and
eventual hopelessness and lead the story into an
inspirational realm. That is talent and Wegley has it ...
Amazon Hall of Fame Reviewer, Grady Harp

Voice of Freedom, **Book 2**

If you love a thriller with non-stop action, this is the book
for you! Americans taking back their country—what can
be more relevant for today?
Diana Austin

When I finished the book, I felt hope stir in my heart!
While I know this is a work of fiction, many actions taken
to uphold the Constitution and call the nation America
again were excellent.
Lisa Johnson

v

CONTENTS

ACKNOWLEDGMENTS.. viii

NOTE TO READERS... ix

Prologue..1

Chapter 1...4

Chapter 2...12

Chapter 3...26

Chapter 4...35

Chapter 5...49

Chapter 6...58

Chapter 7...72

Chapter 8...85

Chapter 9...95

Chapter 10...107

Chapter 11...120

Chapter 12...132

Chapter 13...142

Chapter 14...148

Chapter 15...159

Chapter 16...169

Chapter 17...175

Chapter 18...182

Chapter 19...190

Chapter 20...196

Chapter 21...203

Chapter 22.. 212

Chapter 23.. 218

Chapter 24.. 230

Chapter 25.. 240

Chapter 26.. 257

Chapter 27.. 266

Chapter 28.. 274

Chapter 29.. 295

Chapter 30.. 306

EPILOGUE 312

AUTHOR'S NOTES.. 319

Final Ending to the Against All Enemies Series...... 322

ACKNOWLEDGMENTS

Once again, I thank Susan May Warren, award winning author and writing coach, for her advice and critique of my characters and part of the plot for *Chasing Freedom*. And I thank my wife, Babe, for having faith in this story when I was ready to abandon it or do major, major surgery on it. I appreciate the suggestions of my critique group, Dawn Lily and Gayla Hiss, who helped me work the wrinkles out of the early parts of the story.

Many thanks to Samantha Fury for designing all three book covers for this series. They capture the spirit of these stories and the covers continue to draw praise from readers.

Thanks again to the team at Trinity Web Works/Trinity Press International for preparing this manuscript for publication and incorporating *Chasing Freedom* into my web site.

I thank God for bringing my grandparents to the USA so that I might be born here. They were Americans at heart before ever coming to this nation, the kind of immigrants America needs. May our immigration laws and their implementation by the agencies and courts bring people to our nation who truly want to be Americans and want to protect our way of life, people like my grandparents, and people like the Santiago family depicted in the story, *Chasing Freedom*.

NOTE TO READERS

If you haven't read books one and two, *Voice in the Wilderness* and *Voice of Freedom*, and are starting with the prequel, *Chasing Freedom*, the author recommends that you skip the prologue and epilogue of this story. You will also want to skip the Final Ending to the *Against All Enemies Series*, placed after the Author's Notes at the end of this book. If you do this, *Chasing Freedom* reads like a stand-alone story. The epilogue and prologue are spoilers for books one and two.

If, after reading this story, you choose to read the other two books, you may want to come back and read the prologue and epilogue of *Chasing Freedom* and the Final Ending to the *Against All Enemies Series* placed at the end of this book. The prologue, epilogue and Final Ending are all tightly woven together and can be read in succession. They will help tie up some loose ends in the characters' lives. Also, they were a blast for this author to write.

Prologue

"Oh, crud!"

Allie Jacobs yanked the wheel hard left as her SUV crossed the dirt lot surrounding the Crooked River Coffee shop drive-through. She dropped her coffee cup into the drink holder.

Scalding hot coffee splattered on the door and on her white shorts.

Allie hit the brakes, pushed the gear shift into park, and shoved her door open. Three running strides took her to the ditch by Highway 97 where she lost her breakfast. It took two or three tries, but she got the job done.

As fast as it came, the nausea left.

Great! Right here in the middle of town, the entire population of Terrebonne, Oregon—all 1,200 people—had probably watched her puke.

She turned toward the car door she'd left open and walked back gingerly rubbing her stomach.

Itzy Bancroft's shrill voice shrieked from the back seat of Allie's big SUV. "Mama! Mama! Aunt Allie has Ebola!"

Allie slid into the driver's seat, wondering what Itzy's mother, Julia, would say.

"No, sweetheart. Aunt Allie doesn't have Ebola. She's going to have a baby." Julia Bancroft's hand came to rest on Allie's shoulder. "You doing okay?"

Allie nodded and reached for the open door.

A voice called out from behind her vehicle. "Allie, let me make you a drink that's easier on your stomach. It's on me." The barista had leaned so far out of the mammoth Conestoga Wagon façade that she nearly toppled out the window.

Allie stuck her head out the open door. "I feel fine now, Susie. Thanks, but I'll keep my decaf latte."

Allie glanced at KC Daniels, riding shotgun. "From vomiting to voracious in ten seconds. It's like my body's not sure how to react to having a baby."

"That's what I did when I had Ebola." Itzy's voice had changed from a shriek to a whining complaint. "But, Mama, that's not how they had babies in the village. They had to—"

"She's not having it for several months, Itzy."

"But, Mama, it's not—"

Julia cut her off again. "Let's relax and listen to the story Aunt Allie's going to tell us while we drive to Bend."

"But only if you feel up to it," KC said. "I don't trust the version I heard from Brock. That man's got a wild imagination."

"I'm feeling much better. Coffee actually sounds good,

2

now, even if it is decaf. But, you know, some of this story is R-rated." Allie pulled out of the lot and onto Highway 97, heading south toward Bend.

"Maybe you can give us the PG version," Julia said.

"Yeah, Aunt Allie, the PG version. Because that's what you are, huh?"

Allie watched through the rear-view mirror as Julia took Itzy's chin and turned the small girl's head to face Julia. "PG. Where did you hear that, Itzy?"

"From some 5th grade girls. Did I say a bad word? I didn't mean to."

KC laughed. "I think it's time for a mother-daughter talk."

Aunt Allie to the rescue. "Do you all want to hear this story, or not?"

"What's the name of the story?" Itzy's voice came from the back seat, quieter, filled with curiosity. "It's about you and Uncle Jeff, huh?"

"Yes, Itzy." Allie cranked up the air conditioner to neutralize the scorching July sun while she searched for a title to her story.

"The name of the story ..." Only one name seemed appropriate after all Allie and Jeff had endured. "Itzy, the name of the story is Chasing Freedom, because that's what I did. It starts four years ago, near the mountains, almost 200 miles from here ..."

Chapter 1

Why had Papa picked this rundown, isolated restaurant to rendezvous with her? The Sinaloa Cartel's personal vendetta against him had frightened them all, but Redding, California was a thousand driving miles from their home in Nogales. Surely her family was safe here after fleeing to the U.S. from the border town.

Alejandra Santiago steered the compact car she'd rented in Corvallis into the parking lot of the small restaurant on the outskirts of Redding. Above the mountains to the north, the top of Mount Shasta glowed pink in the fading twilight of the sweltering July evening. What little light remained revealed speckled white walls of a building in dire need of paint.

In his brief phone call, asking if Allie could drive down from the university to see them, Papa had mentioned threats made in Nogales against him and some against her little brother, Benjamin. The cartel was good at intimidation and threatening Benjamin would certainly accomplish that.

Allie, tell me again how this drug kills the germs.

As Benjamin's voice replayed in her mind, she pictured his large brown eyes expressing wonder at each new biological fact his sharp mind assimilated. But even her pharmacy program at Oregon State couldn't supply enough medical facts to satisfy his ravenous appetite for knowledge.

She loved her family dearly, but Allie adored Benjamin. If the cartel tried to hurt him, she would shoot them all herself. No one, not even their notorious leader, El Capitan, could stop her.

Enough depressing thoughts about a cartel that was a thousand miles away.

Allie got out of her car and walked across the parking lot toward the restaurant, looking for Papa.

She gasped when a sweaty palm slapped over her mouth.

The hand pulled her head back, clamping it against a man's hard chest.

A hot, sweaty shirt soaked through the back of her sleeveless blouse.

Now, another hand grabbed her wrists—rough hands, more like sandpaper than flesh.

She tried to kick the person behind her, but a powerful arm ripped her feet from the ground, hoisting her body upward.

Panic hit. Adrenaline flowed. Energized now, Allie squirmed, writhing like a snake in the arms and hands holding her. She shoved one man from her with her arms but his grip tightened.

Allie was helpless, held in the grasp of three men.

"Do not make a sound, *pollita*." A gravelly voice spoke near her ear. A foul breath carried the words.

The stench sent her stomach into roiling nausea.

Despite her panic, the voice of Allie's self-defense instructor sounded clearly.

Never stop fighting.

Allie twisted her arms now held by a pair of big, sweaty hands. Her arms slipped in the wet hands. She nearly pulled them free.

The wet hands squeezed her wrists until pain shot up her arms. The hands regained their control.

She jerked a leg from another man's grasp and kicked at him.

Hard contact.

The man yelped.

"Stop, *pollita*! Now! Or I will cut Benjamin once for each time you move."

Allie drew a sharp breath, then froze.

Who were these people and how had they found Benjamin? The answer she settled on sickened her. It stole her hopes for a good life in America, for regaining Papa's favor, for getting her PharmD degree from OSU—all gone, replaced with a version of hell on earth that only the Sinaloa Cartel could provide.

Someone slid the hem of her shorts up, exposing her

upper leg. A sharp sting came from her right quad.

What had they just done to her?

The gravelly voice sounded again. "Hold her until she is still."

Allie swam through a wave of dizziness. They had drugged her. Her arms and legs grew weak. The battle was over. She had lost.

Would the drug kill her? It wasn't their intent. They could have done that already. But her drugged, helpless state could lead to something much worse than death.

Whatever they did to her, Allie deserved it. She had committed an unforgivable sin, failing to protect her family. She had only made them more vulnerable by letting these men capture her. Even if Papa could somehow forgive her for this, Allie could never forgive herself.

Her despairing thoughts faded to gray fuzziness ... and the gray to utter darkness.

* * *

Only authorized athletes were allowed to touch what could be a lethal weapon.

Jeff Jacobs trotted across the all-weather running track shared by the high school and middle school in the small, Southern Oregon town of O'Brien. His target, twelve-year-old Samuel Bryant.

Sam carried the old, blue, battle-scarred javelin like he meant to throw it.

Jeff ran in front of the boy and cut him off. Hands on

hips, Jeff turned toward the young athlete. "Sam, put it down."

"Aw, coach. Can I—"

"No. A javelin is not a toy. You know, I saw two freshmen playing chicken with a javelin when I was in high school. One ended up with a spear through the top of his foot. It ended his track and field dreams." Just like a stupid mistake had ended Jeff's dreams in Beijing.

"But, coach, I just finished seventh grade. I'm an eighth grader—"

"And you'll get to throw it next track season when you're actually in the eighth grade."

The lanky, muscular boy begrudgingly handed Jeff the spear, pushed the bushy red hair from his eyes, then looked up at Jeff with a smile spreading cross his freckled face. "Okay, coach. You throw it for us, just like you did—"

"No, Sam."

"But, coach, there's nobody near the throwing range."

"I'm not your coach, only a volunteer assistant."

Sam squinted up at Jeff through the bright sunlight of the hot July morning. He lowered his voice to hushed, reverent tones. "But you're the only one who makes us better at our events and, you know ... the Jesus stuff.'

This kid knew how to push the buttons on Jeff's heart, but he wasn't giving in this time.

"Yeah, Jacobs." Pastor Nelson's voice blared from behind.

What was the pastor doing here?

"Let's see what you've got. Sam and I won't stop pestering you until you throw that spear."

Jeff had been training at home. But, without a sponsor, he couldn't afford to train at a real Olympic facility, nor could he fly his old coach out from Denver to help him. Besides, after Beijing, he would have to apply for re-instatement and there were no guarantees that would happen. Not when the feeding frenzy by the media started again.

Jeff huffed a sharp sigh. "Alright. One throw to get you two off my back."

This track was his home. At least it was the only place left on earth that felt like home. And the javelin felt like an old friend in his hand.

Jeff stepped to the starting mark and looked down the throwing range at the white concentric arcs of lime that contrasted with the lush green turf. He set his sights on a point forty feet beyond the farthest mark for the high school throwers 200 feet down range.

After taking a deep breath, Jeff raised the eight-foot-ten-inch spear over his shoulder and began his run. Ten strides in he twisted sideways, shoved the javelin away from his body and switched to his approach stride.

With adrenaline now coursing through his body, Jeff grunted as he swiveled his hips and whipped his throwing arm over his shoulder. He followed through until the fingertips of his long arm touched the grass in front of his left toe.

The old blue javelin nearly disappeared against the

blue of the summer sky. It quivered and rattled all the way to the apex of its trajectory. With a satisfying *thunk*, the spear buried its head in the turf more than fifty feet beyond the 200-foot mark. Maybe seventy feet beyond it.

Jeff blinked his eyes and shook his head. *No way.* He eyeballed the distance, more carefully this time. About 270 feet. It was a good throw for a world-class javelin thrower, but an Olympic record for a decathlete.

"Holy smoke!" Sam's adolescent voice cracked on "smoke," turning it into a two-syllable word.

Pastor Nelson whistled through his teeth. "Jeff, I came to tell you every member of our congregation believes in you. More than fifty people have told me they want to help you with your training expenses."

Believed in Jeffrey Jacobs? They were the only people on the planet who believed in him after the disgracing debacle two years ago. "Pastor, I can't accept it. I'd only be stealing from the people who really need help."

Jeff turned and walked toward the javelin 270 feet away.

Jeffrey, get re-instated. Go back and win gold. Do it for your father.

His mother's voice had come weak and raspy between gasps as she spoke the words shortly before dying two months ago.

... for your father.

Now Dad's words pricked the sorest spot in Jeff's heart.

The empty spot in our trophy case isn't for my medals. It's for you, son. For Olympic gold. You were born for this, not me.

If the truth were told, Jeff didn't just want to win for his father. Jeff loved the applause of the crowd. He loved hearing the roar when the big screen displayed his name after he'd won the decathlon. Jeff's decathlon was supposed to have ended with the Star Spangled Banner in Beijing. But it didn't.

Did he want the glory for the wrong reasons? He chose not to answer the indicting question.

Keep your nose clean, dude. Maybe Rio.

Maybe. But Jeff doubted it. He would try to regain eligibility. How could he not? But, just like his father warned him, there would always be someone who wanted to stab him in the back. And they always came when he least expected it.

Who's it going to be this time?

Chapter 2

The moment the forest went silent, Jeff sensed it. It came as an unsettling feeling more than anything audible. The sensation crept up his spine to the back of his neck.

He shivered then shook off the feeling as he slowed to a stop near a stand of tall Ponderosa pines on the dusty, Southern-Oregon logging road. He adjusted his headband to catch the drops of perspiration from a hot, July evening training run before they became stinging instruments of torture to his eyes. And he listened.

Barely audible, a noise came, one that didn't belong to the forest.

It sounded again. A wheezing cough?

He waited, trying to identify the sound.

The hoarse wheezing grew in volume, now accompanied by a syncopated rhythm of running feet.

With that gate, somebody needed to work on their stride.

Thankfully, it wasn't either of his two worst fears— timber rattlers or cougars.

A slender figure emerged from the small overgrown side road ahead, turned onto the main logging road and ran toward him. The person sounded like someone desperately trying to finish a marathon. Someone who wouldn't.

A young woman. She half ran, and half stumbled, toward him with her long, dark hair waving behind. Her face held wide eyes that contrasted with the dust and perspiration coating her cheeks and forehead.

She ran straight at Jeff, then stumbled and reached for him, her large brown eyes filled with terror.

"Help me! Please!"

Help her? With what?

Off balance now, her eyes closed and she pitched forward.

He leaped toward her, trying to scoop her upper body and stop her face plant.

Jeff's hands slid under her arms.

Her falling body took him to his knees.

He rolled backward, pulling the young woman.

She landed on top of him.

The back of Jeff's head slammed against the dirt road.

His left knee screamed a sharp, stabbing complaint after it folded under him. The back of his head throbbed from striking the road.

Jeff rolled onto his side, easing the woman's body onto

13

the ground. When he straightened his knee, it stopped complaining. And he could deal with the headache, but how should he deal with the woman?

Her gasps for air had turned to deep, steady breathing, and those brown eyes that displayed terror moments before, remained closed.

She must have passed out.

Her perfectly sculpted face was at the very least pretty. Without the dirt mask, maybe beautiful. Black hair with a few gentle waves framed a dark, well-tanned face with high cheekbones. Her lips might have been dark red if they weren't so cracked and parched.

Where had her terror come from?

Angry voices and the sounds of running feet sounded in the distance near where the woman had emerged. "Which way deed she go?"

"I dunno."

"You better find her, Barto, or we both *muerto*."

Whatever it was, the young woman's danger had already become Jeff's.

The pounding of running feet and the voices grew louder. "Do we take her alive, amigo?"

"Si, alive."

Jeff gathered the woman in his arms, scanning the area around him for a hiding place.

She roused and gasped. "What are you doing? Put me down."

"Quiet. Whoever's chasing you is nearly here. We've got to hide."

"No. Put me down. I can outrun them."

"No. I can. You can't."

His words drew a laser look that burned straight through to his heart.

Gasping for breath again, she struggled in his arms to get free.

"Stop it. You're safe, now. And I'm not letting you down."

"Don't feel ... safe ..." Her eyelids fluttered. Her voice grew weaker with each word. Her arms went limp. "If they find you ... you won't be ..."

She stopped moving.

Out again. At least it would keep her quiet.

Jeff scanned the area around them. On the creek-side of the road, a bushy Madrone tree had grown up from the stump of its parent. He carried her behind its dense foliage, trying to avoid stepping on the dry Madrone bark and leaves that lay ready to betray him with their incredibly loud crackling sounds.

As he peered through a small opening between branches, two swarthy men ran out onto the main road.

At the sight of their assault rifles, Jeff stopped breathing.

His act of kindness had morphed to a matter of survival.

The two men stopped.

The forest remained silent, except for the occasional buzzing of grasshoppers' wings ... and the young woman's heavy breathing.

He pulled her face against his neck, trying to muffle her respiration while he studied the men for any indication they had heard her.

The gunmen scanned the road both directions as if unsure which way she had gone.

Two of the three available roads led back into the mountains, the place she had been running from. The men would soon conclude she'd been running toward the small town where he lived, visible in the distance. Obviously, from this location, she had no other good option.

One of the men gestured toward town with his gun, and the two hurried away.

Jeff also needed go toward town. The tiny town of O'Brien lay two miles down the road. Hiding her there was the best solution, better than going straight to the police. The two gunmen could take out the entire O'Brien police force with one burst from their weapons, even if all three officers were on duty.

Jeff's house, on the edge of town, was the first place of refuge he would reach. Surely he could hide her on his home turf if he reached his house unseen.

Maybe he should follow the creek, hidden by the bushes and trees lining it. But the creek meandered all over the small valley. Following the stream would make this a three-mile trek, and if she didn't wake up soon, a three-mile trek carrying a 120-pound woman. He'd already run four miles in the ninety-degree heat.

Could he do this? Yes. He was Jeffrey Jacobs, Olympic decathlon, gold-medal contender. The words mocked him. Maybe he wasn't a contender anymore, but he *would* carry this young woman to safety.

When the men had run two hundred yards down the road, Jeff turned toward the creek. He sidestepped a patch of blackberry vines, backed through the willows lining the creek, and stepped out onto its rocky bed.

The stream was running low, channeling only a small flow of water that wouldn't impede him. The smooth, flat rocks would provide a hidden path where he would leave few tracks.

It was a good plan, but he needed to hurry, to get as far down the creek as he could in case the men returned to look for tracks. No telling what kind of trail he had left in the dust where he fell down with the girl.

But what if the gunmen waited on this side of town, trying to prevent her from entering it to reach help? They might cut him off from his house, certainly from John or Brady, whoever was on patrol this evening.

As he trudged along the creek bed, Jeff explored every plausible scenario he could think of—take the girl to his house, hide her in the root cellar, take her to Pastor Nelson's house. No. That would endanger the pastor and his family.

In the end, there was only one safe course for the girl and him, let God lead. Jeff took that course, praying softly as he followed the winding creek bed.

He prayed for the strength and the wits to carry this young woman to safety and for wisdom to determine what he should do after that.

Leaves and twigs crunched loudly a short distance behind him.

The men were coming to check the creek.

He broke into a labored run, trying to round the next bend before the goons with the guns emerged. His heart shifted into its highest gear. Adrenaline shot through his body.

Jeff ran hard. As he ran, he prayed that he wouldn't stumble. He prayed that the men wouldn't hear his heavy running steps and the clattering of rocks as he carried the young woman down the creek bed.

Who was she? Why was she in serious danger?

Jeff glanced down into the dirt-smudged face bouncing against his shoulder as he ran. She wasn't awake to explain any of it.

She was completely dependent on him. That thought pressed hard against his heart. He pulled the young woman tightly to his chest, looked up into the blue sky, and prayed her words.

Help me. Please.

* * *

Allie's eyes opened. Panic knotted her stomach. She gasped, her gaze darting over the area around her. It was a house. Neat, clean and homey. Best of all, no gunmen. She was lying on a couch near a man. The knot in her stomach tightened.

Her face. She touched it. The dust caked on by perspiration and miles of running down dusty roads was gone. He must have ... The knot became a nauseating cramp.

She clenched her jaw, raised her head, and examined her denim shorts and the buttons on her sleeveless blouse. She was clothed just as she had been when—she must've passed out after she argued with the man who now sat in a chair only a few feet away.

She studied him.

He sat, hands clasped in his lap, eyes closed, but his lips were moving. Was he praying? Yes, he was. A lot of good that would do. But a man of faith, if he was genuine, she would be safe with him.

Allie's gaze lingered on his sandy blonde hair, then moved to his powerful arms and shoulders. He had a pleasant face with a strong chin. Had his eyes been light blue? Yes. And they added the finishing touches to one of the most handsome faces she could recall seeing.

Girl, you've got way too many problems to even think such thoughts.

What about Mom, Dad, and her little brother, Benjamin? Would the cartel kill them because of her? Where were the gunmen? This man must have seen or heard them because they weren't far behind her.

She pushed down on the couch with her hands, trying to sit up. Pain racked every muscle in her body. Her joints ached from the abuse she had inflicted on them during her long run.

When she glanced at the man again, she drew a sharp breath.

His eyes were open, staring at her.

He looked safe, but she would divulge as little as possible. "Where am I?" She hardly recognized her hoarse, raspy voice.

"Let me get you some water." He left the room, then returned quickly with a large glass of ice water and handed it to her.

She took a sip, then a big guzzle. She took a breath, then another gulp.

"Whoa. Slow down. You'll make yourself sick."

He had avoided her original question. "Where am I?"

He sat down in his chair. "You're in my house."

"Am I safe here?"

"For the time being, we're safe."

We're safe? Why had I become we?

She fought through the aches and pains and sat up. "Who are you, and where is your house?"

"We *are* a little overdue for introductions. My house is on the outskirts of the small town of O'Brien. My name is Jeff Jacobs."

"Mr. Jacobs, where are the two men who—"

"You know, it's polite to reciprocate after an introduction." He smiled and propped an ankle on his knee.

That was a good sign. The gunmen must not be near or there would be no smiles, no relaxed posture, unless he was working with them. No. That didn't make sense.

Didn't make sense or maybe you just didn't want it to make sense?

He cleared his throat.

She needed to answer. Providing her name wouldn't add to her danger. If he was one of them, he probably already knew her name. "My name is Alejandra Santiago."

"That won't do."

Proud of her Spanish name and heritage, Allie glared at him.

He pulled his head back as if she'd struck him. "I mean it's a beautiful name, but if I'd tried to say it when they were chasing us, we wouldn't be—it's too long. I'll call you Allie."

"Mr. Jacobs, you can't just change my—"

"I'm Jeff, you're Allie. For survival purposes. Deal?"

She stared at him, meaning to glare again. But the gentleness and warmth in his eyes defused her anger. "Okay. It's a deal ... Jeff." She met his gaze and gave him a weak smile.

So now I'm Allie.

Normally, she only let her family call her Allie. But normality had died forty-eight hours ago in Redding.

She started to protest, then drowned his presumptuousness in another gulp of cold water. "Allie thinks Jeff should tell her what happened after she passed out. And she wants to know where the two gunmen are."

Jeff stood and walked to the couch.

Girl, don't let a stranger move in on you like that.

Again, she started to protest, but his smile and relaxed posture didn't seem threatening. Besides, she needed help from someone she could trust. Maybe Jeff Jacobs was that person.

Don't do what you're thinking. Would you like a long list of serial killers that other women thought were handsome, charming, and safe?

Allie squelched the snarky voice inside and tried to relax by looking away from Jeff through the sheer, living room curtains. Outside, the twilight had turned the mountains to dark shadows with a yellow glow above. Twilight meant Jeff had been with her for two or three hours and who knew what dangers he had faced. Maybe his familiarity came from some bond he felt between them, a bond she didn't feel.

She stiffened when Jeff sat beside her.

"Allie ..." He turned toward her and paused until she met his gaze. "I caught you when you fainted. You must've run a long, long way. I've never seen anyone so exhausted. Then the two gunmen came after us. I carried you. I prayed a lot, and we got away."

"You got away while carrying me? I'm a strong runner but they chased me through the mountains for fifteen miles, maybe more. I couldn't shake them. How did you—"

"Let's just say I'm a stronger runner." A shadow flickered across his face.

Was it sorrow or maybe regret?

The shadow disappeared and he met her gaze. "Or, maybe you wore them down for me."

Allie scanned Jeff's muscular arms and his powerful-looking legs, showing below his running shorts. She looked up from his body to his face.

Her face grew warm when she noticed Jeff tracking her gaze. She needed to stay focused, because the cartel's plans for her had probably changed from catch to kill. How should she tell that to Jeff?

Jeff's smile returned then faded. "Rumor has it they grow marijuana in the mountains south of here. Who are those men?"

The expression on his face said he'd already answered to *his* satisfaction. So how much should she share?

And there were other issues. One appeared to be drawing Jeff's curious gaze to her black hair.

"Have you notified anyone?"

He pursed his lips and shook his head. "Frankly, I didn't know what to do until I heard your story. You look like you're, uh ... maybe ..."

"Do you mean am I illegal? Chased by coyotes all the way from the border?"

"No. It's just that—"

"I *am* Hispanic. My home is in Nogales, Mexico." Or ...

it was.

Jeff nodded slowly, cautiously.

"But I'm not illegal, Jeff. I'm here on an international scholarship to Oregon State University."

His face relaxed.

"So now you know."

Yes, Jeff knew. But was she really safe here? If this man failed her, they would both wind up dead. Probably her family, too. Allie would die before she let that happen.

* * *

As Jeff pondered Allie's story, he had questions. Her situation didn't compute. She was an incredibly beautiful young woman. He noticed that while washing the dirt from her face. She was intelligent, educated, but she had been chased through the mountains by people who were likely drug cartel thugs.

He would have called the police immediately, but he feared she was here illegally, and since he had eluded the two men, he decided to wait. But he couldn't wait any longer. He needed to know more of her story. "I'm glad that you're here legally. But, Allie, we barely escaped from two men who wanted to kill us."

His voice grew louder as sounds of the shooting echoed through his mind. "Why did these men shoot at us? You need to tell me the whole story. I can't help you if I don't understand..." Jeff's voice trailed off and he looked down at the floor.

When he looked up at her face, the smile was gone,

and tears trickled down her cheeks. She looked so hopeless that he struggled to keep from wrapping her up in his arms. Instead, he reached out a hand.

She tensed.

But, when he brushed the tears from her cheeks, she collapsed against him. The tears returned, gushing from her deep, guttural sobs. "They're going to kill my family, Jeff. And I don't know what to do."

Chapter 3

Family was all a person had on this planet, and abandoning hers, letting them down, was the worst thing Allie could possibly do. Several hours ago, it's exactly what she had done. Though what she had faced was a horror worse than dying, it was no excuse.

Allie would never abandon her family again. The only way she could hope to redeem herself was to save them. But she didn't know how, and that shattered what was left of her heart.

Her sobs wouldn't stop. She despised weakness and didn't consider herself a weak woman, but the physical and emotional trauma of the previous forty-eight hours, combined with her betrayal, had been too much for her to handle.

Right now, Jeff's arms were the only source of comfort she had. Though she refused to dwell on that subject, they *were* comforting.

"Allie?" His hand stroked the back of her head. "Can you talk now? Who wants to kill your parents, and where are they?"

"The men at the marijuana plantation." She sat up and wiped her cheeks. "They're part of the Sinaloa Cartel."

"Cartel? Then we need to go to the police now."

"No. The cartel will know it if we do. Then they'll *have* to kill my family. They're probably scouring this area looking for me."

"But you know that, ultimately, contacting law enforcement is the only way to stop them." He pulled out his cell phone from his shorts pocket.

Allie grabbed his arm. "You can't do that!" She reached for the phone.

He deftly moved his hand out of her reach. "Whoa. Relax. I'm not going to call anybody right now." He slipped the phone back into his pocket and raised both hands. "See? Obviously, I don't understand what's going on. Maybe you should start from beginning and tell me the whole story."

She couldn't risk going to the police and hadn't a clue what to do next. Like it or not, she needed this man's help and, as he said, he *was* willing. He had even complied with her request about the phone call.

She studied his eyes, his face. He looked curious and concerned. There was much more to Jeff's looks. Her friends at school would be clamoring for a date with this man. But what she wanted from him was a plan to free her parents. That meant telling him enough of the story so he understood the extent of the problems ... and the dangers.

He had faced danger at least once when he saved her. Allie drew a deep breath, then took his hand, squeezed it, and peered into his bright blue eyes. They drew her in, calmed her. The look in his eyes was intense but not harsh. It spoke of strong character. "For whatever reason, Jeff Jacobs, I trust you. I won't smash your cell phone like ..."

He squeezed back. "I believe you meant that. But you've got a lot of emotions running around inside right now. Probably more than I can imagine." His crooked smile lifted one corner of his mouth. "So the cell stays tucked away in my pocket for safekeeping until we agree on how to use it."

She nodded. "Okay. Where to begin? Like I mentioned, I'm a third-year student at Oregon State in their pharmacy program. I thought with a PharmD degree I could work in any city in Northern Mexico and earn enough to help my family out of their situation."

"What do you mean by *their situation?*"

"When I left for school three years ago, the cartel controlling our area had just begun demanding protection money from the business owners. Each time I went home on break, the problem had grown until the cartel was demanding more than most businessmen could afford. A couple of months ago my father grew desperate. He tried to organize the business owners to protest or to bring in the law."

Jeff frowned. "Did your family have to leave after that?"

"Yes, but I didn't know about it at the time. When the death threats started last month, Dad made plans for them to leave if matters got worse."

"I take it they got worse. Where's your family now?"

"I'm getting there, Jeff." She glanced down at their hands, still clasped, resting on Jeff's knee. Holding onto something solid in her dangerous, unstable world, helped her maintain what little of her sanity remained.

"A few days ago, Papa ... Dad called and said they had fled Nogales. He had found someone who could obtain work visas for them. It wasn't a permanent solution, but he said it was too dangerous to stay in Nogales. I knew what he meant. The cartel was going to kill him."

"I've heard that law enforcement is unreliable in northern Mexico, but could the cartel just—"

"Yes. They can do anything they want. The police are either on the take or trying to stay alive by not interfering with them. Their leader, El Capitan, is the most feared man in all of Mexico. To some he's a terrorist. To others he's a folk hero."

Jeff motioned toward his living room window, facing the mountains to the south. "Your family is up in those mountains, isn't it?"

Allie nodded. "Dad told me they were going to work in Northern California, farm work near Redding. Summer break was starting, so I said I'd meet them, and we set up a rendezvous. I drove down to Redding, but they didn't show. It was dark when I got there and some men grabbed me ... I think they drugged me. I woke up at the marijuana plantation in the mountains. Dad, Mom, and my little brother, Benjamin, were there. No visas, just slave labor, growing and harvesting marijuana for, guess who, the Sinaloa Cartel."

"Why did they want *you*, Allie?"

"Because they overheard Dad's phone call to me and didn't want anyone knowing my family's whereabouts, especially a concerned family member."

The terror of those first waking moments among the men at the marijuana grow site brought a shudder. "At first, I thought they might kill me. I heard them arguing about it. One man wanted..." she cleared her throat, "...to keep me and use me." She stopped and took a drink of water.

Anger, like a fire, blazed in Jeff's eyes, eyes which were now focused on the window facing the mountains.

"Another man had a different idea. He suggested they sell me to one of the traffickers who might pay as much as $200,000 for someone like me. Unspoiled goods, he called me." Her anger pulsed through her like a bolt of lightning and she squeezed Jeff's fingers.

"Ouch! That's quite a grip you've got." He blew out a sigh then met her gaze with contempt glaring in his eyes. "I can't imagine what it feels like to be considered subhuman, nothing but merchandise."

"I'll tell you how it feels. I wanted to kill them. To take one of their guns and turn it on them."

She took another swallow of water and set the glass on the coffee table.

Jeff wrapped both of his big hands around hers. "How did you get away?"

"Dad said I should try to escape that night, before they could take me away to sell me. He helped me, and I broke out of their makeshift jail. Dad fought one of the men, and I ran out of the camp while two of the men got on their ATVs to run me down." Describing how she had abandoned her family brought the searing guilt to her mind and heart.

Jeff's eyes widened. "So you outran two ATVs?"

She looked up into his eyes, eyes that transitioned between anger, concern, and something else that she couldn't interpret. "I didn't outrun them; I just ran where they couldn't go. Actually where I *hoped* they couldn't go— through rocks, dense brush, up steep banks."

She paused as the terror of that chase and the periodic hiding during the night brought another shudder to her shoulders. "They eventually abandoned their ATVs and chased me on foot, yelling for me to stop or my whole family would be tortured to death, starting with my little brother."

She stopped and brushed away the tears that overflowed her eyes. "Before I escaped, Dad said I should keep running no matter what they threatened, no matter what I heard. So I ran and listened to their threats as they chased me."

She looked up at Jeff. Could he see the guilt in her eyes? Did he think she was a coward, too?

There was no condemnation in his eyes. He simply nodded for her to continue.

"I'm a strong runner. When they realized it wouldn't be easy to catch me, they changed their threats. They said if I went to the police to consider my family dead. Then, eventually, they were too tired to yell anything at all. But they didn't give up. The cartel leaders must have threatened to kill them if they lost me."

She looked up into his face and gave him a weak smile. "And then I ran into you and passed out."

He cupped her cheek, looked into her eyes, and shook his head. "That you did. If the grow site is where I'm thinking, I'd bet you ran twenty miles. You didn't have another step left in you, Allie. You were falling when I caught you."

"I was out by that time." She shrugged. "Don't even remember you catching me."

He removed his hand from her cheek and rubbed his chin. "You know, there were shorter ways out of the mountains. But any one of them would've led you to, at best, a remote farm or ranch. Not to the police and not to a good place to hide."

"You mean a place like your home? You said this is your house, didn't you?"

"Yeah." Jeff slumped down on the couch. "It became mine two months ago, when Mom died."

"I'm so sorry, Jeff."

He looked up and gave her a tight-lipped smile. "We knew she was dying, so we were prepared."

"We? Is your father around?"

"No. Dad died ten years ago. 'We' was just Mom and me. But you know something? I don't believe in coincidences."

"Call it what you will, I'm just glad I didn't try some

other way out of the mountains. I wouldn't have made it, and I wouldn't have found you."

What did you mean by that line, girl?

What did Jeff think? She met his intense gaze, then looked away. When she glanced back at his face, he wore a puzzled frown. Probably trying to attach some significance to her statement. She'd better clarify it before he got the wrong idea. "Jeff ... thanks for saving my life."

"After what you just told me, I'm not sure I've done that yet. We need a plan that keeps you safe and gives us a good chance to free your family. This would be a good time to pray for some wisdom."

"We don't have any time to waste."

* * *

Prayer a waste of time?

Apparently Allie was an agnostic. When Jeff had a chance, he would probe deeper, find out what she really believed. In the meantime, she had given him another really important reason for keeping this beautiful, young woman alive. Agnosticism was hard to live with, long on doubt and short on hope. He had something much better to offer her.

His eyes scanned Allie again. The few times she smiled, he'd noticed that she was more than just beautiful. She fit his picture of a Spanish rancheros' daughter, the one all the cowboys fought over, a stereotype he had formed from watching old Western movies. A very nice stereotype.

"Jeff?"

33

"Huh?"

"Where did you wander off to? We really don't have any time to waste. Were you praying?"

"No, just thinking."

"I like to be kept in the loop. Would you care to think out loud?"

Not at the moment.

When Allie slipped her hand from his, he realized he'd been holding it for the past twenty minutes. He realized he'd never sat beside a woman with this kind of beauty, and he realized he needed to get his head back in the game or he wouldn't like how the fourth quarter ended. Jeff prayed silently so it wouldn't upset Allie. The gist of his prayer—that the game would end with Allie and him ahead and that it wouldn't go into sudden-death overtime.

Chapter 4

Allie had seen that look in men's eyes before. Jeff was thinking about her, about how she looked. Maybe she was wrong to place her trust him.

Like I have a choice.

She studied his face. Jeff appeared to be back from la la land, or wherever it was that a man's mind went when he gawked at an attractive woman. "Can the police force here protect us from three or four men with AK-47s, men bent on killing us?"

"The quintessential question. No, Allie, I'm not sure they can even if they call in all their people. This is only a small town with a minimal force."

"It will be dark in another forty-five minutes. Can you sneak me out of here in your car and go to a larger town?"

"Since we both believe they're watching the town. I don't think that would work."

"If you hide me, why not?"

"They would probably recognize me."

"What makes you think that?"

Jeff emptied his lungs with a long sigh, like he was struggling with a decision. Finally, he reached across to his left arm and slid his T-shirt sleeve up to his shoulder.

She gasped when he uncovered a large bandage on his upper arm. The lower edge of the dressing had been painted dark red. The wound was still oozing a little blood.

"Your head was cradled in that arm." He pointed to the wounded limb. "Two inches lower and—"

"That's enough, Jeff." Her breathing turned to panting. Allie tried to breathe more slowly, but she couldn't. Jeff's wound was raw, real, and bloody, highlighting the reality of the danger and exposing how close Allie had come to death. She wasn't sure about God, but she *was* sure that she wasn't ready to face death or possibly Him. Allie had far too many unanswered questions and fears ... and more guilt than she could possibly atone for.

Shoving the guilt aside for the moment, one thing had become clear. If the cartel thug would shoot a bullet near her head, saving their marijuana crop was worth a lot more to them than capturing her. They weren't trying to capture her now, just kill her before she could talk.

"Allie, I turned around to see if I could spot them. That's when one of them fired the burst at us. Fortunately, the guy wasn't a very good shot. He shredded everything in the area but us. But I am sure he got a good look at me."

"I'm sorry." She shook her head. One failure after another. That seemed to be the story of Allie's life. "I've brought you so much trouble. I should just—"

"No, you shouldn't. I'm already in this, and we've got a better chance to save ourselves, and your family, by working together."

"Whatever we decide to do, we need to hurry and do it. If the cartel thinks they need to leave the plantation, they will probably kill my parents. Benjamin is only eleven. They'll sell him to the traffickers."

"Then we should pray for them, for God's protection."

"I told you what I think about that."

"Why are you so opposed to prayer?"

"Where I grew up a lot of people went to church. But the reasons they went—it was all superstition, superstition used for centuries to control our people. They were afraid *not* to go to church. If they didn't perform their duties, it would bring bad luck."

"Maybe part of what you observed was true, but I doubt it represents the beliefs of all the people. Is that what you think about me?"

She looked at Jeff's intense eyes and thought of all he had done since she met him. She wouldn't challenge him on this issue. It didn't apply to Jeff. But how *should* she classify him? "We don't have time for this. We've got to decide who to go to for help."

Jeff's stared at her for a moment then looked away.

Was that pity in his eyes? She didn't want his pity.

He stared across the room, out the window toward the mountains. "We've got two problems to solve. First, how to keep you and me safe, and second, how to free your family. Except for some Navy SEALs, there's only one organization I trust to do both."

"You must be talking about the FBI."

"Yeah. They are the people you call to handle human trafficking and organized crime. But that raises two more problems. How do we contact them, and then how do we convince them to come to O'Brien in the next few hours?"

She studied Jeff's face. He was deep in thought. "Jeff, where is the nearest FBI office?"

"Medford, I think. But it's just a small office. Let's get online and see what we can find." He stood and headed down a hallway.

Allie followed him into a small study. An easy chair sat by the doorway and a computer desk with an office chair sat by the window at the far side of the room. She scanned the walls on the right and left sides of the room. They were lined with bookshelves from floor to ceiling. The shelves held books on philosophy, theology, Christian apologetics, and several on the subject of epistemology. One small section held English books, writing books, and several works of Shakespeare.

She thought Jeff was just a jock. A handsome jock, but it surprised her that he was also a deep thinker. Arguing with this man about his beliefs, or her lack of them, was probably not wise.

When Jeff sat down in the computer chair at the desk, Allie moved behind him to look over his shoulder.

He launched his web browser and typed in the search terms "FBI field offices" and pushed the enter key. The first page of links quickly painted on the screen.

"Look, Jeff. There's a by-state listing of all the field offices."

He had already selected that link and pulled up the Portland office, the only field office in Oregon. "Well, like all of the field offices they've got a SWAT team. And here's a 24-hour contact number. I hope it's not just a recording."

She pointed at the bottom of the screen. "But there's a satellite office in Medford. That's closer."

He hovered over the Medford office information. "It's a link. Let's take a look before we try Portland."

She read the screen over his shoulder. "It says it's a resident agency. What's that?"

"I'm not sure, but it's probably a small office with nobody manning it 24-7. We need a real FBI SWAT team."

"But maybe an agent in Medford would carry more weight than us when we ask for a SWAT team from Portland."

He swiveled his chair to face her. "Allie, even if we reach someone there, we would have to tell our story to one agent in Medford and then have him tell it to someone else at a different office. Too much time and too much room for miscommunication. I say we plead our case with Portland right now."

When Jeff reached for his cell, Allie felt a growing panic. She grabbed his arm. "Jeff, wait! Can they really save my family? I mean, do they have the capability?"

"Yes. They're trained for hostage situations and for taking on organized crime. This is a complete team with all the skills, equipment, and weapons that they need."

"But things could—"

"Yes. Things could go wrong, because the cartel won't just give up your family. It will take force. It will take a SWAT team."

As she stared at Jeff flashbacks played in her mind of her panic as she ran for her life. The belching of automatic weapon fire. The taunts they yelled at her. The endless running. She was breathing hard but not getting enough air. Her feet and hands tingled now, and she felt lightheaded. She was panting. Allie's head buzzed.

Jeff's eyes widened when he looked at her. In an instant she was wrapped up in his strong arms. "I think you're having a panic attack. Breathe deeply, but more slowly. It's going to be okay, Allie."

She pressed her head against chest. Soon the tingling stopped. Her breathing slowed, and she relaxed in his arms as his hand stroked her head. She could hear his heart beating. Jeff's very life, the life he had risked for her.

He spoke softly, "We're doing our very best. If we can get the FBI here, we couldn't do any better for us or your family. There's nothing more we can do but pray for the situation."

She tensed at the word pray. But Jeff was a praying man and she couldn't stop him from doing what he believed best.

Jeff's voice came soft and soothing as he spoke like a child to his daddy. She relaxed and listened to his words, words asking for comfort, protection, and wisdom to guide them in their thinking and their actions.

She didn't remember how it happened, but when Jeff finished praying, her arms were around him too, holding onto him as if her life depended on him. Earlier in the day, it had, and he had not failed her. For now, she would trust Jeff and the sincerity of his prayer.

Allie would make no accusations against Jeff's God. She would simply hold on because, at the moment, this man's comfort and caring were clearly what she needed.

"Allie?"

"What?" She didn't move. Didn't want to move. Not yet.

"Like my prayer … uh, your panic attack is over."

She released her bear hug on Jeff, letting her arms drop to her sides.

He put his hands on her shoulders and held her at arm's length, studying her face with concern in his light blue eyes. "Are you okay now?"

She nodded slowly. "Jeff, I… I didn't know it could be like that." She stepped close to him, leaning against his chest and again listening to his heart.

Allie Santiago, what do you think you are doing?

She ignored the question and the accusing voice inside her head.

Jeff put his hand on the back of her head. "Didn't think it could be like what?"

"Like talking to my dad. Asking him to take care of me. I didn't want it to end." Who was *this* speaking? It wasn't the Alejandra Santiago she knew. For the moment, she didn't care.

41

"It doesn't have to end, Allie. It's best if it never ends. The conversation can just continue on into eternity."

Jeff, his God, her father—aspects of all three, love, security, tenderness, strength, authority—seemed to blend together until they were impossible to distinguish, except for one discriminating factor, Jeff's arms around her. Those arms brought out deep-seated emotions Allie had never felt before, and she wasn't at all sure what to think about that.

She gave him a quick hug then looked up before stepping back. His face was only inches from hers. The warm, caring look in his eyes pulled her across a line she had never before crossed. Allie rose onto her toes and pressed her lips to his cheek, softly, briefly, then she stepped back.

Her face was warm, probably flushed. Jeff would notice. That thought embarrassed her.

Jeff simply smiled and said, "I think this would be the perfect time to make that phone call."

She nodded, still wondering what had just transpired. Wondering where Alejandra Santiago had gone. Maybe she had been replaced by a girl that Jeff called Allie.

Jeff turned to the computer screen to read the phone number and pulled out his cell.

She tried to gather her wits and think through the process of describing their situation to the FBI. The reality of her situation came storming back in all of its urgency. "Jeff, once you get them on the line and tell them why we're calling, would you please give me the phone?"

When he finished keying in the number, Jeff held his

thumb over the call icon. "You sure, Allie?"

"I'm sure."

"Good. Because you'll be a lot more persuasive than me. You already have been."

"What are you insinuating?"

"Well ... you almost persuaded me to break my..." His voice trailed off and stopped.

It was an impulsive, stupid thing for her to do. "I hope you don't think that I ... Jeff, I've never, ever ..."

He pressed a finger over her lips, rescuing her from her stammering. "I see. You mean you don't make a habit of kissing strangers on the cheek?"

She shook her head.

"You know, I made a vow that I would only kiss the girl I was going to marry. But I ..." Jeff stopped talking, pushed the button on his cell, and placed it against his ear.

Though he hadn't said it, Jeff had implied that she had tempted him to break a vow that was very important to him. Or was that only her wishful thinking?

Get a grip, girl.

When she came to her senses, Jeff sat at his desk and he was speaking to someone. Reality, her reality, pushed the fantasy from her mind.

"We're in danger, her family too ... Yes, they are cartel members ... Because they have assault rifles. Look, they shot at us, and they're all over town looking for us."

"Give me the phone, Jeff."

"Gladly." He pursed his lips and shoved his cell at her.

* * *

Jeff shook his head in disgust at the difficulty he had in convincing the person on the other end of the call that their situation was serious. He doubted Allie would have any better luck penetrating the man's wall of questions obviously designed to keep people out.

Allies voice came soft, but filled with emotion, as she described the slavery of her family, the marijuana plantation, the Sinaloa Cartel thugs, her long flight for her life, and Jeff's intervention, including his bullet wound.

How could anyone refuse that plea? This was real distress and a very real damsel. If they could only see Allie, that would be the clincher.

She paused and gripped his hand. "I'm on hold. They're getting two other agents and going into a conference room where there's a speaker. How do you put your cell on speakerphone?"

He covered her hand with his. "You were amazing, Allie. If I was them, I would've caved after your first sentence." He smiled and pressed the speakerphone toggle on the side of his cell. "You take the lead and I'll jump in if I'm needed. We made it through the first hoop. Let's pray we get through the second one, and that these guys are willing to take some action."

She touched his cheek. "You pray. It seems that you get results when you talk with ... Him."

After a half-hour of intense discussion with two

agents, including an almost brutal interrogation of Allie, the other end went silent. They had been muted.

Jeff took Allie's hand. "I think they're making a decision right now."

"You were praying, weren't you?"

"Yeah. Especially when Agent McCheney was grilling you. If he had been in this room talking to you like that ... pow." Jeff pounded a fist on the desk.

"Don't be angry at them, Jeff. They were just doing their job."

"And interrogation is a large part of our job." The voice came from the speakerphone.

Great. The agents had heard their conversation, including his words and sound effects about pounding McCheney.

"No offense taken, Jacobs, yet. Changing the subject— your information dovetails with some sketchy intel we have regarding cartel marijuana-growing activity in the mountains along the California border. We'll need pictures of you two so we can recognize you when we arrive."

When they arrive?

Allie's arms clamped around his neck. "They really *are* coming, Jeff."

Jeff leaned down near the phone in Allie's hands. "Have you got an email address, McCheney?"

"Yeah. Portland at IC dot FBI dot gov. It's a big catch-all e-mail box. I'll monitor it until we get your pictures, so they don't get lost."

"Okay, I'm taking pictures of Allie and me now. I'll send them to you in a few seconds."

Fifteen minutes later, Jeff and Allie got the official word. An FBI SWAT team was coming via helicopter.

McCheney's voice came through the speaker. "I'll be leading the team. You'll know who I am. I'm the big, ugly guy ... unlike Ms. Santiago."

"From the sound of your voice, I'd say polar opposites."

"Jacobs, you just keep Miss Santiago inside and out of sight and I'll overlook your insults."

"I've got my eyes on her, Mc Cheney."

"I'll bet you have. Look, I know what you said about tipping our hand, but I'm going to get some local police protection for you two."

Allie's eyes widened. "But if they figure out that—"

"Don't worry, Ms. Santiago. We'll make sure the locals are discreetly watching your place. They'll drive by every few minutes and will only stop if you're in immediate danger. Stay put. Our team's ready and the chopper should arrive at your location in about ninety minutes. Jacobs, our satellite picture shows a big field to the east of your house. That looks like a good place to set down."

"It's old pasture land. Flat as a table and no obstacles except a dry irrigation ditch."

"Sounds good. You've got my cell number, the local sheriff's number too, right?"

"We've got them."

"See you in about an hour and a half. At first light, we'll go looking for that plantation."

After ending the call, Jeff stood and added McCheney's number to his contact list.

Allie's hand came to rest on his arm.

Jeff looked up from his cell.

She had a major frown on her face as she stared out the window. "Jeff, what if they did find us before the FBI gets here? Do you have any way to protect us?"

"You mean a gun?"

"Yes."

"Only an old lever-action .22. It's no match for an assault rifle. If they show up here we've got two choices. First—"

Footsteps sounded on the porch. Then a knock on the front door.

Allie gasped.

"Go into the kitchen while I see who's out there."

Reluctant to stand in the center of the doorway, Jeff leaned in from one side of the door until his eye aligned with the peephole. A sharp blast of air left his lungs when he saw a swarthy man standing with both hands behind him. He was obviously holding something out of sight.

Like maybe an AK-47?

Jeff didn't recognize this man as one of the two who had chased Allie and him. But Jeff's description would probably have been given to all of the cartel thugs who were out hunting for them.

Bluffing the man could cost him his life, leaving Allie alone. He turned and hurried into the kitchen. "It's one of them. We need to get out of here." He clasped her hand. "Follow me."

"Did he have a gun?"

"I didn't ask, Allie."

Chapter 5

The knocking on the front door turned to pounding. Jeff took Allie's hand and pulled her to the basement doorway.

"Where are we going." Her voice dropped to a whisper.

"We're going to the basement, and then to the root cellar," he whispered back.

The hand Jeff held pulsed with each beat of Allie's heart.

They stepped through the door and scurried down the narrow stairway toward the basement. "This house was built before electricity was available here. The root cellar was the fridge. It has two entrances, one from the basement and another from outside, just behind the garage. I don't think these guys will spot the one behind the garage, not when they're so intent on spotting us."

"But what if they *are* watching it?" Allie's whisper came as a harsh blast of air.

She was terrified but still following him, not causing any delays.

"Unfortunately, I won't know that for sure until I look out. It's a chance we have to take. I'll be careful opening the door."

They scampered from the stairway across the basement to another door. He opened the door, pulled Allie into the small room, and yanked the door closed behind them.

Allie gasped when total darkness enveloped her.

"It's okay." His hand found the emergency flashlight he kept on a shelf inside the doorway. When he turned it on, the room lit nearly as bright as day. He quickly covered it with his hand before his eyes adjusted to the light.

"You wait here while I look out the door."

Jeff climbed up a ladder and cracked the door a few inches. It creaked.

He stopped and waited. In a few seconds, he lifted it a little higher and, through the narrow slit, scanned all three directions. Voices sounded from near the front of the house and the flashing of lights occasionally lit the area between the house and the detached garage. But there was no one behind the garage.

A loud thump sounded from the front of the house. Then another, followed by a loud crash. They had kicked in the front door.

Jeff lit the ladder behind him with the flashlight. "Come on, while they're looking inside the house." He took her hand.

After Allie climbed out, Jeff lowered the door and

pulled her beside him, their backs against the rear wall of the garage. He leaned close and whispered in her ear. "We're going to enter the garage through the side door on my right. There's no front door on the garage, so we have to move quickly in case they look in. I backed my truck in when I parked it today. We're going to blast out of here, so move to your door, open it when I open mine, slide in and buckle your seatbelt. Don't close your door until I hit the ignition. Then hold on tight." He paused. "You ready, Allie?"

"I ..." She squeezed his hand. "I'm ready."

Jeff slid to the corner of the garage and inched his head around it. No one.

A flashlight split the darkness when it shined around the corner. Someone had rounded the corner at the front of the garage.

Jeff reared back, bumping into Allie.

He nudged her farther back behind the garage and stopped, trying to slow his panicky breathing.

They waited a few seconds and the dancing light finished its exploration of the side of the garage, then disappeared.

The two slipped around the corner and through the side door of the garage, pulling it shut, and moved beside the doors of his midsized truck. Jeff gave her the signal to open her door. Both doors opened quietly and they slid in.

Allie's seatbelt clicked.

As they closed their doors, Jeff hit the ignition. When the motor started, he slammed the gearshift into drive and punched the gas pedal.

The wheels of his V8-powered truck squealed as they spun across concrete garage floor.

Directly ahead, the gunmen's large pickup blocked the driveway.

As his pickup rocketed toward the gunmen's truck, Jeff cranked the wheel hard to his left. He crossed the side lawn and drove into an open field. But a deep ditch lined the road. If he challenged the ditch, he would likely roll his truck.

A bigger concern was that he and Allie were headed away from town and away from the police.

Afraid to slow down and climb the ditch at a sharp angle, Jeff yanked the wheel hard right. The pickup hit perpendicular to the ditch. They caught air as the truck shot the ramp onto the road.

Jeff jerked the wheel back to the left and accelerated down the road.

Until now, the garage had shielded them from the front of the house where he suspected the goons were. When he heard the first burst of gunfire, Jeff palmed the back of Allie's head, like he would a basketball, and shoved it nearly to the floorboard.

"Stop shoving me around, Jeff! My head's not a basketball." She tried to raise back up.

Jeff squeezed more tightly and pushed harder.

Allie clawed at his hand but couldn't break free.

Another burst of gunfire. The rear window of the cab

exploded. Shards of glass, sprayed the cab, cutting his right cheek.

Allie stopped resisting.

Jeff let go of her head and mashed the pedal to the floor. When he glanced across the cab. The passenger side window had been shattered, too. The spray of bullets had passed through the space occupied by Allie's head seconds before.

She raised up and glared at him. "Like I said, my head's not a bask—" Allie seemed to freeze in the seat beside him, staring at the shattered glass.

"Allie, if I hadn't treated your head like a basketball, those AK-47s would have let the air out."

"So now I'm an airhead?" The words were accusing, but her tone had mellowed.

"You're anything but an airhead."

She studied his face as he drove the straight stretch of road. "You're face. It's bleeding."

"Yeah. Cause I'm not an airhead either."

At seventy miles-per-hour, the air coming through the broken windows whipped Allie's hair. She swept it from her face and pulled a tissue from the box Jeff kept on the floorboard and dabbed at the blood on his cheek.

Now, his truck flew down the dirt road at more than seventy-five miles-per-hour. They were nearly a half mile from the house, out of accurate gunshot range.

"Jeff, are we safe yet?"

"Out of easy gunshot range, yes. But safe? That depends upon who you think is in control." He flashed a glance at her, but his eyes caught a light in the rear view mirror.

"You're in control, Jeff. I trust you."

Allie still didn't get it. He was just a man. And most people didn't think he was a good example of one.

The gunmen's pickup lights came on and the truck spun a one-eighty in front of his house, then accelerated toward them. Farther back toward town, the lights of a second vehicle appeared in the rear-view mirror. It also raced their way. More goons and more guns.

"Allie, they've got us cut off from town. Our only option is to take the dirt road into the mountains, but there's no way to get back to town, to the police. The roads get continually smaller until, eventually, we have to abandon the truck. My truck is smaller than theirs, and I have four-wheel drive. Maybe we can go farther up the trails than them, get a big lead."

Allie placed her hand on his shoulder. "What about the FBI?"

"The evidence at the house will tell them what happened. But they won't know exactly where we are ... unless we can get cell service. But where we're headed there won't be any."

He accelerated to nearly eighty on the dirt road, heading toward the spot where he had first met Allie.

Far down the road he spotted lights. Reality hit him like a punch in the solar plexus. A third vehicle emerged from one of the mountain roads. It was speeding toward them.

"Another vehicle? They must be communicating, coordinating every move. We're up against an army."

Her words haunted him. "I trust you." He couldn't deliver on that kind of trust. "Allie?'

She squeezed his shoulder.

"Allie, I've gotta focus on driving. Would you pray for us ... for me?"

"Yes. Well, at least I'll try. But, Jeff, I still trust you."

There were limits to what Jeff could be trusted for. Allie needed to aim a lot higher to find the object of her trust. But this wasn't a time for that discussion.

He took the only road left available to them, the road up the mountain toward Bolan Peak. Several roads forked off from the main one. If Jeff could keep his truck out of sight, the cartel punks would eventually make a wrong choice and they could lose them, at least for the night.

Jeff had to make sure *he* didn't take a wrong fork. He needed to stay on the Bolan Mountain road. There were many places to hide on the mountain, and the shelter of the lookout crowned the peak, giving them a view of the entire area for miles in any direction.

The road to the peak was steep and rough, with thousand-foot drop-offs in places and no guard rails. But worse yet, the road had washed out badly last spring. He prayed there would be no slides to stop them.

Regardless, at some point, they would be forced to run up the mountain on foot. Maybe, with a little bit of luck, his cell could pick up a signal on the very top of the peak.

Jeff's pickup bounced across ditches in the road, deep erosions from the melting snow and heavy spring rains. In places the eroded road jerked on the wheel so hard he had to slow down to maintain control.

When the road leveled and smoothed, Jeff could hit fifty-five on some of the straight stretches. By maintaining speeds bordering on disastrous, he should be building up a buffer big enough to shake the gunmen.

The speedometer read sixty when the headlights hit a curve ahead, a much sharper turn than Jeff anticipated. He hit the brakes but entered the turn going far too fast. When Jeff cranked the wheel, the truck slid sideways. The driver's side rear wheel dropped off the road.

"Jeff, we're going over the—"

The rear wheels hit a rock that jutted out of the mountainside, bouncing Jeff out of his seat. His seatbelt yanked him back down.

The truck landed with all four wheels on the road. But the dangerous slide continued, sending the pickup sliding along the edge of the drop-off.

He punched the gas pedal. With wheels churning up clouds of dust, the truck clung to the roadway and inched back into the center of the road.

He glanced at Allie.

Her right hand squeezed the passenger-side handle and her left hand clutched her blouse in the vicinity of her heart. Allie's gaze was locked on the road ahead of them and her lips appeared to be moving.

"That was close. Were you praying, Allie?"

"Does screaming 'help' count as a prayer?"

"Yeah. He's used to hearing that one." Jeff blew out a sigh, trying to calm his racing heart. "When this road dwindles to a trail, we'll have to ditch the pickup. But I'm afraid we'll back to the same place where you started, running through the mountains with those goons in pursuit."

"No, Jeff. It's not the same. This time I have *you* with me."

She was still putting too much stock in Jeff Jacobs. Not a good thing for anyone to do—to rely on someone with disgrace and failure on their permanent record.

Please, help me. I can't let Allie down.

Chapter 6

"Allie, I don't know the roads very well from here on. I want to get as far up the mountain as we can before we have to leave the truck. But I need your eyes. Tell me if you spot anything that looks dangerous."

Allie touched his shoulder. "I'll watch."

"And I'll slow down little."

Jeff's pickup bounced up the rough road, climbing the mountain. The road had obviously seen little traffic in recent years and the forest had encroached, narrowing the roadway.

The headlights lit up a fork in the road. The branch on the right climbed higher up the mountain. It would bring them closer to the peak and the lookout where he planned to spend the night.

From the lookout, he and Allie would be able to see the cartel thugs long before they arrived. He could watch their movements and hide if any of the gunmen got too close. And, if the FBI chopper flew within two or three miles, it would likely spot them.

Jeff turned right at the fork and the road immediately steepened. He shifted into four-wheel-drive and steered around a sharp corner.

"Stop!" Allie's voice pierced his ears.

Jeff stomped on the brakes.

A trestle bridge spanned a deep ravine thirty yards in front of them. The bridge was a relic from the past, from a time when vehicles were much smaller. It was barely wide enough for his truck, certainly too small for the cartel's big pickup to cross.

The real question was could Jeff's truck make it across, safely? The old bridge showed no signs of recent traffic. Crossing it could provide them more protection or put a permanent end to their worries.

"Allie, if we cross the bridge, we can drive a stretch of road that the gunmen will have to walk. We can lengthen our lead. Shall we try it?"

"Can you walk it first. You know, test it?"

"That will cost us some time. Besides I don't think I'd see any more than the headlights are showing us."

"I'm not sure about this, Jeff."

"Then you get out here. I'll drive across by myself. You can run across and join me."

Allie shot him a glaring glance. "You mean, *if* you make it across. If that bridge goes down, I'll be stranded on this side of the ravine, the goons' side, without you. No, I'm going with you."

Jeff pushed lightly on the accelerator and the pickup

crept out onto the bridge. The span was only twenty-five or thirty yards. And he saw no problems. But as he rolled onto the bridge, his truck seemed to be swaying side to side.

"I don't like the feel of this. We're swinging like we're on a footbridge."

Allie clamped a hand onto his shoulder. "Jeff, I think you need to get off—"

A loud crack sounded.

The truck dropped then hit hard, jolting them.

Jeff, instinctively, pushed the gas pedal to the floor.

The truck shot forward.

Another crack.

The rear end of the truck dropped a couple of feet. A harder jolt.

"We're falling!" Allie's voice blasted in his ear. She leaned into his shoulder.

Jeff drove uphill on whatever remained of the bridge, holding the pedal to the floorboard.

His truck exited the bridge with the rear wheels spinning.

Off the bridge now, he stopped and took a calming breath.

Allie had buried her face in his running shirt.

After his evening run, he needed a shower. No telling

what he smelled like. It couldn't be good, but Allie wasn't complaining. She wasn't complaining about anything except possibly being separated from him.

The bond between them had grown incredibly strong for such a short amount of time. Jeff could feel it. Everything that Allie said and did indicated she did, too. But this was not the time to analyze their budding relationship. They must survive or his speculation about them was moot.

Allie pulled her head out of his shirt. "Jeff, you know something?"

"Yeah. I'm ripe as a pomewater. Uh, more like a rotten one."

"A what? Jeff, did ... I mean ... are you okay after that bridge—"

"Forget it. It's Shakespeare, but it was a really bad analogy. And we can't do anything about how we smell, anyway."

"Shakespeare? I think you've lost it," Allie mumbled.

"The only thing I want to lose is those goons chasing us." Jeff opened the door of his truck, stepped out, and shined the flashlight behind them.

The middle section of the bridge had buckled where the trestle gave way. The bridge formed a large V over the ravine. The men chasing them would not be crossing it in their trucks or on foot.

He slid back into the truck.

They drove further up the road. The trees and bushes

now brushed the sides of his pickup. With the windows down, they would soon be brushing Allie and him.

"Is this going to end well?" Allie's shadowy face appeared focused on him.

"End well. What? The road or our ... touché. I get it. Shakespeare." Jeff slowed for a sharp turn.

"Both." Allie spoke softly and rested an arm on his shoulder.

Both? The road? This run for their lives? Their relationship? The softness in her voice said "both" included what was happening between them.

Jeff rounded the turn and slammed on the brakes. A pile of dirt and rocks blocked the old road.

"Well, the road didn't end well. I'm surprised we got this far after the storms from last winter." He took Allie's hand. "How sore are you from your mountain marathon?"

"I'll be alright, as long as I don't have to do this alone."

There it was again, the bond. Would it vanish, replaced by their former lives, once she was safe? Currently, all wasn't well. But this could end well if Jeff did his job protecting her. And, for the first time in years, Olympic gold had a formidable competitor vying for Jeff's heart, Allie Santiago.

Allie and Jeff slid out of his truck. He leaned the seat forward and grabbed his emergency pack. He wasn't sure what might be left in the pack after his last outing, but surely there were some things they could use. Jeff slung it over his shoulder.

The pile of dirt and rocks covered all but a yard of the roadway. They skirted the slide and walked around the next corner. The road ended, abruptly, at a partly collapsed building.

Jeff shined the light behind the pile of boards. A few feet in, a tunnel in the side of the mountain ended in a pile of dirt and rocks. "That explains why there was a trestle bridge this high up on the mountain. This is one of the old gold mines that played out in the thirties."

He took Allie's hand. "The moon's up. Let's see if we can go without the light. We don't want the cartel creeps spotting us if they get around to our side of the mountain."

He glanced at his watch and hit it with the light before turning the flashlight off. "It's 11:30 and we need to get to the top of the peak before we stop for the night. I've never been on this part of the mountain. Only looked at it from a distance. But I think if we cut directly up the mountain, the peak is only a half-mile away. But it's a steep half-mile." He squeezed her hand. "Are you up to that?"

She squeezed back. "If you think it's the best way to go, I can make it."

They climbed the steep slope steadily for fifteen minutes, threading their way through scrubby bushes, clusters of fir trees, and big rocks. Rocks seemed to be everywhere now and weaving around them on a forty-five-degree slope was rapidly claiming both his legs and his lungs.

Allie's breaths came in deep gasps, too. But she hadn't complained. Allie Santiago was stunningly beautiful and as tough as women came. Not a common combination, but

63

one that would make any man proud.

Jeff needed to rest even if Allie didn't. And he needed to focus on more than the woman beside him. "Let's stop and take a look at where we are."

In the valley below them there were no lights, only darkness. "Our friends are probably around the mountain from us and quite a way below. That's why we're not seeing any headlights. Time to go again, Allie."

The climb grew steeper, if that were possible, and the mountainside was now mostly rocks with only a few scrubby trees.

Jeff led Allie through a stand of small fir trees. When they emerged, a huge rock face stood in front of them, blocking their path. The dim moonlight didn't show him if it was climbable. He pulled his flashlight from a pouch in his pack and pushed the switch.

He guided the beam up the rock to the top. "It's at least a hundred feet high."

Jeff shined the light to the right side of the rock face. It didn't end, just wrapped around the mountain. He checked the left side. Same result. "This isn't good."

"What's wrong, Jeff?"

"That cliff has us cut off."

He again studied the top with the light. The corner of a man-made structure appeared on top of the cliff. "So that's where we are."

"And that is?"

Jeff hit the structure with the flashlight beam again.

"That's the lookout tower, Allie. A good place to stop for the night. We'll have shelter and we can see them if they are anywhere in the vicinity." He paused. "How are you at rock climbing?"

"I don't do rock climbing." She stepped close to him.

"That's okay. It's dark. You won't be able to see—"

"Jeff, you're not serious are you?"

"I've never been more serious. I don't see any other way up, and I do see shelter for us at the top. Are you coming?"

Allie put her arms around him. "You need to understand. I'm afraid of heights, acrophobia. I don't flip out or anything. But sometimes I get terrified and I freeze. I'm not sure I—"

"I'll help you, Allie. Each step of the way. If it gets too difficult, we'll back down. But look." He pointed the light at a V-shaped notch in the rock. "I think we can go right up the notch and you'll feel less exposed."

"Just go. I want to get this over with."

"Wait here first, and I'll go up a short way to make sure we can climb to the top."

"Great. We're climbing a mountain that you think may not be climbable. Didn't they make a movie about that? Two people fell and—"

"I won't let you fall. Promise."

He took off his pack, turned toward the rock face, and climbed steadily up to the fifty-foot level. It was a quick and easy climb. But there was one difficult spot about three quarters of the way up the face. They could make it unless Allie froze.

Jeff climbed back down, slipped on his pack, and pulled her toward the rock. He moved beside her and climbed with her, maintaining contact, guiding her hands and feet to good holds.

The first twenty-five feet of the climb went well. Allie began to climb with more confidence.

He stopped her at the three quarters mark. A long slab of limestone had broken loose and wedged in the notch, filling the gap they had been climbing.

Jeff climbed around Allie up to the base of their obstacle. He slipped to the side the slab of rock and was able to pull himself on top of it, a maneuver Allie would probably not be able to replicate. But they could do this if she didn't freeze or freak out.

"It's flat up here, Allie. I want you to come up to the base of this rock, then reach as high as you can with your right arm."

"I'm left-handed, Jeff."

He hadn't noticed, except for the crushing grip on his hand back at the house. "Okay. Stick up your left arm."

"What then?"

"If we can lock wrists, I'll pull you up beside me."

"I can't do that, Jeff."

"Can't or won't?"

"Both!"

"I wouldn't try this if I couldn't hold you. You just keep climbing with your feet as much as you can, supporting your weight with your feet, and I'll pull up the rest of your weight."

"But Jeff, I weigh too—"

"I know how much you weigh. I carried you for three miles. Remember?"

"No, I don't remember. I was unconscious."

They needed to be in the lookout surveying the area for their pursuers, not on the side of a cliff arguing. But the only way to stop her stonewalling was to convince her he could pull her up this stone wall.

"I can hold you, Allie. I can hold all of your weight if I need to. This is no big deal."

"It is to me." She looked up at him and stood silently for a moment. "If I do this, I need you to ... to hold me after I get up there, because I—"

"I'll hold you as long as you need me to." Jeff knelt and reached an arm down to her. "Allie?"

"I'm coming. But you'd better not slip off that rock when I pull on your hand or I'll kill you Jeff Jacobs."

"If I slip, you won't have to."

"That's enough. Why am I even having this conversation with you?"

"Because you're scared."

She stepped beneath the limestone impediment and stood staring at it.

"Allie, give me your hand."

She raised it, slowly.

Jeff grabbed her wrist as soon as he could reach it and pulled.

Allie's feet pawed and dug at the rock She was a runner with strong legs. Only for a second or two did Jeff have to support all of her weight. He gave a final pull and Allie shot over the outer edge of the rock, landing on her knees beside him.

Jeff pulled her to her feet on top of the rock that had blocked them. He took her back into the protection of the V-shaped notch and circled her shoulders with his arms.

Trembling, Allie clung to him, face pressed into his chest. After a few seconds, she looked up at him. "Thank you again, Jeff. I was hanging out over ... nothing. That terrifies me."

"Allie, it's not what you're hanging out over that matters. It's who's hanging on to you."

He couldn't see the warmth in Allie's eyes, but he knew it was there. He sensed it in her warm embrace, her relaxed body.

She slipped her hands behind his neck and gently nudged his head downward. Allie obviously wanted to kiss him.

The question was—no, it wasn't question. It was a decision. Either he would be breaking his vow or making a new vow, one he probably should not make ... yet.

Jeff's hesitation made the decision for him when Allie

raised onto her toes and kissed him.

Allie's kiss was like her, soft and warm.

It surprised Jeff and left him breathless.

She rested her head against his chest and it sounded like she was sniffling.

He cupped her cheek. His hand came away wet. "Allie, are you—"

"I'm sorry, Jeff. I forgot. You know, about your vow." She sniffled again and wiped her cheek. "And this isn't like me. I just wanted to ..."

He waited, but Allie had stopped talking. Now what was he supposed to say? According to what she told him at his house, this was her first kiss ... ever. Now, she was crying about it. He couldn't lecture her or tell her she shouldn't have done it.

Come on, dude. Spin it like a politician.

Maybe the obnoxious voice in his mind was right. But Allie might take this the wrong way. "Please don't cry, Allie. *You* kissed *me*. I didn't break any vow."

"You didn't?"

"No, I didn't."

"Then I'll make you a deal. After that overhanging rock, I'm not sure I can keep climbing up this cliff." Allie looked down at her feet. "If you can get me to the top, without scaring me to death, I ... I'll give you another one."

"Okay. It's a deal."

The dim moonlight revealed a weak smile on her face. "Only if you deliver on your part."

Jeff put his hand under her chin and lifted. "Now let me show you something."

He shined the flashlight into notch above them. "Tell me what you see."

Allie's mouth dropped open and her gaze locked on him. "Jeff Jacobs, you took advantage of me."

He put the light on Allie's full lips. "That's not the way I see it. You took advantage of me."

Allie pulled herself loose from his hand and disappeared into the darkness above.

Jeff stepped up beside her and shined the light into the gap in the rock ahead of them. "A nice little trail all the way to the top. No more climbing."

"You knew about this, and you tricked me."

"I'll let you out of the deal if you want me to."

She turned to face him. "I keep my promises, Jeff."

"And I'll remember that." He slipped an arm around Allie's waist. Her body was shaking. "Getting cold?"

"Yes, a little. It's a lot colder up here than in the valley."

"We're both wearing shorts. We're almost to the top of Bolan Peak. It gets chilly at sixty-two hundred feet. Let's move up to the top and check out the building."

She started up the steep trail through the notch.

He took her hand and pulled her to a stop. "Out of curiosity, when do I get to collect on my end of the deal?"

Allie didn't answer.

He hit her face with the light beam.

Her coy smile disappeared. "Can we talk about something else?"

"Yeah. But I won't forget, Allie."

She charged ahead, nearly pulling him off his feet. "Let's go. It's cold out here."

It was definitely cooling off. Probably for the best. He needed to focus on the danger they would face in the morning, once the cartel gunmen found his truck and deduced where they had gone.

Allie could run. That was a good thing because, come morning, they could be running for their lives.

Chapter 7

The heavens surrounded Allie, a surreal, three-dimensional picture filled with sparkling glitter, a large silver disc painted against an indigo sky, and a milky streak that ran through the middle of it all, from horizon to horizon.

Half way across the rocky top of Bolan Peak the shadowy silhouette of the lookout tower blotted out a rectangular area of stars. Allie tugged on Jeff's hand. "Wait a second. I've never seen the sky like this. It's so beautiful."

He scanned the sky, then her moonlit face. "So precise in its movement, so spectacular in its beauty. But like you, Allie, it's just the product of time and chance."

"That's not fair. I never said I believed that nonsense. Look at it. It had to be created, just like you and me."

"So you believe in God, but not in a good and faithful God?"

"I'm not sure what I believe about God. Can we go inside? I'm cold."

There was something very special happening between her and Jeff, but now he had placed God between them, a God that wasn't so special.

The near side of the tower was level with the ground, the other side supported by posts.

Jeff walked across the rocky ground to the tower door. "I think they rent this place out to hardy souls who want a getaway that's adventurous and romantic."

Romantic. If it weren't for the cartel gunmen, and a certain subject Jeff was sure to bring up again, this would be the first real romantic night of her life. Being with someone she trusted completely, who was handsome, and whom she felt drawn to, was a much more powerful experience than what the Hollywood movies provided. And Hollywood movie directors were experts at creating powerful emotional responses.

She shivered and stepped close to Jeff, while he fiddled with what looked like a lock.

"What are the odds of that, Allie? The lock wasn't pushed in enough to catch. We don't have to break-in, just walk in. God is good, isn't he?"

That was debatable, but she wasn't in the mood for a debate with Jeff. "Maybe He was good this time." *But you can't count on Him.*

Jeff pushed the door open, stepped in, and took her hand. "C'mon, let's warm you up. You feel cold."

Warm her up. If Jeff only knew how much warmth a simple touch from him generated she—

Come on, girl, get a grip. You're almost twenty-one

years old, not a giddy fourteen-year-old.

Allie followed Jeff into the lookout tower. The residual heat from the sunny afternoon left the glass-enclosed room almost too warm. She walked to the middle of the room and turned a full circle. The 360-degree view of the star-studded sky again overwhelmed her.

Jeff closed the door and moved beside her.

When his arm slipped around her, Allie laid her head on his shoulder. It seemed natural, the proper place for Allie Santiago's head. She wouldn't even have considered behaving like this a few days ago. How could a few hours make so much difference?

He kissed her forehead, then pulled her toward the moonlit side of the tower. "Come over here, Allie. I want you to see this."

He pointed down the mountain.

She sighted down his arm to a small, flickering light near the base of the mountain. Or was it on the adjacent mountain?

"That's the cartel men's campfire. It looks like they took the wrong fork in the road and they're camping in the canyon near the base of the mountain. I'll bet they left somebody at the fork to prevent us from backtracking. But we're safe for tonight."

"Listen, Jeff." A distant noise grew louder. "Is that the FBI helicopter?"

Jeff looked toward the north side of the building. "They know we're not at the house and they're looking for us. Unfortunately, they're looking near town."

He pulled his cell from his shorts pocket and it lit up. "No bars. I'm going to walk around the perimeter of the tower and see if I can catch a signal from some cell tower."

"Be careful."

"It's okay, Allie. We're safe for the night. No goons, no grizzlies, and no ghosts up here. And Bigfoot's just a myth. Be right back."

"Don't tell me you used to believe in monsters."

"Yeah. So do you. The Sinaloa Cartel. But you're in the heart of Bigfoot country. Too many sightings in this area to count. But that was mostly fifty years ago."

She watched as Jeff left the building and moved onto the deck encircling the tower.

He moved slowly along the deck, stopping to hold up the cell every few feet. After Jeff circled the tower, he came back inside shaking his head. "No luck. I'll try again before it gets too light in the morning."

"What do you think the FBI will do, Jeff?"

"They'll check out the evidence at the house. That trail of rubber I burned on the garage floor, evidence of shooting, along with the goons' absence from town—they'll have a good idea what happened and they'll come looking for us tomorrow. We need to be ready to signal them. There's a mirror in my pack we can use. My pack. That reminds me, you're probably thirsty."

"Parched. And hungry too."

"I've got some energy bars in my pack, but let's check the little pantry." He hit the small, doorless pantry with the flashlight beam. "There are some water bottles. Let me check them before we get too excited. I may have to go out looking for water."

She followed him toward the water. "How many bottles are there?"

"Six. And they haven't been opened. The expiration date is sometime next year. They were probably left by the last guests who stayed here."

"Jeff, there's a book on the table. It looks like a log. Maybe it will tell us who they were and when they stayed here." She reached for the book.

"First, you need to get some water in you." He tossed her a bottle.

In the dim light, she bobbled it, then grabbed it before it hit the floor. "Bring the flashlight over here." She stepped to the log, opened her bottle, flipped the lid, and sucked hard. That literally wet her thirst. Allie began guzzling.

"Whoa, whoa. Do you always drink like that? You'll make yourself sick if you don't slow down."

She gave him a mock frown and closed the lid on her bottle.

Jeff put the light beam on the book.

Allie opened it and flipped pages until she found the last entry. "June 29. That was two weeks ago. It says, 'You may not believe this, but Eric and I (Brenda) spent our wedding night here. The most romantic spot on earth. It was incredible! I hope you enjoy it here half as much as we did'."

Allie closed the log. "I think that's enough of that."

"Allie?" Jeff stepped close to her, slipped a hand under her arm and gently turned her to face him.

Was Jeff going to claim the prize he tricked her into offering? The thought was enticing and frightening at the same time. He had no idea how strongly his closeness affected her.

"Yes?" The word caught in her throat and then escaped, sounding like a bullfrog's croak.

"I don't know how to tell you this in a diplomatic way, so I'll just say it plain. You are so beautiful, and when I'm with you, unless we're running for our lives, I can't ... I just ..."

Jeff was being honest. She should be, too. "I think it's called chemistry."

"Yeah. But you and I can't afford any explosions. So ..." His nervous, hesitating voice sounded completely out of character for the confident man she was coming to know.

"I'm glad you told me."

"You are?" His voice broke, sounding like an adolescent boy.

She understood. But how does a person admit something like that, something she'd never experienced before? Her face grew warm. Allie was blushing. Maybe Jeff couldn't tell in the dim light.

Jeff cupped her cheek, then pulled his hand back. "Great. We're spending the night in Eric and Brenda's honeymoon cottage in the most romantic setting I've ever been in and with the most beautiful woman I've ever met. She owes me a kiss that could well, ... you know. And a half-dozen armed thugs are camped near the base of the mountain, making plans to blow us away in the morning. They may be too late."

"Jeff, you make it sound so wild and crazy and—it's not *that* bad. Well, not quite that bad. Maybe it's..." But it *was* that bad.

Tears overflowed her eyes. It was a stupid, immature response. Allie wiped the tears from her cheeks.

Jeff noticed and his arms curled around her. "You know, if you and I were brought together for a purpose, I believe the same God that brought us together will make sure we have some time for this relationship to grow in a good way."

Jeff had made a big assumption about them. And why did he have to insert God between them again? "You mean the same God I don't believe in?"

"That's not how you really think about Him. I've heard you, and I understand where you're coming from. You're just not sure you can trust Him enough to put your faith in Him. Just try Him. He'll prove Himself to you."

She stepped back from Jeff. "There's nothing provable about your faith. Nothing a person can count on. And you certainly can't count on ..." Memories flooded Allie's consciousness, memories of desperation and darkness.

Allie took a calming breath. "When I was nine, my grandmother got sick, really sick. I prayed for her so hard that I got sick. Prayed for a miracle. Evidently, God doesn't care about the prayers of little girls. So I stopped praying."

"I'm sorry, Allie. Can I show you something?"

"I have the feeling you're going to show me anyway. Go ahead."

Jeff pulled a folded piece of paper from his pocket.

Allie recognized it immediately. When things looked hopeless at the marijuana plantation, she had written a complaint against whoever was in control. Maybe a complaint against God. Maybe a complaint against life.

He unfolded the paper. "When you were unconscious on my couch, I wanted to know who you were, so I looked—"

"I was helpless and you searched me? How could you do that, Jeff?"

"Allie, it wasn't like that. I only searched for some ID."

"You mean like birthmarks?"

"No. A driver's license. But this paper was sticking out of your shorts pocket. I read it and ... let me read it again."

Jeff shined his light on the paper and read. "I've cried for help until my voice is gone. I've looked for help until my sight is nearly gone. Who will hear and help? Will anyone answer my cries? These people hate me and plan to destroy me for their own profit. What have I done to them?

"They have made me work as a slave for them. I didn't take anything from them. I owed them nothing. I'm not perfect, but do I deserve this? Is there any hope anywhere?

"Will anyone answer my questions? *Can* anyone answer them?"

He looked up at her.

Allie promised herself she wouldn't cry again, but once again tears overflowed her eyes and trickled down her cheeks.

Jeff turned the paper over. "After I read your words, I realized I'd read them before. So I opened my Bible and—"

"You're not going to preach to me, Jeff. I won't listen."

"I would never preach to you. I just want you to hear someone else who cried out with words identical to yours."

"Yeah, sure. Someone, two or three thousand years ago, was captured by a drug gang, and they tried to mow him down with an automatic slingshot."

"Just listen, please. Here are King David's words from Psalm 69. I'm paraphrasing them in modern English."

Allie shrugged. Her shoulders lied about her interest, but she wasn't going to tell Jeff.

He began reading his words.

"I am exhausted from my calling out for help; my throat is parched and burning. And my eyes are failing from looking for you, God."

She drew a sharp breath. Those were her words.

Jeff continued.

"My enemies hate me and they don't even have a reason. I have countless enemies, enemies without cause and they want to destroy me. They force me to give to them what I did not steal.

"You know all of my failings, O God. They are not hidden from your eyes."

Allie blew out the breath she'd been holding and looked away out the window. "I ... I don't understand. How could someone else—"

"It's called the human condition. The ugliness of living on planet Earth that every worldview or philosophy tries to explain. And, yeah, David's complaint was identical to yours. But there *is* an answer to the human condition, Allie."

"Probably somebody else's answer. I'll bet it didn't satisfy David." And it wouldn't satisfy her.

Jeff studied her face for a moment. "That's where you're wrong. The answer comes in David's own words. Even though he complained, here's his answer. It's what he believed. I'm paraphrasing a couple of verses from Psalm 59."

"I'm going to sing about your power. This morning I'm going to sing about your great love for me. You, Lord, are my fortress. You are my refuge in the times of trouble. You are my Strength and so I'll sing praises to your name. You, my loving God, are my fortress."

Both of those poems or psalms, as Jeff called them, came from the same man. Somehow, he could complain to God and yet praise Him. Was that even allowed?

When Allie asked the question, immediately Jeff's prayer from earlier in the evening came to mind. It had sounded like a young child talking to his daddy. A child can complain to their dad, ask for help, and get it. Just because trouble came a child didn't run from their dad. He was their fortress. He protected them.

The defensive walls Allie had built to protect a hurting, doubting heart all crumbled in an instant. There was nothing left to hold them up, not even her stubborn will. "Jeff, I ..." Her voice caught and she looked up into Jeff's face in the moonlight.

The tenderness in his eyes said he understood the change in her.

And she *had* changed. At some point in Jeff's reading, the switch was flipped and the lights had come on in Allie's soul, or spirit, wherever the real Alejandra Santiago existed.

In a huge explosion, the light breached the dam holding back a flood of emotions Allie had held inside, emotions that had been shredding the place in her heart where faith and hope resided. The flood was freeing but frightening in intensity. And it demanded something of Allie, something she felt inadequate to give. "Jeff, hold me please."

"You're not going to explode on me are you?"

"I've already done that. I ... I need you to pray for me. Tell God I'm sorry. So sorry. I blamed Him without even giving Him a chance."

"He would love to hear it from you. He loves to have conversations with the people he created, even if they complain sometimes. Go ahead. Tell Him."

While Jeff held her, Allie tried to find the right words. But once she started, the words poured out from her heart in a continuous flow to Someone she *knew* was listening.

For the first time, Allie understood the real nature of her problem—her rebellion and lack of trust—so the cross took on its proper role in her mind and heart. Her offenses against God had been paid for. She didn't have to condemn herself for complaining to Him. She only had to realize that He understood. He would help her, not desert her just because she didn't understand.

When her tears stopped, Jeff took her by the shoulders and held her in front of him so the moonlight lit her face. He studied it.

She returned his gaze and smiled.

"Alejandra Santiago, I believe God just took your heart. Stole it the way you ran into my life and stole—"

"Jeff?"

"Yeah?"

"Just call me Allie. I like it much better."

"But you gave me such a bad time for—"

"Only because I thought you were being presumptuous."

"I was just being a guy. We don't do four syllables. We invent shorter names. But, you know something? I'm hungry. How about you?"

"Starved."

"Let me get you a couple of energy bars from my pack. Then you need to get some sleep. I'll keep my eye on that camp for a while."

"Standing watch, huh? Wake me up in a couple of hours and I'll take my turn."

"If I get sleepy, I'll wake you up."

He probably wouldn't. She would have to wake herself up. "Jeff, what do think is going to happen tomorrow?"

"The goons and the FBI both go on a treasure hunt."

"Treasure?"

"Yeah, treasure. You, Allie."

But I've never thought of myself like that."

"But I have."

She had stopped Jeff while he tried to tell her she had stolen his heart. And, now, he had alluded to his feelings for her in more than just chemical terms. It was time for her to reciprocate. He needed to know how deeply she had begun to treasure him.

Allie finished her energy bar, took a drink of water, then curled up on the flat, board platform meant for sleeping bags with air mattresses. The moonlight created a profile of Jeff as he sat near the window watching.

Despite the impending danger, she was at peace. As she sought the right words to describe to Jeff her real feelings toward him, she drifted into a warm, secure place...

Allie awoke with a start and sat up on her wooden bed.

Chapter 8

Something had pulled Allie from her deep sleep. Sitting on the wooden bed frame, she brushed a strand of hair from her face and scanned the cabin of the lookout tower. Darkness filled the lower part of the room beneath the windows. But the moon, now in the western sky, created a silhouette of Jeff's head, a head which had already nodded twice in the few seconds she had watched him.

Maybe she had awoken because Jeff needed her. Where had that thought come from? He certainly looked like he needed rest and she needed to stand watch. Did God actually do things for people like waking them up?

If you want to know something, ask and I will answer you and show you wonderful, mysterious things that you don't yet understand. Didn't I use your own words to draw you to me?

She rubbed her arms. Goose bumps. The temperature had dropped in the lookout, but that didn't account for all the bumps on Allie's arm. They came from the awesomeness of communicating with the Creator of the universe, her God, something she couldn't recall ever happening before.

And if it had happened because Jeff needed her—Allie slid her feet onto the floor and approached him.

Jeff's head nodded downward, but this time it stayed down.

The flashlight stood on end in the window sill. She took it and shot Jeff's watch with the beam. 4:30 a.m.

She bent over and kissed his forehead.

Jeff raised his head. "What time is it?"

"Four thirty. You need some sleep, Jeff. I'll watch now."

She led him to the wooden bed.

He sat down and rolled onto the hard wooden boards, then raised his head. "It gets light about five thirty. The cartel gunmen and the FBI will probably set out about that time. Wake me up."

Jeff lowered his head and within a few seconds the deep, easy breathing of a sleeper came from the wooden bed.

Allie sat down in the chair by the window and looked toward the east where the precursor to sunrise painted an orange line on the horizon. Above the line, lay a royal blue semicircle which darkened to indigo farther up in the sky. But the valley below lay blanketed by darkness.

An hour passed and, on the eastern horizon, yellow joined the strange, cloudless rainbow, heralding the coming sunrise. Far below Bolan Peak, lights of one vehicle came on. Very faintly, in the stillness of the dawn, Allie heard an engine start.

She stood, moved beside Jeff and sat.

His deep, regular breathing had soothed her while she watched. But this tranquil night was ending. Allie shivered at the certainty that danger would come with the day. She shivered again at the uncertainty of what the danger would bring and how it might change her life ... or how it might end it.

"Jeff?"

His eyes opened, and he smiled at her. The smile quickly disappeared when he studied her face. "What is it?"

"They started one of their trucks. It's all beginning and it frightens me."

He sat up and slid over beside her. "Don't worry. We can watch their movements, so they can't surprise us. If we need to, we can run down the other side of the mountain to escape. But remember, the FBI's going to be moving out too."

"There's something else ...you haven't actually been to this lookout before, have you?"

"No. Why?"

"If I wasn't so worried about the gunmen, I might take back my offer."

"Whatever it is I did, I'm sorry, Allie."

She tried to give him a smile. "It's more about what you didn't do. Now that it's light, look out the window to the south and tell me what you see."

Jeff stood and stepped to the south side of the square

room. "Are you talking about that steep slope with all the rocks?"

"You mean that walkable slope that we could have used if we had circled the cliff last night and approached from the south." She shook her head. "I didn't have to be terrified by that rock face. We didn't have to climb anything."

"It does look a little easier."

"No lie." She paused. "But forget last night."

Jeff placed a hand on her shoulder. "What if I don't want to?"

"Jeff, listen. What if the gunmen try to come up from the south? They can just walk right in on us."

"But they don't know that. The rock face looks like the only way up here. If they try to climb it, I think we can stop them. We let them climb part way up, then we roll some rocks on them from the top. They'll never make it up."

"Eventually, they'll get tired of being brained with boulders and some of them will try the southern route."

"There are rocks to roll there, too. But you're right to be concerned. We probably couldn't stop them."

"We need to leave now, Jeff. There's a drivable road that comes within fifty yards of the lookout on the south side. Do you know where it goes?"

"Yeah. It comes off from Highway 199 a little south of the California border. The goons would have to know about that, drive for an hour to reach the road, and then another hour to get up here. They won't come that way. They'll arrive from the north and we'll see them coming."

"We could use that road to run down the mountain for help."

"It's a long run. Probably fifteen to twenty miles. I would've thought you had enough of running through the mountains yesterday. Think about it, Allie. The FBI chopper will be all over these mountains this morning, looking for us. And we're in the best possible place for them to spot us, on top of the highest peak."

Allie walked to the opposite side of the lookout. She gasped. "Lights, Jeff. What are they doing?"

He hurried over and draped an arm over her shoulders. "It's the third pickup. They probably left it guarding the fork in the road last night so we couldn't drive back down and escape. It's coming up the mountain toward my truck. They'll find it and it won't take them long to figure out the rest."

"You said yesterday they must be communicating with each other."

"Yeah. Bet they have two-way radios. If so, they'll be swarming all over this peak in another hour."

Swarming all over this peak. Allie shuddered. "Whatever happens, Jeff, promise me one thing." She put her arms around him and pressed her cheek into his chest. "Don't let them get me, even if you have to force them to shoot me, don't let any of those filthy people touch me."

"Get you? First, let's concentrate on getting away. I'm not ready to make any plans to throw in the towel, not by a long sight."

"We need to pray, don't we?"

He lifted her chin and smiled at her. "This must be the new Allie talking."

She nodded. "Also the scared Allie. Will you do it, please? I just want to hold on to you and listen."

Jeff wrapped his arms around her and prayed for protection from the gunmen and wisdom for all the decisions they would have to make. His words asked for help, but his tone was expectant, as if he thought God really would provide for them.

Would Allie Santiago ever be able to pray with that kind of confidence? To face life concerned but without terror and its paralyzing fear? If she could spend enough time with Jeff Jacobs, she would learn.

Jeff brushed a wisp of hair from her face. "I need Allie Santiago to come back from wherever she went. It's time to get busy."

She dropped her arms to her sides and heaved a sigh.

Jeff picked up his pack, rummaging through it until he found the small mirror. He slipped it into his pocket. "From now on, we need to make sure they can't see us, and we have to assume they have binoculars. We'll only expose ourselves to signal the helicopter if it flies near us."

Allie gasped and dropped to her knees. She peered over the window sill on the south side of the lookout. There was movement a few hundred yards below the cliff. "I think I saw two of them below the big rock face."

"Then they must suspect we're up here. They found my truck and, since they farm marijuana in this area, I'm sure they know about this lookout tower. They won't do anything until the rest of the men show up. But I'm not sure what they'll try then."

"Jeff..." Allie tapped the window with her index finger. "Look toward town. Even with the mountain tops."

"The chopper's airborne."

"But it's flying toward the marijuana plantation. That's at least fifteen miles from here."

"We've got a decision to make right now. Either we run down that road on the south side, and try to disappear into the forest, or we hold on here until the chopper spots us."

"Jeff, I think we should leave and—"

"Keep in mind that once the chopper arrives, we're safe. If we start running, we aren't safe until we reach someplace where there's adequate police protection."

Allie pressed a hand over her heart, now pounding out a presto beat. "You want to wait here, don't you?"

"Yes. But if that frightens you too much, I'll run with you."

"You prayed." She took a calming breath. "You prayed for protection. The FBI helicopter, with a SWAT team onboard, is the only sure protection for us. I'll stay."

"You are an incredible woman, Allie Santiago. I... I want to ... uh, need to tell you..."

She placed her fingertips over his lips. "Save it for

91

later, Jeff. When we're safe, then you can tell me whatever you want to."

* * *

Jeff drew a sharp breath when movement caught his eye. Something had moved in the trees 200 yards below the rock face. More movement. "I think the cartel army just arrived. We need to buy ourselves some time for that chopper to fly our way."

Allie looked up at him. The intense look in her eyes no longer held fear. There was a fierceness Jeff had never seen before. "If they're stupid enough to try climbing the cliff, Jeff, we could give them some real headaches."

"I climbed the cliff, too. If you're calling me stupid, what about that stupid deal you made with me?"

She gave him a weak smile. "The kiss? That was a crazy deal, Jeff." The smile grew stronger. "Crazy like a fox. Let's go give them a rocky reception."

"We'll go, but only if you promise to keep your head down. I don't want anything happening to—"

"Shhhh. You're supposed to be helping me learn to trust, not giving me more reasons to be afraid."

She followed Jeff out of the lookout.

As they moved away from the tower, Jeff took her hand and pulled down on it. "You're supposed to be staying as low as you can." He turned away from the sun and pointed ahead. "Let's go around the west side of the rock. From there, we can get to the top of the rock face without being seen."

"Jeff, if we walk down into that notch, we can get right on top of them."

"No way am I letting you go near that notch. One burst from their automatics and bullets would be ricocheting all over inside that gap."

"I see what you mean. The notch would guide the bullets to—"

"To us, Allie." He led her to a high point on the cliff above the notch and stopped behind a large rock. "Stay here until I locate them."

Jeff crept around the rock toward the edge of the cliff.

Muffled voices and the sounds of shoes scraping on the rock came from far below. The gunmen were coming up the notch.

He scrambled back to Allie's position and scanned the area around them. "See the rock about ten feet from the edge?"

The men's voices grew louder, excited voices.

Allie's eyes widened. "That rock's as big as a refrigerator."

"Yeah. But if we can roll it toward that little dip on the right, it will drop straight into the notch they're climbing."

"I hear them coming. We've got to hurry."

Jeff moved forward, sat on the ground, and rolled back. He placed his feet against the side of the rock. "Allie, push on the top with your hands. Push as hard as you can. On three."

The clattering of metal on rocks sounded a short distance below them. The first climbers were nearly to the top.

"One, two, three..."

Allie leaned hard into the rock. He pushed with all his leg strength.

The rock didn't budge.

It was too late to run. The gunman would clear the top and mow them down before Allie and Jeff could reach the road on the south side of the peak.

They were out of time and out of backup plans.

Chapter 9

With the cartel gunmen approaching the top of the rock face, Jeff's mind was a blender full of pureed thoughts. None of them lasted long enough to latch on to before they were chopped and swirled into a useless mixture.

He looked up at Allie.

She still pushed on the upper portion of the block of limestone. "Jeff, help me! We've only got a few more seconds."

He stood and put his hands near the top of the rock. What had he been thinking? He had more leverage pushing at the top, even if his legs were four times stronger than his arms. "Allie, ready ... push!"

Allie grunted with her effort.

Had the rock moved?

"Again, Allie. Ready ... push."

The rock tilted and inch or two, then rocked back to equilibrium."

They're almost on top, Jeff."

"This time, we push, then let the rock come back, then push again when it rocks forward. We increase the amplitude each time."

Allie looked at him, wide-eyed. "Rock'n roll?"

"Yeah. Like a rolling stone." Any other time, Jeff would have laughed at their pun.

"I am coming, Alejandra." Words yelled from the cliff below ended all thoughts about humor. "Soon you will be mine." The man lapsed into Spanish.

"What's he saying?"

"Don't ask, Jeff. Just don't ask."

"Then let's shut his big mouth. Ready to rock?"

"Yes. Right onto his head."

"Ready, push."

They found the right rhythm and the amplitude of the rocking grew from one to six inches.

"Keep it rocking, Allie. We need to rock it over the square corner."

Twelve inches. Eighteen inches.

"Push with everything you've got on the next one."

Jeff roared out his fury as he dealt the rock a savage shove. The boulder reached its tipping point and slowed to a stop. "Shove again!"

The rock slowly pitched forward, headed down the

slope. With a grinding sound, the monolith smashed smaller rocks. It accelerated and tumbled over the edge, then dropped like a two-ton hammer head guided by the notch in the rock face.

Allie clenched her jaw. "Take that you scrawny little—"

A scream came from a short distance below.

More yells and loud crunching noises reverberated between the rock face and the adjacent mountain.

A deep boom echoed through the mountains when the rock hit bottom.

Something moved in the periphery of Jeff's vision. He grabbed Allie's shoulders and pulled her down behind a nearby rock protrusion.

The staccato belching of assault rifles sounded and two lines of flying dirt and rock fragments passed by them on either side.

Though the gunmen on the cliff were stopped for now, the two men approaching from the lookout tower had Jeff and Allie at their mercy. They had found the way around the cliff.

Jeff grabbed a baseball-sized rock to use as a weapon. He shoved Allie flat on the ground with his other hand. He raised to throw the rock, but dropped to the ground when the boulder proved too short to protect him.

With Allie squirming under his hand that still pinned her to the ground, Jeff had run out of options for defending Allie and him.

Jeff's gaze darted back and forth between the notch on

the cliff and the approaching gunmen. He couldn't stay crouched by the rock letting the gunmen shoot him and come for Allie.

He drew his arm back in throwing position and waited for the men to move closer.

A loud whoosh followed by a whirring sound turned his head toward the northwest.

From the next ridge over, a helicopter shot up into view and rushed at them a half mile away.

Somehow in the confusion of the battle, the chopper had spotted them and snuck in behind the mountain to the northwest. Now it turned broadside to them and several guns jutted out the door.

Jeff raised his arm and waved at the chopper.

The two gunmen by the tower started a loud, heated discussion.

One of the men raised his gun and fired a short burst at them.

Fragments of rock stung Jeff's hand. He pulled it down, ducked behind the rock, and glanced at the bleeding cuts.

Allie tried to sit up.

He couldn't let her become a target. Jeff shoved her head down to the ground and pinned it there.

She twisted her head beneath his hand.

Jeff yelped as pain shot through his hand.

Allie had bitten his finger.

"Don't shove me around again. Leave my head alone. Do you understand?" Allie's voice had become deep, growling at him with a Spanish accent.

Great. One hand was bleeding from being hit by flying fragments, and he'd nearly lost a finger on the other hand. But he'd learned one of Allie's hot buttons. Don't mess with her head.

At least the gunmen hadn't shot again. Jeff raised his head a few inches and glanced their way.

The men by the lookout had started a shouting match in Spanish.

Jeff raised his head higher to see what was happening.

The two men ran by the lookout and headed south still in an intense argument.

A long burst of gunfire from the helicopter ended the argument. One of the thugs fell, then jumped up and ran out of sight. The other man limped away headed the same direction his luck had gone … south.

"What were they saying, Allie?"

"I'm sorry." She cupped his cheek.

"They weren't sorry for trying to kill us."

"I mean I'm sorry for biting you. I wanted to see what was happening, but you kept shoving my mouth into the dirt." She pulled her hand from his cheek and stuck a finger in his face. "No one shoves me around and gets away with it, Jeff Jacobs. Do you understand me?"

He retreated from her accusing finger. "Yeah. I understand. Like the mob, you lose a finger for every transgression. Now, what were they saying when they ran over the peak? It was something about the poodle."

"Not quite. It was meant for you, Jeff, but I won't translate it. I don't talk that way and, about you, I think just the opposite."

"Come on, Allie give me a—"

Suddenly the helicopter veered sharply away. A boom sounded from the base of the cliff, followed by a whooshing sound. The fiery tail of a rocket streaked across the blue sky, barely missing the chopper.

A quarter of a mile away an explosion of fire and smoke appeared against the powder blue sky. The report seemed to resonate in Jeff's chest when it pounded him.

"What the—the goons have RPGs! Let's run down the trail to the notch and watch this, Allie."

"So now that there's a war to watch you just forget about me?"

How could he keep up with her mood changes? And he wasn't doing very well at anticipating their causes. "As long as I live, Allie, that's something you don't have to worry about. We can watch from here."

The words were out before he thought about their implications. It didn't matter. As best he knew, they were the truth, no matter what the future held for them.

When Jeff looked up into the blue sky, the chopper had swung broadside toward the cartel men.

They had quickly abandoned their attempt to climb the rock face and now focused on the helicopter.

More guns protruded from the chopper and the noise of gunfire sounded for several seconds, kicking up dust all around the cartel gunmen.

One of the goons yelled and fell.

The rest ran away.

Jeff made a quick tally. He counted five who had gotten away safely. The two who had run to the south were wounded, but still loose. The one who had taunted Allie was squashed by the boulder and two men lay still after being hit by FBI gunfire.

Ten men had come in three trucks to get them, even after the cartel knew Allie had contacted the authorities. Why did they want her so badly? He didn't like the answer he came up with. It was pure vindictiveness. They were evil and bent on revenge, the same kind of revenge that left limbs and heads along Mexican roads.

There was no safe place for Allie as long as there were cartel members alive who remembered what she had done to them. What she had done to them—he looked at Allie and smiled. She had broken their hold on this whole area. In the process, she had gotten a firm hold on another area, an area that included Jeff Jacobs' heart.

His musings ended when the chopper hovered over Allie and him.

Allie's hair blew behind her in long, dark wisps, that made this beautiful, brown-eyed woman look like a model at a photo shoot, not a woman who had spent a night on the mountain without a bath and without makeup.

A voice blared over the PA system of the chopper. "This is the FBI. Jeff Jacobs and Alejandra Santiago, you're safe. We can't land on the peak, so we'll lift you. We're sending someone down to assist."

A man in a harness dropped out of the chopper.

Allie stepped close and circled Jeff with her arms. "I can't do this ... just hang out there in the air."

"You'll be in a harness. There's no way you can fall."

"But I—"

"I'll explain to the guy coming down. He's probably dealt with acrophobia before."

After touching down, a large man in what looked like a camouflaged military uniform unhooked himself and approached them. "I'm Special Agent Nelson, FBI. Let's get you two out of here. Ladies first, Ms. Santiago."

"Nelson, she's afraid of heights. Have you—"

"Got just the thing for you." He pulled out something resembling a scarf and fashioned a blindfold, then tied it around Allie's head."

"What are you doing? I'll know when you lift me and not being able to see will only make me—"

"We won't go until you're ready, Ms. Santiago. But let me get the harness around you." He buckled Allie in and secured the harness. But Nelson clipped himself on the line, too. "Now, we'll just lift you a few inches off the ground to let you get the feel of it. I'm right here beside you. How does it feel?'

"Uh ... not as scary as I thought. But please wait a

minute before we go any higher."

Jeff watched as Allie was lifted up ten feet, then twenty feet.

Clipped on beside Allie, Agent Nelson talked to her until an arm reached out of the chopper and pulled the two inside.

A loud yell sounded above the whir of helicopter blades. A man's voice.

A few moments later, Nelson came back down. After he hit the ground he limped toward Jeff.

"What happened to you, man? Did you bump your leg getting in?"

"You might say that. She kicked me in the shin when the blindfold came off. Called me a liar. Well, at least she's safe."

Jeff grinned. "Yeah. She's safe. But I don't know about you when you go back up. She's a runner. Has strong legs. FYI, she nearly bit my finger off when I shoved her face in the dirt to keep her head from being shot."

"Beautiful but violent." Nelson frowned. "Is she always like that?"

"Not when she kisses you."

"Kisses you? You're a lucky guy, Jacobs." Nelson secured Jeff in the harness. "How did you manage that?"

"I still haven't figured that out. But if I do, I'm not gonna' tell anybody."

The line tightened and Jeff went airborne, swinging

gently as he rose to the wop, wop beat of the chopper.

A man built like an NFL linebacker pulled Jeff into the helicopter and removed the harness. The big man shoved a huge hand at him. "Jacobs. I'm Agent McCheney."

Jeff took the hand. "At last, the big, ugly guy in the flesh. A minute later, McCheney, and you might have been too late."

"We had our eye on you, Jacobs. And you need to be careful who you're calling names. Your girlfriend here's a lot nicer than you."

"Girlfriend?"

Allie whirled toward him, frowning at his reply.

"How did you come up with that assessment, McCheney?"

"Told you we had our eyes on you ... for quite a while. See." He lifted up a powerful pair of binoculars.

It was time to get serious. "So what can you tell us about my girlfriend's family?"

Allie's frown disappeared and she scooted close to his side.

The chopper turned and headed toward town.

"Her family. I was hoping you could help us there." McCheney sighed. "We found a plantation early this morning, but it had already been abandoned. It was partially harvested and it looked like the *farmers* left in a big hurry."

"You didn't find any ..." Allie's voice trailed off.

McCheney's voice grew soft. "No, we didn't. Everyone appears to have been moved. We'll talk about that after we get you back to Jacobs' place. We're arranging protection for you there—for both of you, if you don't mind staying at Mr. Jacobs' house, Ms. Santiago."

"Please call me Allie." She smiled at Jeff. "No, I don't mind. Uh ... we'll be chaperoned, won't we?"

"By the best U.S. Marshals that your tax dollars can buy." McCheney stared intently at Allie. "Well, the best money that U.S. tax payer's money can buy."

Allie returned McCheney's look, staring with equal intensity. "My parents were fleeing the cartel and thought they were coming here legally with work visas. Instead they were taken as slaves. They're good people."

McCheney nodded. "We'll continue our discussion once we're on the ground."

Jeff met the big agent's gaze. "What about the gunmen running loose on the ground?"

"Don't worry about them," McCheney said. "We've got people on the ground tracking them."

"But you saw what kind of weapons those guys have. How—"

"Like I said, Jacobs. Don't worry about them. We can handle them. What we need to do now, is pick your and Ms. Santiago's brains and come up with a plan to save her family and, hopefully, end the cartel operations in the Ore-Cal border region. We'll round up these cartel peons and hope they lead us up the ladder to—"

"El Capitan." Allie blurted out with disdain in her

voice.

"Yeah. To their leader." McCheney replicated Allie's contempt. "Do you know why the cartel wants you even after you notified us, Ms. Santiago?"

"Yes. Do you mean that you don't?"

McCheney looked uncomfortable. "I just wanted you to realize that ... well, you're still in danger and—"

"Agent McCheney, you think I not know what they want?" Allie switched to a heavy Spanish accent, speaking in broken English. "My head beside r-r-roadway." She reverted to impeccable English. "Revenge. If you cost the Sinaloa Cartel twenty million dollars, as I have, they will make you pay. As long as anyone who remembers you is still alive, you will pay."

Chapter 10

Allie studied the ground near Jeff's house as the helicopter descended. It touched down softly not far from a black sedan parked along the street.

"Looks like I've got a new door, and a doorman." Jeff pointed toward the armed man standing by a door that did not match the exterior of his house.

"He's a new addition to our marshals in the region. One of the best." McCheney boomed out over the whopping of the chopper blades.

"Listen up," McCheney said, as the rotors spun down. His piercing gray eyes sent a chill tingling up Allie's back when those eyes focused on her. "We're going into the house, shortly. You will let our men escort you, but we'll be moving quickly. It's just a precaution. Do you understand?"

Was she going to get special protection? Something like witness protection? The thought of being under the control of the authorities and the resultant loss of freedom was unsettling. But as long as she could be with her family and Jeff, especially Jeff, she could tolerate protection.

Sandwiched between FBI agents, Jeff and Allie scurried to the door and stepped inside the house.

The armed man guarding the door turned toward her and Jeff. He was medium height with a muscular build. Probably mid-30s. He shoved a hand at Jeff. "I'm Marshall Wes Smith."

Jeff grinned. "Wes Smith... Smith and—"

"Okay. That's enough fun with my name." Wes returned Jeff's grin.

"I'm Jeff Jacobs and this is—

Wes cut in. "Ms. Alejandra Santiago." Wes focused on her. "Your, uh, fame precedes you, Ms. Santiago."

"Just call me Allie, please."

Her request drew a smile from Jeff. He slipped his arm around her.

Wes's eyes darted back and forth, looking from Jeff to her. "I'm seeing a picture here. Are you two like ... a couple?"

Allie waited.

Jeff didn't reply.

She looked up at Jeff. "Well, aren't you going to answer the man?"

"After what we've been through, Allie and I have grown close, really close. Yeah, we're a couple."

"I see." Wes raised his eyebrows. "If you two youngsters need a chaperone..."

What was Wes insinuating. "Jeff's an honorable man, Mr. Smith."

"But, Ms. Sant—"

"Just Allie."

"Uh ... Allie, I was only trying to—"

"That's enough, Reverend Smith." McCheney's voice of authority brought the room to attention. "Wes likes to play the father role. In this case, he's nearly old enough to—"

"I turn twenty-one in a couple of weeks, Agent McCheney. He's hardly old enough to be my father." She didn't like being discussed in this manner. "I am an adult, and in matters of the heart, quite able to look after myself."

"It wasn't your heart I was worried—"

"Enough, Wes." McCheney sighed and met Allie's gaze. "Wes means well ... let's move to the dining room table. We have a lot to discuss."

While they walked into the dining room, she whispered in Jeff's ear. "If he tries to tell me what I can or can't do with you, I'll—"

"Kick him in the shin like you did Nelson?" Jeff said as he grinned at her.

"If anyone kicks one of my men, I'm going to arrest them for assault." McCheney's voice boomed from behind them.

Was he serious? She glanced back at McCheney's face.

Allie couldn't decipher his expression but didn't feel inclined to challenge the man.

She sat down beside Jeff at the table, and scooted her chair close to his.

McCheney sat directly across the table from her. "Miss Sant—, uh, Allie, you told us on the phone about your family's situation in Nogales and what happened after they entered the United States. We need some descriptions. What is your father's full name?"

"Full name? Our lineage goes back to the Spanish Conquistadors."

"We don't need your whole family tree."

"Rafael Santiago, my dad, is forty-five. He's about five-foot-ten, medium build—a handsome, dignified looking man."

"What about your mother?"

"Lorena Santiago. She's forty-one, five-foot-five, slender ... a pretty woman."

Wes turned from the living room window. "No surprise there."

"This is my show, Wes. Just watch the window," McCheney said. "You'll get a turn later. What about your little brother?"

"Benjamin's eleven. A wonderful, bright boy. I'm afraid they'll sell him to the traffickers."

"You try your best to help us, and we'll do everything

110

humanly possible to make sure that doesn't happen."
McCheney had lowered his voice and he met her gaze.

For the first time, a softness appeared on McCheney's face and in his eyes.

So her family members were real people to this FBI agent. Not just descriptions. It gave her hope.

"You said you were only held for a few hours at the marijuana growing site. Did you hear about any other plantations in the area?"

"They mentioned another marijuana site to the south, or the southeast, about fifteen miles away."

"Any other locations of any sort that you heard them mention?"

"Yes. A more remote location maybe thirty miles to the south. I don't know if it was another marijuana farm or not. It was north of the Klamath River, but that's all I remember."

"Anything else you can tell us?"

"Yes. Find them, McCheney."

"We will, Allie." McCheney wrote in his notepad for several seconds, then looked up at Jeff. "Jacobs, you said they shot at you on more than one occasion. I need some details if we're going to charge these guys."

"You mean that RPG they shot at you wasn't enough?"

"We want all the charges. You don't want these guys ducking charges and roaming the streets or the mountains again, do you?"

Jeff shook his head and sighed. "Yesterday, when I was carrying Allie, they shot at me." He lifted his shirt sleeve, revealing the wound.

McCheney whistled through his teeth. "You are a lucky man. An inch further in and that bullet could have ripped your arm off."

"An inch lower and it would've hit Allie's head."

After Jeff's comment, McCheney's face turned red and he blasted out a crude description of the cartel members and a place he'd like to send them. "I want these guys! This isn't Mexico! The law is in control here. Our laws are enforced, and it's—sorry, Jacobs."

McCheney's rant ended. "Were any more shots fired at you?"

"They shot up my truck. Allie was leaning down in the seat, or the burst would have hit her in the head. Then they shot at us this morning on the mountain, just after we rolled that rock on—"

"So that's what squashed the short, scrawny perp." McCheney rubbed his chin. "How big was that rock?"

Jeff pointed a thumb at his large refrigerator.

"Holy moly!" Nelson's eyes widened.

McCheney stared at the refrigerator, then looked at Jeff. "How did you move a boulder that size?"

Allie took Jeff's hand. "Rock 'n roll."

Jeff grinned. "You know what they say about that old time rock and roll?"

"It didn't soothe that thug's soul. Too bad you didn't squash a few more of them." McCheney stood. "Nelson, assemble the team. We're flying south in five minutes. I'll coordinate with the San Francisco office while were en route."

He turned to Wes. "Take good care of these two. When does your buddy arrive?"

"He'll be here before dark. Got it all covered, McCheney."

Wes stepped outside the front door as the SWAT team hurried to the chopper.

Allie stood beside Jeff in the kitchen and curled an arm around his waist. "We need to pray for them Jeff, and for my family. I'd like to try ... if you'll help me."

"Pray, Allie. You'll do fine."

Allie poured her heart out to the God she had refused to trust twenty-four hours ago, to *her* God.

Jeff's prayer added the few things she had missed.

By the time the chopper took off at three o'clock, they had covered all the bases with their prayers. It was now time for the cleanup men, the FBI, to hit a grand slam, finding her family alive and well.

Since they were confined to the house for the rest of the afternoon, Jeff fielded her questions about his family. He showed her some of his mom's things around the house, antiques, family pictures, and a big music collection. But he said little about himself as an adult. And he avoided a glass hutch with trophies and sports paraphernalia.

Jeff had secrets he was guarding. But he was a good man. What could there possibly be that he wasn't willing to tell her? His mother died two months ago. Some of the memories might be too painful to talk about.

Shortly after five o'clock, Wes stepped outside to check the perimeter of the house. Jeff's phone rang a few seconds later.

He stared at the phone, as if reluctant to move toward it.

Allie nodded toward the phone. "Aren't you going to answer it, Jeff? It could be important news."

He grabbed the phone and pressed a button. "Hello." His eyes narrowed. "Alejandra? ... Wait a minute, I'll have to get her."

Jeff muted the receiver with his hand. Someone wants to talk to you, Allie, and they're trying really hard to speak good English, without an accent. I don't think you should—"

"Give me the phone, Jeff. No one can hurt me through a phone line."

Jeff slowly pushed the phone at her. "Be careful. We'll need to tell Wes about this."

She took the phone and walked a few steps from Jeff. "Hello."

"Is this Alejandra?" A gravelly voice spoke with a heavy accent.

"Yes."

"Does Alejandra wish to see her family with or without

114

their heads?"

She gasped.

"I think that means *with* their heads. Come to the forest at the eastern edge of the field behind Jeff Jacobs' house at precisely 11:00 p.m. If you don't, we will kill your family. Do not tell the police. Do not tell anyone about our conversation, including the man who answered. No tricks. As I speak, we have a knife to your little brother's throat. Remember you are being watched. Eleven o'clock at the eastern edge of the field, do you understand?"

"Yes."

The man hung up.

"Allie, it was one of the cartel goons, wasn't it?"

Jeff knew, but she couldn't let him know everything. "It was them. They're trying to frighten me, keep me from talking, or ... or testifying. But I promised them nothing." It wasn't a lie, but it *was* deceit.

"We have to tell Wes about the call. They'll probably want to trace it, maybe bug the phone, or whatever they do in these cases."

"I'll let Wes know when he comes back in."

"Let me know what? About the phone call you just receive from some cartel thug?" Wes had entered through the back door.

"Wes, how did you know?" How much had he heard?

"It's my business to know if I'm going to keep you safe. We weren't set up to record it, but we already traced the call. It went to a public phone. A deputy sheriff has been dispatched, but he won't find them when he gets there."

She looked at Wes and shook her head, glad the FBI couldn't bug her brain. Allie replayed her words from the phone call. "Yes." Then she had gasped followed by another "yes." She hadn't given her plans away to anyone. But fooling Jeff wouldn't be easy. It wasn't something she wanted to do. If he knew, he would physically stop her from doing what she must do.

Between now and eleven o'clock, she had to look normal, raise no suspicions. But what she planned to do would hurt Jeff, hurt him deeply. That thought shredded her already aching heart. How could she soften the blow? If they found her body like the cartel would leave it—she couldn't let her mind go there. Nothing could soften that blow.

Maybe she shouldn't soften any blows. That would only cause Jeff to follow her. Maybe the blow needed to be a knockout punch, one that took him out of her life. That might keep him safe, and it was a small price to pay for a woman who was probably about to die.

Just before nine o'clock, a knock sounded on the front door.

"It's my partner, Cliff," Wes said.

Jeff stood beside the couch where he and Allie had been sitting. He took her hand and pulled her to her feet. "Let's meet the rest of the team. We're probably going to spend a lot of time with these two."

A tall, muscular man in jeans and a sport coat entered. His gaze settled on Allie, and he smiled.

Wes glanced at Allie, then back to his partner. "Cliff,

this is Allie Jacobs ... whoops, I mean Allie Santiago."

Allie gave Jeff a quick glance. Their gazes locked.

Jeff smiled.

Allie couldn't return it. Her heart had been ripped from her chest by thoughts of the price she must pay for her decision to go and the manner in which she must leave.

Cliff's hand reached out to greet her.

She took it, trying to look calm though her heart played a wild percussion solo in her chest.

"I'm Cliff Johnson. Glad to meet you, Allie."

She nodded, afraid her voice might betray her.

Jeff reached out a hand. "Jeff Jacobs. How do you do, Cliff."

There were two marshals now. More scrutiny. Could she pull this off?

Cliff and Wes excused themselves and walked into the den.

Allie plopped back onto the couch.

Jeff sat down beside her. "Something's wrong, Allie. You're ... well, acting strange."

This was much harder than she anticipated. "I'm worried because we haven't heard from McCheney, and it'll be dark soon."

Her words were all deceit. And lying to the man who had captured her heart seemed to drown her in a sea of guilt. Allie hated what she was doing. But, if she loved Jeff, she had to steal her heart from him or he would die, too.

"Yeah. It's almost dark," Jeff said. "I've been thinking about that too." He took her hand.

She interlaced their fingers. The feeling of Jeff's strong hand intimately intertwined with hers brought tears to her eyes. She tried to blink them back. It was useless. The dam had been breached again, and the reservoir poured down her cheeks.

Jeff's free hand pulled her head snugly against his neck. "It's going to be okay, Allie. You'll see."

It *wouldn't* be okay. It would *never* be okay. Her silent tears turn to sobs. She clung to Jeff for the last time.

After Allie's sobbing ended, she didn't want to let go. She pulled Jeff into a fierce hug.

Wes cleared his throat as he approached Jeff and Allie.

Allie sat up and released Jeff's hand, then wiped her cheeks.

"What did you do to her, Jeff? If you hurt this young lady, you'll answer to me." Wes stood in front of them, hands on his hips.

Wes meant well, but she needed to set him straight. "Jeff was only trying to comfort me ... about my mom, dad, and brother, Benjamin."

"Oh. I wanted you to know, the guest bedroom, Allie's room, is off limits to us men. House rules."

Jeff looked up at Wes, who was hardly ten years older

than Jeff. "Yes, Dad." He gave Wes a thin-lipped smile. "You keep Allie safe by doing your job, and I'll keep her safe by doing mine."

"Touché." Wes grinned. "Okay, let's get back to work, Cliff."

Allie's heart sank as she thought about these people so dedicated to her safety. She was betraying them. Maybe she was betraying God. At that thought, her stomach roiled. She ran to the bathroom and retched. Once. Twice. It wasn't going to stop anytime soon.

How could she do this to Jeff, the marshals, the FBI, to herself?

"Are you okay, Allie?" Jeff's voice came from just outside the door.

"I'm okay now. Just an upset stomach."

She rinsed her mouth, washed her face, then glanced at the small bathroom wall clock. It said 10:20 p.m. Almost time. She opened the door and found Jeff waiting in the hallway.

"I'm not feeling well. I'm going to bed now." She hugged Jeff and kissed his cheek but didn't meet his gaze. "Good night, Jeff."

"See you in the morning, Allie."

"Yes, in the morning." She lied again.

Chapter 11

Allie closed her bedroom door and sobs came, deep guttural groans, the sounds of a soul committing suicide. She curled up on the bed and buried her wet face in her pillow to mute the mourning of a heart broken beyond repair.

She had lied to Jeff. Deliberately deceived him. After what she had done, Jeff would never understand, would he? Maybe she could leave him a note and try to explain.

Allie wiped her eyes and surveyed the room. There was no desk, but the top drawer in the dresser by the bed contained some writing materials. She pulled out a notepad and a pen, then sat on the edge of the bed, seeking words to explain the unexplainable.

The words wouldn't come, so Allie simply wrote the truth. Now her words flowed with ease. True words from a person's heart were far more easily composed than cruel lies.

She finished the note to Jeff and re-read it.

Please forgive me, Jeff. I lied to you. It literally made me sick to do it, but I didn't know what else to do.

They said they would kill Benjamin if I didn't agree to meet them in the forest at 11:00 p.m. I know they won't let me or my family go, but I'm praying I can buy some time, so we have at least a small chance for the FBI to find us.

In case that doesn't happen, there are some things I need to tell you. These words can't possibly say it all, but I will try.

You are a good man, Jeff Jacobs. I love the way you gently pointed me toward God. I love the way you have protected me. I love the way you comfort me, especially the comfort of your arms. I love your soft kisses on my forehead. What I'm trying to say is love doesn't come from the time, but from the knowing. After what we've been through together, I know you, Jeff, and I love you.

Please pray for me.

Allie.

What was she thinking? Allie couldn't give this to Jeff. After reading this message, no power on earth could stop him from following her. It would get him killed.

She ripped the page from the notepad, threw it beside her on the bed, and sought words that would end their relationship, words that would keep Jeff safe.

Tears blurred her vision while she struggled to write her cruel lies. When she read the new note. She wanted to tear it up, to run to Jeff and tell him everything.

Allie trembled as she tore the new note from the pad.

Tears came as she placed it on the pillow.

You have to do this, girl.

Her body rebelled. It wouldn't move from the bed.

Allie needed to leave now or she would start retching, again.

The alarm clock by the bed said 10:55 p.m. Out of time, Allie stood to leave and gasped. She'd almost left her first note on the bed. She grabbed it.

The room would be searched. There was no safe place here for the note. She stuffed it into the pocket of her shorts.

Allie walked softly to the door, opened it a crack, and peered out. No one in the hallway.

She opened the door farther and looked down the hallway to the living room.

Shadows moved across the floor. The marshals. But they stood near the window, not where they could see her.

Allie took a deep breath and exhaled slowly, trying to calm her volatile stomach. She tiptoed to the end of the hallway and slipped out the back door of the house.

She ran to the fence behind the house and stopped beside three strands of barbed wire. The enormity of her lies to Jeff ripped her conscience like the barbs on that fence would rip her skin if she wasn't careful.

In the wake of her damaged conscience, a dark cloud settled over her. Nothing good lay in Alejandra Santiago's future, now. Perhaps one bleak hope remained, that her future, and the pain in it, would be short.

Girl, you need to get a grip and get across that field before they hurt Benjamin.

The field directly behind the house was a pasture with short grass. The marshals might spot her crossing it. If so, they would stop her.

In the adjacent field to the north, the profuse growth of tall grass and weeds reached nearly to her waist. Allie walked along the fence to the northern field, slipped through the strands of wire, and crouched low as she scurried through the moonlit field toward the forest.

Halfway across the field, Allie looked back over her shoulder at the house. No lights flashed on in her bedroom, no loud voices. They didn't know she had left. But, if anyone came out of the house, she would drop to her knees in the tall grass.

Now beyond the reach of the house lights, Allie ran eastward toward the trees, holding her queasy stomach with her left hand while her right hand, pressed to her chest, held a broken heart. The deed had been done. Irreversible damage.

When Allie entered the forest she slowed and glanced around her. Had she misunderstood the man who called?

Beams of moonlight, filtered by the forest canopy, lit parts of the forest floor. She stopped and scanned the area around her. But there were no signs of—

A hand clamped over her mouth and sweaty arms pulled her against damp clothing. A foul breath blew against the back of her neck, causing her stomach to churn. "Be quiet or you will die on this spot." A man's voice hissed the words.

She stiffened and fought the urge to drive her elbow into his stomach and run back to Jeff. She fought for control until a sharp prick stung her back. Allie gasped.

"Can you feel the knife against your back, *pollita*? Do not make a sound or this knife will sever your spine. Do you understand me?"

She nodded slowly. Her dipping head caused her lips to press against the disgusting hand.

"I am going to remove my hand and you are going to remain silent. Do we agree on this?"

Again she nodded.

The hand jerked from her mouth.

Another hand slapped a strip of duct tape over her mouth.

The tape pinched her lip against her teeth, cutting the soft tissue inside Allie's lip. That brought the salty, metal taste of blood.

A powerful hand gripped her wrist.

She breathed furiously through her nose. Not enough air. With the tape over her mouth, she couldn't catch her breath. She would suffocate.

Allie had to breathe, now. She reached for the tape.

"No, *pollita*." The man yanked her arm down. He pulled her steadily toward something sitting in a dark spot under a tree. An ATV.

Choking, hurting, suffocating—Allie's stomach roiled. Bile rose into her throat. She swallowed hard and tasted more blood, gagging on it.

A short, stocky man with long hair climbed onto the ATV seat.

The man holding Allie lifted her off the ground and set her on the seat behind short man.

"Hang on to Hector and do not try any tricks. I'm driving behind you and watching, you worthless little...." The man's vulgar names added to the contamination of touching his sweaty body.

The greasy tresses of the goon in front of her, Hector, turned Allie's revulsion into full-fledged nausea.

She ripped the tape from her lips.

Hector's filthy hair lashed her face and flew into her mouth.

Allie's stomach erupted. Whatever was left of its contents splattered onto Hector's neck and back.

He bowed his shoulders and arched his back, crying out like he'd been stabbed. Hector swung a leg off the ATV, whirled, and slapped her face.

Allie ignored the sting of his slap and tried to catch her breath.

The foul-breathed thug from the other ATV approached and tried to slap another strip of tape over her mouth.

"No! I'll vomit and choke," she managed between breaths.

"Shut up," he hissed. "From now on you answer only

by nodding. That is all you need to do, because the correct answer will always be yes. Do you understand?"

She nodded. With the threat of the tape gone, her breathing slowed.

He dropped the tape to the ground. "See how accommodating I am? But if you make a sound, I will peel your little brother alive in front of you, then your mother, and then the fun really begins. Have I convinced you to keep quiet?"

In an instant, Allie's panic fled and her fear morphed to seething anger. But she could not let them see her defiance. She needed to appear intimidated.

"Are you convinced? Answer me, now."

Allie lowered her gaze from the man's face to the dark forest floor and nodded.

"We have wasted far too much time on you."

Two engines started and revved.

In a few more seconds, Allie flew through the forest. The greasy hair of the unkempt, uncouth man flew in her face, brushing her lips. Her urge to vomit came again. She fought it off by picturing herself grabbing Hector's head and gouging out his eyes. The fear that they would hurt Benjamin stopped her.

They would likely kill her if she tried anything and she had to stay alive long enough to reach her family, to know they were alive. Until then, she would pray the FBI could find and rescue them.

And Jeff? After what she'd done to him, Jeff belonged

to her past, not to whatever remained of Allie's future.

* * *

Jeff stayed up with Wes and Cliff after Allie went to bed sick. He waited with the marshals hoping McCheney and the helicopter would return with news about her family.

Cliff's cell rang. He answered, exchanged a few words, then hung up. "The chopper is returning, but it's still several miles out."

"Why are you still up, Jacobs?" Wes asked. "If you had any sense you'd go to bed like Allie."

"Do you always insult your clients?"

"Clients?"

"Yeah. I pay your salary."

"Well, why don't you get some rest and let me earn my salary?"

Jeff had no reason to stay up now that Allie had gone to bed and the chopper was going to be later than they expected. "See you guys in the morning."

His bed felt good to Jeff's tired body, but sleep wouldn't come. Worries about Allie kept him awake. Why had her mood become so gloomy? Was it only because she felt ill?

He prayed for Allie, for her family, and for the FBI in their search. The peace that usually followed praying eluded him. So did sleep.

The same uneasy feeling that crawled up his spine

before Allie ran out of the woods returned. Though the marshal's house rules restricted Jeff from entering Allie's room, he couldn't sleep until he knew she was okay.

Jeff opened his bedroom door, walked down the hall to Allie's room, and reached for the doorknob.

"Sorry, Jeff. That's off limits. You can survive without Allie until morning. You saw what she went through this evening. She needs some sleep."

"There's something wrong here, Wes. If you're not going to let me go in, then you check on Allie."

"If it'll shut you up, I'll look in on her."

Jeff stepped away from the door.

Wes knocked softly and waited.

No response.

Wes cracked the door and looked in. His eyes widened. He pushed the door open farther, then hit the light.

Allie was gone.

"Maybe she's in the bathroom," Wes said.

"She's not, Wes. The door's open." The thumping of Jeff's heart became a wild drumming.

Wes ran down the hallway toward the living room. "Cliff, call the local police and the Sheriff. Allie's gone. I'll call McCheney. Then you and I need to start searching for her."

Both marshals were busy in the living room, so Jeff stepped into Allie's bedroom looking for clues as to what happened. His gaze locked on a sheet of paper folded in half on Allie's pillow. He stepped to the bed and picked it up.

When he unfolded the sheet of paper his eyes stopped at the first word written on the page, "Jeff."

He continued reading.

I have something that I must do for my family. In fact, I've finally come to my senses and realized that whatever passed between us was only a brief infatuation that came from my moments of weakness and vulnerability.

It's my family that matters most to me and you are not part of it. Our relationship would never have worked, anyway. My father would never allow it.

Thank you for saving my life. I will be forever grateful. But that is all.

Goodbye, Jeff. I wish you well.

Alejandra

He stared at the sheet of paper. Her cold message came like a stunning blow. Could Allie have written this? Not the woman he knew. Or was it that he didn't really know her? After all, how well could he know another person in less than forty-eight hours?

Where she had signed her name, large, swollen circles marred the paper. Allie's tears.

Mixed signals. It didn't add up.

The phone call? It must have instigated all this, both her message and her leaving.

The reason she gave for leaving ...

I have something that I must do for my family.

Allie was sacrificing herself for her family, or trying to. At that thought, something stirred so deep in Jeff's heart that it frightened him. In the next instant, all fear was gone, replaced by a resolve to find Allie, no matter the difficulty, the danger, or the cost. And he would not accept the message in her note until she repeated it to his face.

Jeff stepped out of Allie's bedroom and looked down the hallway toward the living room.

Wes had his cell glued to his ear, and Cliff punched buttons on his phone.

If the cartel had used the phone call to coerce Allie to meet them, the meeting place would probably be in the edge of the trees across the field to the east. That was the nearest hidden approach to the house.

The front of his house was well lit. She wouldn't have gone that direction. But the back of the house ...

Jeff slipped out the back door, leaped the fence, and sprinted across the field, his powerful legs ripping the sod with each stride.

A few seconds later, Jeff's heart thumped hard as he slowed to enter the trees. If she came this way, Allie might still be in the vicinity.

Jeff stopped and brutally willed his oxygen-starved body to stop breathing. He managed to create enough time between two breaths to listen. The brief silence was broken by the sounds of two engines droning through the dark forest. Two small, four-cycle engines.

The cartel goons had taken Allie on an ATV.

Jeff looked into the trees, toward the sounds of the ATVs. Somewhere in the distance, a light flashed through a gap in the trees.

He turned and looked toward his house.

Jeff clenched his jaw, turned toward the forest, and sprinted into the dark shadows toward the sounds of the ATVs, toward whatever danger lay ahead, and toward Allie.

Chapter 12

Jeff ran with reckless abandon toward the sounds of the two ATVs. He hurdled logs and leaped small bushes, fearing losing the ATVs more than anything the night or the forest might hold.

Knowing the general lay of the land helped. This was the dry side of the valley, sheltered from much of the rain.

He flew through the widely spaced Ponderosa pine trees covering the mountain slopes and weaved through several stands of white oak and Madrone trees. The sparse vegetation allowed moonbeams to light the ground. It was enough for Jeff to run.

Dense patches of Manzanita dominated the areas burned by forest fires in previous years. The current path of the ATVs would soon bring them to such an area. The ATVs would have to circle around the Manzanita, while Jeff could plow through it. Slicing off distance at every opportunity was the only way he could hope to close on the ATVs.

Jeff's biggest disadvantage, he didn't know the ATVs destination. Were they taking her to a car or truck? If so,

Allie was—he refused dwell on that possibility.

But, if Jeff caught them, what could he do? The truth was, he'd probably get shot. He shoved that depressing thought from his mind and focused on running the fastest mile he'd ever run. Pictures of Allie being held captive by such depraved members of humanity sent Jeff into a sprint.

During the assault on Bolan Peak, she had begged him not to let the cartel thugs have her. Now, the cartel had her and, once again, Jeffrey Jacobs was a failure. Regardless, this time he refused to run from his failures. He *would* get Allie back.

After a half-mile of hard running, Jeff's deep gasps for air forced him to settle into a slower, steadier pace. He needed to run smarter, not harder.

Thankful that the ATVs sounded no farther ahead, he sought ways to close on them. Jeff turned toward the northeast.

The ATVS had headed toward a deep ravine where a creek flowed down from the mountains. The cartel thugs would have to cross the creek well below the ravine if they planned to continue going northeastward. Riding double with Allie, they could not cut straight across.

But I can.

Jeff ran into an open area and stopped. Here the ravine became a narrow canyon. A protruding boulder provided a launching ramp that might enable him to jump the twenty-foot-wide gorge. If he could leap across it, he could gain a quarter mile or more.

The long jump wasn't his best decathlon event, though

he had leaped more than twenty-five feet. But did his tired legs have a twenty-foot jump left in them?

Jeff stopped and studied the distance in the moonlight. It was a downhill jump. That would help.

He would either make the jump and have a chance to catch up to Allie or, if he didn't clear the ravine, he wouldn't have to listen to disparaging remarks about Jeff Jacobs anymore. But the consequences of failing to make this jump sent adrenaline surging through his veins.

Full of energy now, Jeff backed up several yards and sprinted toward his long jump board, the boulder.

Jeff gathered himself for the jump. When his left foot hit the outer edge of the rock, he launched his body out over the chasm. His legs pedaled, churning the air with the form of an accomplished long jumper. His body flew through the moonlit area and into the darkness of a shadow cast by a large pine tree.

Jeff's feet hit and dug into the dirt. He had made it across. He drove his arms backward, propelling his body forward so he wouldn't fall back into the gorge.

His chest slammed into the trunk of the tree. Jeff fell on his rear. Sitting on a bed of pine needles, he shook off the stunned feeling and jumped to his feet.

A loud buzz came from his left side.

Jeff leaped hard to his right.

He pulled his feet up to his body while he flew through the air.

A long, dark form shot toward the spot where he'd

been standing, then blended with the dark forest floor.

When his feet hit the ground, Jeff jumped farther to his right and sprinted eastward.

Behind him, the big timber rattler continued its buzzing complaint.

Jeff didn't mind snakes, only the poisonous variety. If he'd been bitten by a large rattler, he would've had to stop running or the venom would kill him.

A defensive rattler should have been able to bite him. In spite of Jeff's disgrace and failure, he had been protected. That thought encouraged him as he continued running toward the sound of the ATVs.

The ATV engines labored, lugging down. They must be climbing the mountain ahead. If the climb took its toll on the machines, it would take an even greater toll on his body.

He ran up the small mountain taking shortcuts wherever possible, but the sounds of the engines said he wasn't gaining. His lungs burned from the abuse, but Jeff stumbled ahead on rubbery legs.

The steep grade slowed him to a walk as he climbed the last few steps to the top of the mountain. He stopped. Something had changed.

No ATV engines.

What did that mean? Were they loading Allie into a car?

He summoned the strength to run from the mountaintop down to a clearing that provided a view of the valley shrouded in darkness.

Below, in the small, sheltered valley, a light flickered. A campfire.

Would they be so careless as to build a fire?

He had crossed several hills and a mountain. The camp lay several miles from civilization, hidden in a small valley. At 1:00 a.m. in such a remote place, they probably felt safe. And, obviously, they were not expecting a visitor.

As Jeff descended the mountain toward the light below, he sought a plan, any kind of a plan, to free Allie and to stop the ATVs from carrying her away again. He had ruled out stealing an ATV. That was too risky. But neither did he want armed thugs chasing Allie and him on those machines.

The camp lay only fifty yards ahead now, beyond some bushes and trees. The sound of running water came from the other side of the camp, and above the sounds of the brook, the murmur of voices.

Maybe the running water would cover some of his noises, but he needed to avoid—a sharp crack sounded. He had stepped on a dry branch.

Jeff stopped.

So did the voices in the camp.

How could he have been so careless? The only redeeming thing about his miscue was his distance from them. If they came looking, they probably couldn't find him before he slipped away.

Jeff waited and watched.

Two men stood and turned slowly in a full circle scanning the surrounding darkness. When they finished, one of them shrugged. The other sat.

That was strike one. He couldn't afford another.

After a couple of minutes, the murmur of voices in the camp resumed.

One man walked to a vehicle beyond the firelight. A pickup. He pulled what looked like several sleeping bags from it and carried them back toward the others near the fire.

Jeff needed to spot Allie now and to get an accurate accounting of both men and vehicles.

He circled toward the pickup, keeping the vehicle between him and the men. There were two four-wheel-drive pickups and, only a few yards away, lay an old logging road. The overgrown road appeared to end at this spot. Probably the site of an old logging landing.

One thing was certain, he could not let them put Allie into one of those pickups. They would head down that road and he would never see her again.

Between the trucks and the fire, partially hidden by bushes, sat two SUVs.

He circled the camp until he was between the brook and the fire. Where was Allie?

Thoughts of what they might be doing to her broke his concentration. Jeff's stomach churned. If he didn't spot her soon, he was going to lose it, do something crazy, and get himself killed.

As he often did during track and field competitions, Jeff brutally stuffed his emotions and stuck to his task, studying the camp.

Four men sat near the fire, one less than the number who had escaped uninjured from their battle at Bolan Peak. One man must be tending to business elsewhere.

Three of the men had dark hair and skin like most Hispanics. The fourth was definitely Caucasian.

Jeff listened to their words. They often started sentences in English then transitioned to Spanish.

When the Spanish words began, the Caucasian man launched a complaint. The three others switched back to English. If the pattern held, Jeff could follow most of their conversation.

He moved closer, not more than twenty-five yards from the men. He surveyed the perimeter of the lighted area. Allie!

He tried to muffle his gasp.

She sat facing a tree only fifteen or twenty yards in front of him.

Allie's profile, silhouetted by the firelight, showed her hugging a Madrone, apparently tied with her arms around the tree.

His gaze remained locked on Allie, studying her. How did she really feel about Jeff Jacobs?

The men's words yanked his attention back to them.

"She knows too much and has cost us far too much, already. Today the FBI took over the second plantation.

They killed Gustav and Leonardo. Of course, they were already wounded, not much use to us. We even had to..." The goon walked over to Allie and stroked her hair, "... to move papa, mama, and little brother Benjamin..." He yanked on her hair.

Allie groaned then swiveled her head toward the men.

Jeff could imagine her fierce glare.

"We need to move them to the last plantation," the tall man said.

"I think we need to kill them all, cut our losses, and leave these mountains. They are cursed." The stumpy goon with the long hair turned toward the other three by the fire. "Do you want to rot in a cell for the rest of your life because of what *una pollita* knows? If we are caught, that's what will happen, because she knows far too much."

The Caucasian man appeared restless. His foot tapped out a snappy rhythm on the ground. He leaned forward, holding his hands near the flames. "I joined you for the money."

The long-haired man sneered at him. "You did not join *us*. We chose *you* and made the offer. Do you think you could've refused it? No, gringo. We kill those who refuse."

"Regardless, I'm in it for the money. We've lost over two million dollars because of her and our losses are growing." He pointed toward Allie. "If we keep her away from the pimps, we can sell her to one of the big-time dealers. If she's unspoiled goods, she'll bring a good price.

"You're right about *una pollita*. If she is, as you say unspoiled, the international traffickers operating near

Portland might pay as much as four-hundred thousand dollars for one like her. They could double their money in a year. And maybe a hundred thousand for her little brother. It's not two million, but if we ..." he looked at Allie, "... work *papacito* and *mama* until they drop, or until we are forced to move, we might recoup half our loss. Perhaps we would stay in favor with El Capitan's son. That would probably save our heads."

Hearing the man speak of Allie as mere merchandise lit a raging fire inside of Jeff. By the time he had doused the fire, his body shook. He was breathing too hard and too loud. Jeff covered his face with his hands to muffle the sounds.

The stocky, greasy-haired man approached Allie. "So, *mi pollita*, am I looking at unspoiled goods? Answer me!"

"I would not dishonor my family." Allie's words dripped with disdain. "So what do *you* think?" She spat on him.

The man drew back a boot to kick her.

"Cool it, Hector!" The tall quiet one's voice spoke with authority. "Both unspoiled and undamaged is what brings top dollar. Surely you can find other ways to vent your frustration than kicking *una pollita* in the face. In fact, I will help you. You stand the first *two* watches tonight. And leave the girl alone. Do you understand?"

Hector snorted a reply in Spanish, then retreated to the fire.

"Good. It is settled. We take the girl with us and sell her at the first opportunity. Now, we should all get some sleep ... except for you, Hector. *Buenas noches.*"

With one man standing guard, maybe he could free

Allie. A plan had been perking in his mind since he surveyed the vehicles.

Hector plopped down on a log near the fire, folding his arms and apparently moping over the redress from their leader.

If only he would mope himself to sleep.

Jeff fished through his shorts pocket until his fingers wrapped around his knife. He smiled and began to mouth the words of a lullaby, words that Jeff hoped God would relay to the mind of the long-haired thug on the log.

Then, Jeff waited.

Chapter 13

Jeff's heart drummed in a wild percussion solo. Raw nerves churned his stomach to nausea. Could a man without a weapon steal Allie from armed thugs, men who faced danger on a daily basis and prevailed?

Dude, if you muff this, you don't even want to think about what will happen.

Jeff squelched the annoying voice in his mind and focused on the guard.

Hector's head had slumped forward three minutes ago. His eyes hadn't glanced at Allie for at least five.

Jeff crept closer to her, feeling the forest floor for the dried leaves and bark of the Madrone trees, the early warning radar of Southern Oregon forests

His hand stopped on a cluster of dried Madrone berries. Perfect.

Jeff scooped up the berries and squeezed to crush the brittle stems. The berries rolled into his palm. He picked out several of these pea-size Madrone seeds.

Only ten yards from Allie now, he studied her silhouette. It showed her hugging a tree trunk, trying to use it as a pillow.

She shifted from cheek to cheek against the tree.

That picture of her discomfort ripped at his heart. But, if he couldn't free her, mere discomfort didn't compare to the plans the goons had made for Allie.

Jeff moved closer, positioning himself so the lingering flames of the fire lit his face for Allie without giving Hector an angle to spot Jeff through the tree branches.

He held up his hand in the firelight and studied it. Even in the dim light of the dying fire he could see the flesh tones in his fingers. Allie should be able to see him, but would she know it was him? And, after the note, how would she react?

He slid forward, gently pushing the layer of dry leaves to the sides ahead of him. Soon he had created a trail bare of any leaves or bark.

Now only a dozen feet from Allie, he pinched a berry between his thumb and forefinger. He aimed as if throwing a dart and launched the tiny missile at Allie's arm.

It bounced off the tree below her arm and landed quietly on the ground.

He adjusted his aim and tossed another berry. It hit the tree beside her head.

Allie moved her head and adjusted her cheek against the hard pillow.

He aimed and tossed two berries in rapid succession.

The first found her arm, the second bounced off her head.

She pulled her head back and looked around her.

The next berry hit her between the eyes. Her gaze followed the berry's trajectory until Allie gasped. Her head turned. She shot a glance at the dozing Hector, then focused on Jeff's face. Now her body shook in spasms.

Was she crying?

He shoved a closed fist at her then popped it open displaying five fingers while he tapped his watch. He mouthed the words, "Five minutes."

Allie gave him a quick nod, then glanced back at Hector.

When she looked his way again, Jeff mouthed the words, "Don't worry, I will save you, Allie."

She nodded again.

He flashed five fingers again then backed away, using his approach path.

Unable to reach her face with her hands, Allie rubbed her cheeks on her upper arms, wiping away tears.

But what emotions had brought the tears? Guilt? Gratefulness? At this point, it didn't matter. The only thing that mattered was getting Allie safely away from this scurvy crew.

Jeff turned and hurried toward the vehicles. He had to wreak as much havoc as possible in five short minutes while remaining silent.

The fire had died down to glowing coals. He could

move more freely without being detected as long as he was quiet. After circling back to the pickups, Jeff crept ahead to the ATVs.

Somewhere in the distance the whop, whop of a helicopter rotor sounded in the night sky. It passed by far to the south.

McCheney must have finished his other task and was heading back to Jeff's house. That would not be a pleasant place to be when McCheney found that the marshals had lost both of their witnesses.

Jeff opened his small knife and reached under the first ATV until he felt the engine. His fingers walked up the warm engine to the top. The rubber tube they encountered felt cool against his skin.

He grasped the tube with his left hand, pulling it taught, and slit the ATV's throat. After cutting the other end of the fuel line, he pulled the segment of hose out and cut it in half to prevent reuse. To be safe, he would hide the pieces of fuel line where the goons wouldn't find them.

The air had cooled considerably in the mountain valley. The low-level inversion trapped the pungent odor of gasoline near the ground. Soon Hector, or one of the other men, would smell trouble and come to investigate.

He needed to hurry.

After another slice with his knife the second ATV oozed its life onto the engine, where it puddled before dripping onto the ground.

After killing the ATVs, Jeff circled back to the creek. Now the odor of gasoline was strong, maybe strong enough to wake them.

Jeff stopped at the spot where he had thrown the Madrone berries and studied Allie.

She held her cheek against the side of the tree and stared back onto the darkness, toward him.

Fifteen feet of dry Madrone leaves and curled bark slowed him. He carefully ran his hands under the leaves, like a plow, and pushed them to the sides to clear the way to Allie.

When he reached her, he touched her cheek. It was wet.

She avoided his gaze. Whatever her reasons, it hurt to see the woman he loved doing that.

Jeff pushed the knife into the dim light of the dying fire.

She looked at the knife for a moment, then pulled her hands apart, stretching the bands taught against the tree trunk.

In a quick, satisfying motion, he cut Allie's slavery.

Jeff glanced at Hector.

The man was out, breathing heavily.

Jeff guided Allie around the tree to the path he had cleared, then slipped behind her.

With his hands on her waist, Jeff guided her silently toward the brook.

At the water's edge, Allie stopped and swiveled toward him. Severed nylon bands brushed his skin as her arms circled his neck, squeezing with surprising strength. The sobbing began again.

He needed to get her away before someone heard her.

Something pulled Jeff's attention from Allie.

The air reeked of gasoline, burning his nostrils with each breath.

"Follow me, Allie. Be quiet and hurry."

She took his hand. "I was a fool. They weren't going to take me to my family ... just sell me to—Jeff, take me away from here. Please." Her soft whisper had grown more intense and far too loud.

He pulled her toward the creek without replying.

"Through the water?" She whispered.

"You'll understand in a few—"

"*Gasolina! Gasolina!*" Hector's frantic voice.

"*La pollita se ha ido!*"

Chapter 14

What had the goon's last few words meant? "I understood the gasoline part, but—"

"He said that I was gone," Allie whispered.

Jeff and Allie splashed through the water. He stepped ahead and pushed through the willows on the far side of the Creek, creating an opening for her.

Jeff climbed a few feet up the steep bank on the east side of the creek and pulled Allie up beside him.

The muffled rumble of ATV starters turning the engines repeated several times.

"Did you do something to their ATVs?"

"Yeah. I murdered them. Slit their fuel lines."

He trudged up the steep hill holding tight to Allie's hand. "What does *pollita* mean?"

"I told you they were referring to me. But don't call me that, Jeff. You probably have a lot of things you want to call me right now. But maybe sometime, if you'd like, you can call me *mi novia*."

148

This was interesting. Though he didn't know what *novia* meant, Jeff understood *mi* and that lifted part of the weight from his heavy heart.

He pulled her over the top of the rise and descended the hill, putting a more comfortable distance between them and the camp.

"Okay, *mi novia*. Enough Spanish lessons. We need to circle around to the west and try to get back to Wes and Cliff. Did you hear the chopper fly by?"

"I heard it."

Jeff stopped. "Listen." He paused. "They started one of the pickups."

Allie stepped beside him. "Do you think they're leaving?"

"Not all in one truck. My guess is that two or three of them will track us, even if they have to wait until daylight."

Jeff turned south, parallel to the slope, and picked up the pace. "You haven't had much sleep for several nights. How are you doing?"

"You're here. I'm fine."

They had a lot to talk over, but the clues Allie kept dropping gave him reason to hope that it would be a good conversation when it happened.

"Jeff, where do you think the pickup is going? I'm worried about my family."

"I don't think it's headed to that third plantation."

She moved up beside him. "So you overheard their conversation?"

"Yeah. I don't think that gang will do anything about your family until they deal with us. We're their greatest threat."

Allie sighed sharply. "I don't feel like a threat, only threatened."

"Whoever's in the truck probably has orders to cut us off from the house. There's a forest service road about five miles due west of my place. From there, he can cut us off from the east or circle around to the Bolan Peak road and cut us off from the south."

"But..." Allie looked up at the moon in the western sky, "... we're headed south. Why not north?"

He pulled her to a stop on top of a flat ridge. "I'll answer your question if you'll answer mine."

She stared up into his eyes. The moon lit her face and her eyes sparkled its reflection. "Okay."

"We can't go north because that's where the first pickup is headed. If the other one should leave, too, it would have to start out to the north. The terrain there is flat. If we were up there, they could even drive off-road to chase us. They'd run us down."

"Then south it is."

They walked along the ridge line for nearly a mile. When it curved to the southeast, Jeff led Allie off the ridge and down the slope into a sparse pine forest.

"What about your question, Jeff? You haven't asked—"

"Don't worry. I won't forget to ask it." The note, why she wrote it, what she really felt— it was sure to come up when they had a chance to talk.

Jeff glanced at his watch. 3:00 a.m. In another hour or so, the early dawn would send the cartel gunmen out looking for them. Unless the goons were good trackers, he should be able to get Allie to his house even if he had to carry her. But the man who left in the truck concerned him.

So did Allie. She was obviously tiring, slower stepping over obstacles, struggling up small banks. Her breathing grew louder and more labored.

He stopped. "I could use a rest."

She stepped close and leaned on him, pressing her head against his shoulder. "Thank you, Jeff. I was really getting tired."

This didn't jive with the note. Thanking him. Her head pressed into him and her arms around him. It went far beyond mere gratefulness. Like her words, Allie's actions would need some explanation.

"There's a big boulder ahead, and it looks flat on top. But wait here and let me check it out. I already ran into one timber rattler tonight." He checked the rock and waved Allie up.

"Timber rattler? Cartel rattlesnakes. Jeff, you took too many chances coming after me." She paused. "How did you leave? Wes wouldn't have let you just walk out."

"Maybe I should be asking you that question."

Allie backed away from him and wiped her eye.

He took her hands and lowered her onto a seat at the edge of the rock and sat beside her. "Wes is probably still kicking himself for letting me sneak out, especially after you disappeared."

She hooked his arm with hers and leaned her head against his shoulder. "Cliff wouldn't have encouraged you either."

"Encouraged me? Your note did that." He draped an arm around her shoulders. But even as he held her, the words from Allie's note ripped through his heart like a dull jigsaw blade.

"Jeff, that note was supposed to discourage you. It was—" Her voice broke and she cried softly for a while.

"The note was all lies. I lied because I didn't want to endanger you. But there's no excuse for lying." Allie looked up at him. "Can you ever forgive me? Please, wait before you answer. You need to know the *whole* truth." She slid a hand into the pocket of her shorts and slipped out a crumpled sheet of paper. "This is the first note, the one I couldn't leave, the one that tells the truth."

Jeff took the paper from her hand and unfolded it. "Allie, it's too dark to read a note. Maybe in another hour—"

"No. It's got to be now. I ... I'll read it to you. I've played it in my mind so many times tonight that I know it by heart."

Allie began reciting the note in voice that was soft but heavy with emotion. "Please forgive me, Jeff. I lied to you. It literally made me sick to do it, but I didn't know what else to do."

She continued, pouring her broken heart out to him through words she'd penned several hours earlier.

As Jeff listened, her words shattered his heart then they repaired it, piece by broken piece.

Allie slowed as her message concluded. "After what we've been through together, I know you, Jeff, and I love you."

He drew a sharp breath at her confession.

"Please pray for me, Jeff. Allie." She stopped and wiped her cheeks.

He tried to lift her chin, to see her face in the moonlight.

She resisted. "I lied to you. Knowing how we both felt, and I still lied. I love my family and would do anything to save them. I guess I'd even lie to someone I loved."

"The most important thing isn't the lie. It's that you're sorry, and that I forgive you, completely. It never happened, Allie."

"How can you say that after what I did?"

"Forgiveness doesn't always have to be earned."

She pulled her head from his chest and looked up. "You mean like ... *expiacion.* You know, the Jesus thing."

"Expiation? Maybe. But I can't do what he does *mi novia.*" He kissed her forehead.

"But you have, Jeff."

No, he hadn't. But this was no time for a theological

debate with Allie. "You know, you still haven't told me what *mi novia* means."

"It depends."

"Depends on what?"

"On the context."

"Okay. What does it mean in the context that I used it?"

She didn't reply.

"C'mon, Allie. We've got a lot of ground to cover before daylight."

"It could mean my girlfriend or ... my fiancé."

Jeff pulled Allie's head back against his chest. "I see."

How could he ever have doubted this incredible woman?

Dude, she lied to—

He choked the accusing voice into silence, hoping he had killed it.

"Jeff ..." Her voice came in a hoarse whisper. "It was a stupid thing to do."

"You mean writing a note to discourage me? Yeah. I guess it was."

"So you think I *am* stupid?"

"Allie, it was stupid to think a note could stop me from following you."

"At the time I couldn't think of anything else to do. But it's more than just the note. Leaving like I did was stupid and it didn't help my parents. I should have known the cartel men were lying to me."

Jeff touched her cheek. His hand came away wet. He wiped Allie's tears away. "When you left, it scared me so much that I almost ... never mind that. But you did accomplish one thing. You spread the cartel members in this area so thin that they can't do anything, effectively. Maybe not even guard your family."

"I think you're just trying to make a moron feel better." She looked up into his eyes.

He looked down at Allie's face. In the waning moonlight, he couldn't see all of her features. But Jeff knew Allie's face. Vivid memories replaced the shadowed places, creating the most beautiful face he had ever seen. "Do you feel better?"

"Some. But I need you to understand something. To really believe me. I'll never lie to you again, Jeff. Never. You have my word."

"I believe you, Allie. I—"

"No. Don't say it until you feel it. Then you can say that to me."

He nodded. And waiting was probably best, because there were things he had to tell Allie before this relationship could go any deeper.

He would wait. Not because of what Allie had done. The truth was, Jeff trusted her a lot more than he trusted himself. "Okay. I'll say it to you, then. But we need to go, now. If I'm right, in about two miles we'll be close enough to my house and the Forest Service road to start worrying about that pickup."

Jeff stood and pulled Allie up beside him.

She gave him a fierce hug, took his hand, and whispered. "I'm ready now, *mi amor.*"

Mi amor?

Allie had just moved their relationship to a new level and placed him on a pedestal he didn't deserve. There were things she needed to know before those words reflected reality. Maybe someday he could become *mi amor*, but only after she knew the truth about him. And after she heard it, only if she still felt the same. Until then, he wouldn't reciprocate.

Jeff took her hand and led her from the rock across the clearing and into the trees below.

The light of dawn brightened the horizon to the east and the hilltops ahead of them.

The terrain looked familiar. Recognition sent that unsettling tingling up the back of his neck. They were only one hill from the Forest Service road, and it was light enough for the cartel gunmen to spot them.

They trudged up the hill, hand-in-hand. But, near the top, the tingling sensation came again, stronger this time. Jeff stopped.

What is it?" Allie asked.

"Did you hear anything?"

"No. Nothing."

"Allie, let's listen for a minute before we go down to the road."

Allie looked up studying his face. "Are we listening for the cartel's pickup?"

"I'm not sure what I heard. Let's just listen."

She draped an arm around his waist.

He rested an arm on her shoulders.

Even with danger lurking, it was hard to concentrate on anything other than Allie's presence. But with only a mile or two to reach his house, he couldn't afford to walk into a trap.

They waited another minute, but there was only silence.

Jeff took her hand and they descended the hill moving cautiously toward the road, working their way around clusters of Madrone. A few yards above the road, he stopped behind a small tree.

To their left dirt and rocks tumbled down a steep bank only a few yards away. Something, or someone, had climbed up that bank.

Below them, a man ran out from behind a bush. He held a long object.

Jeff dropped Allie's hand and leaped with all his leg strength, launching his body out over the man.

"Jeff, no!" Allie screamed.

The impact of Jeff's body drove the man to the ground. Jeff grabbed the long stick from the man's hand and raised it like a club.

The man drew back a foot to deliver a kick.

"Stop it!"

Jeff hesitated. What did Allie mean?

Air exploded from Jeff's lungs when Allie landed on top of him.

She grabbed the stick. "Stop! Both of you."

An engine roared as a pickup raced toward them.

"The cartel!" Jeff pointed up the road.

The other man motioned up the hill. "Mama and Benjamin."

Allie's father? Had Allie's family escaped?

Jeff grabbed Allie's and the man's hands, yanking both of them to their feet.

The pickup slid to a stop on the dirt road.

"Go! Go!" Jeff pushed the two up the hill.

He glanced back at the truck.

A gun jutted out the window.

Chapter 15

"Over here." Jeff motioned for them to move behind a stand of trees on the hillside. "Go straight up the hill. Keep the trees between you and the gunman. Go down the other side. At the bottom, turn right and head due south."

He glanced at the trees. Good. The gunman still had no clear shot at them. "I'll keep this guy busy for a few minutes, then catch up with you."

Allie hugged him. "Be careful, please."

"Allie?" Her father's frown deepened. "Who is he?"

"It's okay, Papa. He saved my life, more times than I can count."

Jeff watched as they ran up the hill, keeping the trees between them and the pickup.

The goon backed up the truck several yards.

Not a good development. Allie's family was still on this side of the hill. Jeff couldn't let the man in the truck spot them.

A gun now stuck out the passenger's window of the rolling truck. There were two men inside.

Jeff grabbed a baseball-size rock, stepped out from the cover of the trees, and let it fly. As he dove to the ground behind a rock outcropping, a cry sounded from the truck followed by cursing in English and Spanish.

A burst of gunfire sent dust and shattered rock flying into the air all around him. After fifteen long seconds, the burst ended. The shooter must've emptied the magazine.

This might be Jeff's only chance. He rose to all fours, then leaped for the cover the trees and sprinted up the hill.

Two pickup doors slammed in rapid succession.

More gunfire.

Shredded vegetation exploded above his head and the bitter smell of wet madrone bark filled the air. Thankfully, the tree trunks had held their own against the cartel's deadly pruning machines.

In five more seconds, Jeff topped the hill and sprinted hard down the backside. He flew down the hill with twenty-foot leaping strides, jumping bushes and dodging trees like an NFL running back in a desperate bid to reach the goal.

At the base of the hill, Jeff cut hard to his right. Worrisome questions plagued him. How far ahead were Allie and her family? Could they sustain a pace that would keep them ahead of the gunmen? Where was the FBI? Was the chopper in the air yet? If so, was it still in the area?

He had no answers, so he focused on running at his

breakneck pace without breaking his neck.

He leaped a patch of Poison Oak.

Movement in the trees a hundred yards ahead.

Jeff slowed and watched the trees. Allie's brown legs and denim shorts disappeared into a stand of trees.

Despite his rapidly draining energy, Jeff willed himself to run faster, driving with all the leg strength that remained.

In another two hundred yards, he caught them.

To make it this far, all four must have run hard. Allie, with an arm around her mother's waist, had evidently stayed beside her mother, helping her.

When Allie spotted him she hurried to his side. "Jeff, are you okay?"

"Yeah. How about your family?"

"They're just tired. I was so scared when I heard the shooting. I didn't stop praying until I saw you." She grabbed his hand and hung on to it.

He squeezed hers. "Have you heard or seen any signs of them?"

"The truck started, the engine revved up, and I heard the wheels spinning. That was less than a minute ago."

"I think I know what that means. They've turned back. They think we're going south, so they're trying to prevent us from circling them and getting to my house."

"Can they do that?"

"Yeah. They *are* doing it. We need to stop, reconnoiter, and rest."

"We *do* need to rest. Mama is really struggling."

"We're safe for a while, unless one of the goons is following me. Allie, we can't afford a bad decision at this point. See the bushes ahead on the left."

She nodded.

"Lead them there. Hide and wait for me."

"Jeff, don't go back. Please."

"I won't go up the hill. I promise. I'm just watching our backside." He squeezed her hand, released it and reversed direction.

He moved behind a large pine tree in a small clearing, stopped, and listened. The only sounds came from Allie and her family. In a few seconds those sounds stopped.

The forest fell silent except for the distant sound of an engine somewhere to the southwest. He had guessed correctly.

Jeff turned and trotted toward the bushes, thankful they were all still alive and uninjured.

* * *

Allie heard Jeff's footsteps. They slowed, then he stepped behind the scrubby madrones that hid them. Her arms instinctively wrapped around him and she pressed her head against his chest. What might her father think? She would deal with that later, after Papa's disapproving glances turned to words.

She looked up into his Jeff's eyes. "Are we okay here?"

"Yeah. They're driving south, trying to head us off at Bolan Peak Road. We've got a few minutes to decide what to do."

Even before she turned to see them, Papa's and Mama's gazes seemed to bore into her back. They wouldn't understand her intimacy with Jeff and would not approve of what they saw. A knot formed in her stomach as she turned toward her parents.

So much was on the line in these initial introductions. She purposely stood close beside Jeff, circled his waist with her arm, and smiled at them, trying to shed any appearance of shame, discomfort, or pretense. Allie might appear calm and comfortable, but her heart pounded a presto tempo.

Papa waited, hands on hips, and a questioning look in his eyes, the look he gave her when she was a child caught in a disobedient act. Papa was reserving judgment on Jeff, but only for the moment. "Papa, Mama, Benjamin, this is Jeff Jacobs, the man who saved my life. The man who just saved all our lives."

Jeff made eye contact with her father.

"Jeff, meet my father, Rafael Santiago." She drew a breath and held it.

Jeff stepped forward and extended his hand.

Allie resumed breathing when her father took it.

"It's good to meet you, Mr. Santiago."

She motioned toward Mama. "And my mother,

Lorena."

Jeff nodded to her mother. "And good to meet you, Ma'am."

"And my brother, Benjamin."

Benjamin rushed to Allie's side, hugged her, then gave Jeff his hand.

Jeff shook it. "Good to meet you, Benjamin."

Benjamin's eyes focused on Jeff's face. "Did you really save Allie's life?"

"I think God played a big role in that, Benjamin."

At Jeff's reference to God, a smile that came to her mother's face, easing the knot in Allie's stomach.

Jeff lifted her chin up until their eyes met. His face held a questioning frown. "Allie? I notice they call you Allie, too. You made such a big deal out of—"

She poked him in the ribs. "They earned the right to shorten my name. But you just took it, Jeff, without my permission."

He gave her a weak smile. "Yeah. Guess I did."

Mama whispered something in Papa's ear.

Papa studied Jeff and cleared his throat. "So you are a man of faith, Jeff Jacobs?"

"Yeah. I'm a Christian. Jesus is my Lord and Savior."

"Unlike my skeptical daughter. Please call me Rafael."

"And to all of you, I'm Jeff." He paused. "But Mr.

Santiago ... uh, Rafael, Allie's not a skeptic. At least not anymore."

Papa's lips parted as if to speak, but he didn't. He nodded slowly, then smiled, a reaction that warmed Allie's heart. Maybe there would be no confrontation with Jeff or with Allie. Her former unwillingness to accept her parents' faith had created a rift that had broken Allie's heart. But that was in the past ... she hoped.

She needed to keep this conversation moving in a positive direction. "Jeff pointed the way for me. His savior is now mine, too."

Before Allie could react, Mama's arms were around her. "*Mi hija esta en casa.* Allie is home. Thank you, Lord" She looked up at Jeff. "And thank you, Mr. Jacobs."

"It's Jeff, Ma'am. Now, we need a plan to get us some help."

She looked at her father. "Jeff got the FBI involved. They came in the helicopter when several gunmen were firing at us. They saved Jeff and me, then they went looking for you at the marijuana plantation."

Her father gave Jeff a long, penetrating look. "If they saved you, what are you doing out here?"

Allie winced at her father's words. "It's a long story, sir," Jeff said. "But—"

"Papa, I made a big mistake and it endangered both of us."

Her mother stepped in front of Papa and pointed skyward. "We saw ...*una helicoptero.*"

"I wish the helicopter had seen you," Jeff said. "It has an FBI SWAT team onboard. We expected to hear it in the air this morning. Since we haven't, I'm not sure where they are. But helping the FBI to spot us is our number one priority."

"Jeff?" Allie shook her head at him. "It's our number two priority. Remember Bolan Peak. Those men nearly killed us before the helicopter arrived. We don't want a repeat."

"Yeah. We've got to keep you and your family as safe as possible and still be visible from the air. I know this area well, Rafael. We should go east, put more distance between ourselves and the cartel thugs. We need to find a place they cannot drive to in their trucks."

Alarms rang in her mind. "But Jeff, the camp where they held me last night is to the east."

"Were not going that far, Allie. Do you remember the rock where—"

"I remember." She'd confessed her love to Jeff there. That wasn't a conversation to have in front of Papa. Not yet. But he was sure to ask questions about her relationship with Jeff. And the look in Papa's eyes said he wouldn't wait much longer.

Jeff leaned toward her and whispered, "How do you say precious treasure in Spanish?"

She pulled her head back and gave him her biggest bug-eyed stare. What was he up to?

"C'mon, Allie. Humor me."

Papa's feet shuffled restlessly. Jeff could be asking for

trouble or ... could he be asking for something else? *"Precioso tesoro,* precious treasure," she whispered back.

He nodded and smiled at her. "Yes, that rock, *mi amor."* Jeff wasn't whispering.

Allie's breath caught in her throat. Papa and Mama hadn't heard all that had transpired between Jeff and her. They wouldn't understand and ... Jeff had never said he loved her. It was more of a mutual understanding. At least, Allie thought it was. She looked at Papa.

He gave Jeff an icy stare. "I do not trust your words, Mr. Jacobs. You are ... *muy intimo* ... too familiar with my daughter."

"I would never dishonor your daughter, Rafael. Allie *es mi precioso tesoro, mi vida."*

"Jeff, that's not what I said. I thought you didn't know Spanish." What kind of game was Jeff playing with her father?

"Just because I asked you to translate a couple of things for me doesn't mean I don't know *any* Spanish."

"Treasure you say?" Papa's intense eyes frightened her. "Men search a long time for such things. *Mi amor* is reserved for those who have found it."

Jeff had taken a bold approach. He was removing all doubt in Papa's mind about the nature of Jeff's relationship with her. His verbal sparring with Papa was now over. She held her breath and waited for Jeff to throw his knockout punch. What words had he chosen?

"What does one do when God places the treasure they're seeking right in front of them? Do I ignore the treasure that God presented to me, the treasure that is Allie? Allie and I have faced death together several times, with only God and each other to rely on. I know Allie well, in a good way. She is a good woman, a woman of faith, and she is my treasure, *mi amor.*"

Papa's eyes grew intense at Jeff's final words.

Jeff met her father's gaze. "Allie can speak for herself about me, but we need to save that discussion for later. Let's move to the east. The hills ahead are small, easy climbs. It's only about two miles from here to the rock."

Papa didn't move. "In following you, I am trusting my family to you, Jeff."

Papa was back to using Jeff again. That was a good sign.

Please don't let Jeff fail. Papa needs to see what I have seen.

Chapter 16

Jeff glanced at his watch. It was nearly 8:00 a.m. Why wasn't the chopper in the air looking for them?

He led Allie and her family across two ridges before he spotted their destination, the rock outcropping. It lay two hundred yards up the next slope, near the center of a large, mountainside meadow.

Allie had held her mother's arm, supporting her for the past mile, while Rafael and Benjamin trudged along behind Allie.

Jeff slowed his pace when the Santiago's fell behind him. The physical stress, lack of sleep, and emotional trauma were taking their toll on all of them. The rock would give them a much needed respite.

As they approached the outcropping, Jeff slowed until Allie came alongside. "Allie, lead them around to the top of the rock. They can rest up where you and I sat."

His words brought a smile to Allie's lips. "Come on, Mama. Just a little farther now."

Rafael took Lorena's other arm and they helped her

make the climb up the hill to where the flat top of the rock protruded from the hillside.

Jeff pointed up the hill, fifty yards above the rock. "I'm going to run up to the top and make sure there are no surprises on the other side."

"Jeff." Allie left her mother to her father's care and took his hand. She whispered to him. "Listen for a minute. I'm not sure, but I think I hear an ATV."

"Quiet everyone. Allie hears something. Let's all listen for a moment."

In a few seconds, Allie pursed her lips. "Yes. It's an ATV. I've heard them enough lately to recognize that sound."

Jeff shook his head. "I still can't hear it. Which direction is it coming from?"

She pointed to the northwest.

It worried him. If they were able to get an ATV running, that left one man to drive the second truck, two in the truck they'd already encountered, and one man on the ATV. A man with an AK-47 might be headed toward them. "That's not good."

Allie's twin frown lines deepened. "Do you think we're in danger here?"

"Yeah. If the ATV is coming from the northwest, he's been traveling over higher terrain to the north of us. From up there, he might have spotted us. And if he did, he could be circling around to sneak in close to us from a direction we wouldn't expect. We need a plan to defend ourselves in case he gets closer." Jeff looked at the rock,

170

then to the northwest.

"No, Jeff. Please don't take any risks." Allie pointed to a thick cluster of trees south of the rock. "Let's all hide in the trees. He won't be able to see us, and if we don't leave any tracks..."

"But if he looked in there, we all would—"

"Don't say it. It's not going to—" She gasped. "It's getting closer."

"You need to take your family in there and hide. It's only one guy. I'll take him out."

"But he's armed."

"I am too. With surprise. Now go. Hurry, Allie."

Hands on hips and steely-eyed, Rafael turned to face Jeff. "A surprise of two has a better chance of success. Since you know how to leap on people like an American football player, I'll leave that to you. What do you want me to do?"

There was another man here now. Not just any man, Allie's father. He would feel responsible for his family. But Rafael's willingness to let Jeff lead was a surprise. This man trusted him.

Jeff glanced toward the thick stand of trees as Allie's arm swept her mother and Benjamin through the foliage and out of sight.

The ATV's engine droned more loudly now.

"He'll enter the clearing from the north and he'll be able to see the base of the rock. If you'll stand there, Rafael, until he gets within fifty yards or grabs his gun, we can lure him in. Before he can shoot, you disappear around the south corner of the outcropping."

"What about you?"

"I'll lay down in a depression on top. This guy will either dismount to run after you, or he'll ride toward you on his ATV. Either way, I'll jump him from on top. After I take him down, you grab a rock and brain the guy."

"Brain him?"

"Yeah."

"Do you mean hit him on the head?"

"Yes. But do it hard, Rafael. Knocking people out is a lot harder than it looks like in the movies. Any questions before—forget the questions. Here he comes. Stay here. I'm going on top."

Jeff drew all the remaining power in his legs to sprint up the south side of the rock. He leaped and slid on his stomach across the top of the rock as the ATV shot into the clearing.

The driver was the man called Hector. He had an assault rifle strapped to his back.

Hector's head swiveled toward the rock where Rafael stood. Hector gunned the engine.

In a few seconds Rafael's head bobbed into view over the edge of the rock as he rounded the corner on the south side. He was safe for the moment.

Jeff tracked Hector's approach.

He veered uphill. Hector was going around the

opposite direction from Rafael.

They hadn't planned for this. Hector would go above the rock. He could spot Jeff, kill him, then get Rafael.

The ATV's wheels ripped at the ground, sending clouds of dust shooting from the tires as it climbed up the hill beside the rock. But the gun was still on the driver's back.

Jeff had only one option, rush the guy and pray for a good outcome.

Rafael leaped out from the south side of the rock, near the top. He had made himself a target.

Hector hit the brakes and reached for his rifle, his gaze locked on Rafael.

Jeff scurried on all fours across the rock. As he rose, he launched his body at Hector from fifteen feet away.

Hector pulled the butt of the gun against his shoulder. The barrel rose toward Rafael. Then it swung toward Jeff.

The staccato belching of the rifle sounded as Jeff crashed into Hector.

Pain seared through Jeff's left side. Lightning flashed in his eyes. In its wake, darkness.

* * *

Allie peered through a small opening in the tree branches.

The ATV roared as it accelerated across the mountainside meadow toward the rock.

The ATV turned sharply toward the top of the rock

where Jeff hid.

Allie opened her mouth to yell a warning. Her cry stopped in her throat when she thought of Benjamin and Mama standing behind her. Allie couldn't draw the gunman's attention.

Papa rounded the rock, exposing his body to the gunman. It was Hector.

Two quick bursts and Hector could kill both Jeff and Papa.

Jeff's body flew through the air toward the ATV.

A burst of gunfire sounded.

Jeff dealt Hector a savage blow, then fell to the ground.

Her father flew at the gunman. The rock in his hand made a sickening thud as Papa dealt a heavy blow to Hector's head.

He slumped over the front of the ATV.

Papa hit him again, harder this time. The fight was over.

But Jeff wasn't moving. He must have been hit.

Allie burst through the tree branches, running toward Jeff, while a slideshow of bloody, mortal wounds played mercilessly in her mind.

Chapter 17

Please, God. Not Jeff. Don't take him now.

Gaze locked on Jeff, willing him to get up or to move, Allie sprinted across the meadow toward him.

Papa pulled Hector's limp body off the ATV, grabbed his gun, then turned toward Jeff.

Hector lay motionless only a few feet from Jeff's body.

Allie reached Jeff and stopped. Her breathing stopped. Time had stopped. But she couldn't let it stop or she would be stuck in this nightmare.

Blood pooled around Jeff's arm and side. Could anyone survive after losing so much blood?

Her sobs started before her knees hit the ground. Deep gasps chopped them apart, preventing them from becoming one long, suffocating sob. On her knees, Allie touched the bleeding area, Jeff's upper left arm and side.

Papa tapped her shoulder. "Allie, I hear the ... *helicoptero.*"

"Signal to them, Papa. I need to help Jeff, try to stop the bleeding." But how?

"Papa, you have on an undershirt. I need your shirt, now."

He pulled his shirt off, handing it to her, then waved his arms to the sky.

Summoning all her strength, in one violent motion Allie ripped the long sleeve from her father's shirt.

The sleeve was dirty, but hospitals had antibiotics. They wouldn't need hospitals or antibiotics if she couldn't stop the flow of blood, now.

When she pulled back Jeff's shredded shirtsleeve, her fingers dripped with the very life of Jeff. The blood came from a large hole about two inches below his shoulder. She wrapped the shirtsleeve around his arm, placing it above the wound.

Allie pulled the makeshift tourniquet tight and tied it.

The blood flow decreased, but only slightly.

She looked around for something to twist the tourniquet. Nothing.

Panic and frustration grew. Allie panted now, hyperventilating. She needed to breathe more slowly or she would pass out.

She scanned the area around her again and spotted the brake handle on the ATV. With it, she could twist the tourniquet tight, but first she had to break the handle off.

A rock the size of a soccer ball lay a few feet away. Allie slid her hands under it, stood, and lifted the rock high above her head. She grunted out her fury and desperation as she drove the rock down on the brake handle.

The metal lever snapped off from her vicious blow. The rock smashed on the ground narrowly missing her toes. A chunk of metal the width of her hand landed on the ground by her feet. She grabbed the broken brake handle, slid it under the tourniquet and twisted hard. Once. Twice around ...

The flow of blood stopped. Allie held the tourniquet, keeping it tight with one hand, tracing the contours of Jeff's face with the other.

She prayed with groanings from her heart or maybe her soul. They weren't even words. Could God hear her? Would He understand?

The staccato sound of the helicopter grew and morphed to a continuous roar. Hair flew into her face and whipped around her neck. Dust blew across the ground in front of her.

But Allie's eyes remained focused on Jeff. And from the depths of her heart she continued praying with an intensity she had never before used when talking to God.

Someone put a hand on her shoulder and knelt beside her.

"I'm Dan, the SWAT Medic. We're going to take good care of him, but for right now, you just keep holding the tourniquet tight."

Dan checked Jeff's pulse, then looked at the wound. "Was he conscious after this happened?"

Other men swarmed around them. From somewhere

near she heard Mama's voice, then Benjamin's, talking to SWAT team members.

"Conscious? No," she said. "He jumped from the rock onto the gunman. When Jeff landed on the man, I heard shots, then Jeff fell to the ground, and he hasn't moved. Is he going to be okay?"

The medic quickly checked Jeff for other wounds. Then he stood. "Pete, Rick, bring the stretcher. We need to get this man to a hospital, pronto."

She grabbed Dan's arm. "Is he going to be okay?"

"He's lost a lot of blood. His pulse is weak. But I'm not sure why he's unconscious. Until we check that out I can't say. But one thing I can say for sure, if you hadn't put that tourniquet on him, he wouldn't be alive."

Dan obviously meant to encourage her with his words. But they didn't make her feel any better.

Jeff had saved her life so many times. This was her turn. But she might have failed him. "I need to go, too. You have to let me come along or I'll..."

"Ms. Santiago, you, your family, and Mr. Jacobs will all be on the chopper when it takes off. About you going to the hospital, that will have to be cleared with the team leader."

Allie looked at the semi-organized chaos around her, at least a dozen men, all performing various duties.

"Who is the team leader?"

Dan nodded toward a tall man in SWAT gear. "Grady. The man talking to your ... uh, father, I assume. Let me talk to Grady. But first you need to let me take care of Jeff Jacobs."

"I'll help you."

"No. You've done enough. I'll take it from here."

"Then I'll watch."

"Fine, Ms. Santiago. You watch."

"And you'll ask Grady when we get onboard?"

"I don't think you're going to let me forget." He paused as he tightened his improved tourniquet and removed hers. "You must really like this guy?"

"No. I love him."

"I see. And how does he feel about you?"

Dan was just trying to keep her mind busy, keep her from losing her sanity. But he was also pushing her beyond exasperation.

Allie's words erupted like lava. "You fix him! Then ask him yourself."

"I believe I got my answer. Jeff's a lucky man." Dan paused and glanced up. "Okay, Pete. Load him up."

She followed the stretcher toward the helicopter, but the leader, Grady, stepped in front of her.

"I haven't had a chance to talk with you yet, Ms. Santiago. There are some questions I need to ask you about what transpired during the past twelve hours."

"Can you ask me on the way to the hospital?"

"If you don't mind yelling ... and everyone hearing your answers. It will be noisy while we're in the air."

"I don't mind, but you have to let me go to the hospital with Jeff."

"Have to?"

Dan clamped a hand on the leader's arm. "Grady, she and Jeff Jacobs are ... " he crossed his fingers, "... like you and Bethany."

"Oh." Grady nodded slowly. "Okay, on the condition that you answer my questions and agree not to run off again. I'll have the two marshals meet us at the hospital because you two still need protection."

"Yes. I guess we do. What about my family?"

Grady pursed his lips. "That's an entirely different matter."

"What do you mean?"

"They don't have visas and your father said their passports were taken. Until their situation is resolved, your family will go to the Immigration Detention Center in Medford."

Her parents and Benjamin in a detention center? That could be purgatory, or worse. "They don't deserve that! They are good people and thought they had valid visas."

Grady's eyes softened. "For what it's worth, I believe their story."

And Grady didn't deserve the abuse she'd given him. Allie's anger cooled.

"Ms. Santiago, I don't make these kinds of decisions. That's Immigration and Customs Enforcement's domain. I'll explain their circumstances to ICE. But frankly, I've only heard of one case where someone from Mexico was granted asylum in the U.S. due to danger from drug cartels. He was a journalist who did an expose on the drug lords."

It was clear that her family's situation would take a while to resolve. In the meantime, she would need Jeff more than ever. But the reality was she had no guarantee that Jeff would still be alive at the end of this day?

Chapter 18

The wop, wop sounded more like a roll played on a bass drum. The drum was Jeff's head. He tried to raise his left arm to hold his skull together. Pain screamed its message down his arm to his fingertips, then reverberated up and down his arm. The warm gray fuzziness began another invasion of his consciousness. He surrendered, willingly.

Through the narrow slits, bright lights stabbed Jeff's eyes. Pain rose to a crescendo inside his head. A vague memory of lightning bolts running through his left arm made him cautious. He wiggled the fingers of his left hand. That slight movement brought immediate regret.

Allie. Some inner sense told him she was nearby.

Her hand took his.

He forced his eyes to open. Less pain this time.

She sat beside him, her chair pulled close to his bed.

So he was in a hospital.

Allie raised her head and opened her eyes. There were tears on her cheeks.

"Hello, beautiful." His words reverberated inside his head creating something like a brain freeze on steroids. What had he called them as a kid? Slurpee tumors?

Funny how stuff from the past crosses a person's mind when—he was probably spaced out on drugs.

She met his gaze and wiped her cheeks with her free hand. "You're awake. How do you feel?"

"Like someone used a jack hammer on my head, then tried to amputate my arm with a dull knife." He tried to laugh, but the soft chuckle brought another Slurpee tumor.

"I was so worried about you, Jeff. You bled so much. And you were unconscious. I did what I could, then the SWAT team arrived, and their medic took over."

"You saved my life, didn't you Allie?"

"The medic thought so. But you've saved mine more times than I—"

"No. You saved mine by running into my arms a few days ago."

"Turning romantic on me. You must be feeling a lot better."

"Better is a relative term. I feel better than a man having a root canal without Novocain. What do the doctors say about me? Am I going to live?"

"You'll live. We're still waiting for some kind of final prognosis from the attending physician."

"I know what would really help this monster headache. You could—"

"Jeff, I've never kissed anyone before you. I would say we got off to a rather fast start. We skipped some things. When you're up to talking, we need to."

"I can talk, Allie. It's not my mouth that hurts."

She studied his face. "Tell me the truth."

"I did. Do you have some questions for me?"

"There are some things I've wondered about. Like ... what you do for a living. You never told me."

"Well, I have a small inheritance from Mom, plus her house. I have an MA in English and I'm supposed to start teaching some college classes online this fall. It was the only teaching position I could find. They'll probably give me freshman composition classes. If I'm lucky, maybe I'll snag a philosophy class." He paused. "What about you, Allie?"

"After all of this ... I don't know if I can go back to school in September."

"But you have a scholarship. Isn't your visa contingent upon being in school and making progress toward your degree?"

"Yes. But school is in Corvallis, and my family is in Medford, in a detention facility."

He tried to digest Allie's information. Immigration detention. He should've expected that. "Worst case, you can see them on weekends. But let's pray about it. We can do some research when I get out of here. Their situation should be resolved long before school starts."

A tall distinguished looking man in scrubs stepped into the room.

Allie straightened in her chair. Waves of dark hair that had caressed her cheeks fell back against her shoulders. "The doctor," she whispered, still holding Jeff's hand.

"So our celebrity is awake. Mr. Jacobs, I'm Dr. Harris."

"Celebrity?" Media attention was never a good thing for Jeffrey Jacobs.

The doctor sighed sharply. "Yes. It's been a media frenzy since the FBI showed up in that helicopter with you and Ms. Santiago onboard. So far our security and the two marshals have kept them at bay. Changing the subject, you are a very fortunate young man."

"Yes, I know, doctor." He peered into Allie's eyes.

"I see." The doctor paused. "You'll live, but you might not feel like it for a few hours. That headache will get better. You have a mild concussion from striking your head on a rock. We'll stay on top of the gunshot wound with pain meds. By tomorrow your pain level should drop and Ms. Santiago's blood will—"

"Allie?"

She pointed to the bandage on her arm and smiled. "We're both O positive, Jeff. Completely compatible."

Dr. Harris chuckled. "You make a lovely couple. As I was saying, you'll feel a lot stronger tomorrow. We've pumped you full of antibiotics and, barring some unforeseen setback, we'll probably send you home tomorrow afternoon with a few pain pills and more antibiotics." He paused again. "Any questions?"

Allie swiveled in her chair toward the doctor. "Is there any reason I can't sleep in Jeff's room tonight?"

"Well, I, uh, have never been asked—"

"I didn't mean ..." Allie's cheeks turned rosy pink and she quickly pointed to the reclining chair.

It was refreshing, cute, highlighting her innocence and her beauty.

The doctor shrugged. "It's fine by me, but security is pretty tight right now. You'll have to take it up with those folks. I'll see you when I make my rounds in the morning. Both of you, I presume." He focused on Allie. "You can sleep pretty well on these recliners. I ought to know." Dr. Harris grinned as he left the room.

A rap on the door sounded and Wes walked in.

"The folks we have to take it up with." Jeff looked at Wes and squeezed her hand.

"We've locked down this place tight as a banjo head." Wes gave a satisfied nod.

"I may have a major headache in progress, but don't you mean tight as a drum?"

"You ever play a banjo, Jeff? Or changed the head?"

"Nope."

"Well, the head's tighter than a drum."

"You sound like Yogi Berra." Jeff shook his head, then winced from the pain.

Allie stroked his head, then shot Wes a glance. "I'm staying here tonight, too."

Wes shook his head. "It would be better if you—"

"No. You have to protect Jeff here anyway, so I won't be a burden." She pointed across the small room. "I'm staying in that chair. It reclines."

Cliff stuck his head in the door. "An overnighter, huh? I'm going to coordinate some things with hospital security, Wes. You can deal with that subject. It's right up your alley."

"Guess I have to chaperone you two, even with Jeff in the hospital suffering from a gunshot wound and a concussion?"

Allie gave Wes a weak smile. "I promise not to run away if you let me stay."

"So you learned your lesson?"

"Yes. You don't bargain with people that you can't trust."

"Well, you must trust me then."

"What do you mean?"

"You just cut a deal with me."

"I did, didn't I?

Wes pursed his lips and gave her a melodramatic frown. "I'm going to regret this."

Allie squeezed Wes's arm. "Thanks. We won't give you any trouble. Promise." A frown formed on Allie's brow. "Any word about my family?"

"No, Allie. Once the immigration folks take over, we're out of the loop. But they'll be safe at the Medford facility."

"Unless they deport them back to Sinaloa Cartel territory."

Wes sighed. "I'm praying that doesn't happen."

"So you ... pray?"

"Yep. In my line of work, it helps to maintain close communication with the Person who watches out for me."

"Then I'm glad it's you watching out for us."

"Probably because I'm a pushover. Well, I'll be outside your door. You two behave, or this little arrangement will get rearranged."

"Wes, I don't know what you're worried about. I can't move my left arm or I'll scream. My head feels like the bass drum in a marching band. Do you really think—"

"Jacobs, maybe I should tell you about the guy who'd been shot three times and his girlfriend came to visit him in the hospital—maybe I shouldn't tell you that story."

"No, you shouldn't. Thanks, Wes. Goodbye now." Allie waved him out the door.

She scooted her chair closer to his bed and sat. "I think we need to talk about us. *We* happened so fast that—I mean, Jeff, you called me *mi amor* in front of Papa. I thought he might punch you. He's very protective and—"

"Allie, I wanted him to know up front that our relationship was serious and that my intentions were honorable. But I didn't have much time to say all that. So I took a chance."

"It worked. Papa admires you. To Benjamin, you're a superhero. And to me you are ... *mi amor.*"

"I love you too, Allie. But I wonder if you'll feel the same when you know the truth about me?"

Chapter 19

With media at the hospital, trying to create a story, Allie was sure to hear something about his past. He had to explain before—

"What do you mean by the truth about you? I know everything that I—"

"Allie, there are things that you need to hear from me before you hear rumors or media gossip."

"It's a closed issue. You know something, sometimes you are your own worst critic. Besides, we have another issue to discuss."

"But, Allie—"

"Jeff, while you were still sleeping, I overheard part of a discussion between the marshals. I think their boss wants them to separate us."

Allie's words, "separate us," troubled him in a dozen ways. Jeff was no law enforcement expert, but any way he looked at it, separating Allie and him would be a stupid move. It would only dilute the DOJ's resources, resources that were probably spread too thin already.

He studied Allie's face, the twin frown lines, the way she crowded close to him—she was worried.

"Allie, we need to ask Wes about this. Would you please go get him?"

She studied *his* face and her eyes grew softer. The frown lines disappeared. "We've kept you from resting far too long. Are you up to this, Jeff?"

"Yeah. I am. My headache's getting better. I'll be fine."

"I hope our discussion with Wes doesn't bring you another one." She leaned down and kissed his cheek. "Be right back."

A kiss. Be right back—it could all end when Allie let him tell his story.

Less than a minute later, Allie led Wes into the hospital room. She sat on the bed next to Jeff.

Wes stood in the middle of the room, hands on hips. "Look. Splitting you two up wasn't my idea. But my boss is pushing Cliff and I really hard in that direction. I think it's what ICE might do that concerns him."

Surely ICE wasn't considering Allie for detention. She had student status.

"I'm the one with the most incriminating testimony against the cartel members." Allie jumped up from the bed. "Tell your boss I won't testify if he separates Jeff and me. Tell him to put that in his cigar and smoke it."

Jeff reached for her hand. "You mean put it in his pipe?"

Allie's cheeks were red. She ignored him, pulled her

hand from his, and clamped both of her hands onto her hips. "Or put it in some other place ... some really—"

"Allie, you need to settle down." Jeff grabbed her wrist and tugged on it. "I think Wes got your message."

She turned toward him, jaws clenched and head shaking. "If they try to separate us, I'll ... I'll marry you. Then they won't be able—"

"Don't you think you need to ask me about that?"

"You wouldn't turn me down. I know you, Jeff. I ... I could convince you."

"And I'll bet she could." Wes raised his hands, palms out. "I'm outta here. I'll give the message to my boss." After turning to leave, Wes looked back at Jeff. "I'd say good luck," he mumbled as he left. "But it looks like you've already got that."

After Wes disappeared out the door, Allie moved back to Jeff's bedside.

He took her hand. "Sit down."

"I'm sorry, Jeff. I was afraid. Then I got mad. Then I just—"

"Just tempted me." He smiled at her. "If I needed to, I'd marry you now. But before we plan something out of desperation, let's wait to hear from Wes."

"You need to know the truth about me, Jeff. I have a really bad temper. Only once in a great while do I lose it. But when I do, you'd better watch out."

"I believe you, especially after your instructions for Wes's boss."

"Please forgive me. I don't use bad words or say crude things ... well, not normally."

"You are a good woman, Allie Santiago. That's what I believe. Now let's concentrate on getting me out of this hospital so you and I can find a way to help your family. If we were back at my house, I can think of several things to try."

"Then let's tell Wes to take us to *your* place."

"You don't need to tell me. You got your wish, Allie." Wes stood in the doorway. "When Jeff is discharged, and rumor has it that's been moved up to tomorrow morning, we're taking you back to O'Brien to Jeff's house. We believe the cartel has left the area, except for the four injured men we have in custody here."

"Four?" Maybe he had lost count after banging his head on the rock. But only three wounded goons were captured. The other one was dead.

"Hector Suarez, survived, barely. He's conscious now and, get this, he swears he had an out-of-body experience."

Jeff waved off Wes's words. "Don't trust him. He's one of the worst of that bunch. I wouldn't believe him even if he cut all of that long, greasy hair off and started asking for a priest."

Wes chuckled. "His long hair's already been cut off. They had to ... lice."

"Oh, gross!" Allie held her stomach. "I actually rode on an ATV behind him and his hair kept whipping my—I'm going to be sick."

"Has he actually asked for a priest?" Jeff asked.

"No. Just the phone number of some publishing company."

After he spent an hour checking Allie's long hair for lice, Jeff tried to sleep. But every hour of the long night was punctuated by a nurse's poking, prodding and questions.

In the reclining chair across the room, Allie slept through most of it. Seeing her relaxed with her permanently tanned face and waves of dark hair, brought back her words, "I'll marry you. You won't turn me down, Jeff. I could convince you."

He was already convinced. It was only a matter of time, spending a little more of it together ... if his past didn't interfere.

Dr. Harris came by on his rounds at 9:00 a.m. As the doctor told him yesterday, Jeff's arm felt much better. It would remain in a sling for several days, but he could already use his hand a little.

After Jeff's discharge, policemen seemed to have taken over the hospital. Uniformed officers stood at every corner, every door, and at the elevators.

Wes and Cliff escorted Allie and Jeff to a waiting helicopter on the hospital's pad, a much smaller bird than the SWAT team used.

After they all climbed in the chopper Jeff turned to Wes sitting in front of Allie and him. "Earlier this morning, I thought you said we were driving to O'Brien."

"That was before the Intel report came in. It seems that

the cartel has moved some people into the area. The helicopter will prevent them from trying anything en route."

Allie leaned forward in her seat. "If the cartel is back in the area, will we be safe at Jeff's house?"

"That's our job," Wes said. "And we're good at it. Don't worry. Besides, there'll be more law enforcement people watching you two than just Cliff and I."

She leaned back as the rotor spun up. "I wonder why they came back. To salvage their marijuana?"

There was only one explanation. He didn't want to worry Allie, but a false sense of security would only increase the danger. "Allie, these guys are vindictive. Not only do they get even, but they like sending out warnings so others will think twice before crossing them."

"You think they came back to kill us, don't you?"

"Cliff and Wes know that. That's why they have more people watching us. If it gets too dangerous, they'll move us. At least that's how I've heard short-term protection works."

Allie hooked his arm and leaned against his shoulder. "Knowing that organized crime is sending people after you to kill you is ..." Her words trailed off.

"Yeah. It's scary, Allie."

Chapter 20

Jeff scanned the mountains to the southwest as the chopper flew through the blue skies of a typical, Southern-Oregon, July morning. But it wasn't a typical morning. New cartel members were arriving. Possibly waiting in those mountains for Allie and him to return.

Allie clung to his uninjured arm, her head against his shoulder. She hadn't spoken a word since they took off.

After they boarded, Wes had remained silent, too.

But the usually quiet Cliff chattered, nervously.

Was everyone worried about returning to his house?

He couldn't let Allie see his concern. She needed some peace in her life.

A few minutes after crossing the green farmland of the river valley, O'Brien came into view. In another minute, the chopper descended and hovered over the field behind Jeff's home.

Two police cars sat along the road in front of the house and a uniformed officer stood on the front porch.

Security had definitely been beefed up. It provided another reason for some of O'Brien's residents to want Jeffrey Jacobs gone.

The helicopter touched down and the rotor began a slow spin down.

Allie's haunted eyes surveyed his well-guarded house. she leaned toward him. "Do you think this was a good idea, Jeff?"

"Do you mean keeping us together?"

"No. Keeping us at your house."

He grinned. "Look. With fields all around it, the house should be easy to defend."

Wes unbuckled and turned toward them. "Jeff is right. This is an easily defended home. And we've added a video surveillance system, modified the phones, and added some troopers to patrol the area. We'll keep you safe, Allie. You two wanted to be together, so relax and enjoy yourselves ... within reasonable limits."

Allie still clung to his arm, but now she looked up at Wes. "Have you ever ... uh, lost anyone?"

"Nope. Had one case where—well, let's just say we're still batting a thousand."

"But so far you've only had to stop the local marijuana growers."

Wes chuckled. "You mean the dregs of the cartel barrel?"

"But they have hired assassins, Wes. Those people nearly killed my father."

"If you don't wander off again, we've made that almost impossible. You'll be safe," Cliff said.

Wes stepped out of the chopper, then stuck his head back inside. "You know the drill. Wait until Cliff and I are ready, then we all hurry inside."

"Home sweet home." Jeff shook his head. "But it's not like it used to be."

"You mean it's not peaceful like it was before I came into your life?"

Was she looking for more assurances? "I wouldn't roll the clock back and try to change anything, except maybe the part where Hector put a bullet through my arm." He patted the sling holding his left arm. "How about you, Allie?"

"I'll go where you go, because that means I'll be where I want to be."

He kissed her cheek and rose to get out.

"Knock it off, you two. We're not gonna stand out here all day just so you can tell your grandkids about the time you parked in a helicopter."

"Wes is cranky today. We'd better go, Allie. You and I have some research to do."

* * *

Allie heard the front door close as she walked into the study.

Jeff sat in his computer chair, staring into the screen of his laptop. "Who just left?" His eyes remained focused on his computer's display.

"Cliff. He went to the store."

"Getting lunch for us, I hope."

"Men. Their minds are either on food or—"

Wow! Allie, you look absolutely—"

"See what I mean?"

"What?"

"You weren't even listening to me, were you, Jeff? That's another thing about men."

"When you saunter into my study looking like you came from a fashion magazine photo shoot, it's hard to listen, hard to think about anything else."

"I rest my case." She stepped beside Jeff's chair. "One of the nurses felt sorry for me and brought me some clothes she couldn't wear anymore. My blouse and cut-off jeans needed to be washed. After sitting behind Hector Suarez, I should have burned them."

He grinned. "Thank the nurse for me if you see her again."

"We're not going to have any more visits to the hospital. Jeff, what were you reading so intently when I came in?"

Jeff grabbed a folding chair with his good arm and deftly pushed it open with his foot. "Sit down." He pointed a thumb at the laptop. "I was looking at the rules for work visa applications."

She sat beside him and scooted the chair a bit closer. "Then why are you reading a message from ... Brock

Daniels? Who's he?"

"He's a friend from Eastern Oregon. We met through his blog. We're both into Christian apologetics. But back to the subject at hand."

His chair swiveled until he faced her.

Allie drew a sharp breath when Jeff's hands clasped around the back of her neck.

"You are so beautiful, Allie. How did someone like me ever—"

"Hush." She stopped his lips with her fingertips, then leaned into his embrace.

Jeff's arms slid around her.

The security and comfort of his embrace and Jeff's handsome face carried Allie's mind away to a wonderful place, a place she prayed lay somewhere in her future, her near future.

Behind her, someone cleared their throat.

Jeff released Allie. "Wes ... your timing stinks."

"That's what the bad guys always say when I arrest them."

"Hey, I'm not one of the bad guys."

"That's a matter of opinion." He cocked his head and eyed them with suspicion. "Am I going to have to separate you two?" His face relaxed into a grin.

She turned in her chair. "Don't worry. Jeff and I will do fine together."

"That's exactly what I'm worried about. My oldest daughter just turned thirteen. Stuff like this gives me ulcers."

"I'm twenty, almost twenty-one. Jeff is twenty-four. We're both adults so—"

"And that's supposed to ease my mind?"

Wes's insinuations had crossed the line. Allie stood and faced him, feeling her cheeks burn and harsh words move to the tip of her tongue. She tried to blow them away with a blast of air. "That's enough, Wes. Jeff is an honorable man."

"He's a man. You got that right."

Jeff reached up and pulled her back into her chair. "Allie, Wes is just trying to do his job. He cares about us. You know that. Besides ..." Jeff grinned, "... I know places in this house where he can't possibly find us."

Jeff's grin distracted and defused Allie.

Wes dismissed Jeff's words with a wave of his hand and turned to leave.

Allie looked down at Jeff's arm. It wasn't in the sling. "I see your arm mysteriously got better just when you needed it to grab me."

"Yeah. Couldn't have you biting or kicking a Federal Marshal like you did Agent Nelson."

"You're never going to let me forget that, are you? Don't answer. Seriously, how is your arm?"

"I can use it a little as long as I rest it before the bullet hole heats up too much."

She stroked Jeff's injured arm. "Wes thought things heated up a little too much between us. What do *you* think?"

"Can I plead the fifth?"

"So, we really *do* need Wes for, you know ..." Two weeks ago, she would have never believed Alejandro Santiago would make such an admission. But now she was Allie, Jeff's Allie. Their chemistry and, at a much deeper level, their emotional bonding, with a spiritual component, was far stronger than anything she had ever experienced.

Jeff had captured her mind and her heart. Nothing could ever change that, could it? Not even Jeff's interrupted revelation, some story about himself that he hadn't yet told her?

Chapter 21

Jeff slid his arm back into the sling, then wiggled it into touch-typing position.

"Wait, Jeff." Allie scooted her chair against his and gently removed the sling from his arm.

"What are you doing? I need to rest my—"

"Relax." She slid her hands under his forearm, supporting it. "Is that better?"

"Do you really want better, Allie?"

The warmth in her eyes derailed his train of thought.

Allie looked down at his arm supported by her hands. "Let's save 'better' for later. Now, try typing."

What had he been ready to do? The search terms. He typed in immigration, asylum, and citizenship then clicked the search icon. "Let's see what this search returns. Both you and your family need to stay here in the U.S. legally. With a little luck, this search will show us all the paths to citizenship."

"Open up the article on political asylum, Jeff. Let's see what it has to say. The SWAT team leader told me about asylum prison, or as he called it, asylum hell."

"I saw a movie about that. An Afghan woman escaped the Taliban. They were going to kill her, but when she asked for asylum in the U.S., the way we treated her almost killed her. Killed her spirit and her hope. Then a lawyer helped her. That's what we need, a lawyer, and I think we may have one."

He reached for the phone.

"Remember, it's bugged."

"So. I don't need to be secretive about this."

She pointed at the laptop display. "Let's read a little more. It will help when we're talking to a lawyer."

He put the phone down and scrolled down the page. "Here's a refugee guide for seeking asylum. Even the temporary protected status it mentions would help. Let's take a look before we throw out this option, because this is really who your parents are, refugees."

"There's a list of approved countries for refugees. But, Jeff, it doesn't include Mexico."

"Then here's another angle. Your family was trafficked illegally, and they will likely be testifying against the captured cartel members. Look at this."

She leaned close to him, trying to read the small print.

The scent of Allie, her closeness, the softness of her hair against his cheek— whatever he'd been trying to show her had been interrupted, swapped out of memory like a program on an overloaded computer.

"Listen to this, Jeff."

Come on, Jacobs. Focus. This is about Allie's family.

"U Nonimmigrant Status visas allow victims of trafficking and other crimes to remain in the United States so they can assist law enforcement authorities in the investigation or prosecution of the criminal activity." Allie looked up at him. "It's not permanent status, but maybe it could get my family out of immigration detention and buy enough time to pursue some other path to permanent residency."

He reached for the phone again. "We've raised enough legal issues that I think it's time to consult a lawyer, and I happen to know one ... well, sort of."

"What do you mean by 'sort of'?"

"He goes to the church I've been attending since I moved back home a few months ago."

Jeff picked up his phone. "Let's see if Larry Wendell can help us." Jeff brought up a phone number list on the laptop, then dialed.

"Hi, Larry. This is Jeff Jacobs, the new guy at O'Brien Community."

"The apologist himself. Thanks for teaching that section of my Sunday School class." Larry's end went silent.

Probably waiting to see why Jeff would call a lawyer. "I've got a question for you, actually some potential clients. Have you ever gotten involved in immigration law?"

"Only once," Larry said. "I helped a visitor who was robbed outside of a convenience store in Cave Junction. Lost his ID and visa."

Jeff gave Larry a nutshell version of the Santiago's situation, including the danger from the drug cartel.

"That's quite a story. Sounds like a good movie plot. Sorry. I didn't mean to make light of your—"

"It's okay, Larry, provided you give us a two-thumbs-up ending to the plot."

"Can you stop by my office tomorrow morning?"

"Uh, here's the thing. Their daughter, Allie, and I are under U.S. Marshals' protection at my place. Allie's family is in the Medford Immigration Detention Center."

"Marshall's protection and detention ... that puts a different light on things.

"Yeah. Tell me about it. But Allie and I found information about U Nonimmigrant Status visas. We wondered if her family would qualify. If so, would that visa get them out of the detention center?"

Larry didn't respond immediately. What was he thinking?

"Jeff, do they have passports?"

No, their passports were taken by the people who abducted them."

Larry launched into an explanation of immigration regulations, using acronyms unfamiliar to Jeff, ending with a proposal to visit the Santiago's in Medford.

Jeff sensed he was smiling when he hung up the phone.

So was Allie. It was good to see her eyes light up. "What did he say?"

"He handled one immigration case a couple of years ago and he would be glad to help, but he needs to do some review. He mentioned CFR and INA, whatever they are. He needs to do a little research, and then talk to you and your parents."

Allie took his hand. "Do you think we can trust this Larry Wendell? I mean *really* trust him?"

"From everything I've heard about him, I would trust him. He's a good father, husband, and a good man."

She sighed. "Maybe the light at the end of the tunnel isn't a freight train roaring at us." She stared at the hand she held, the one attached to Jeff's injured arm. "I'm sorry. I got so excited I forgot about your arm." She slid her hands under his left arm.

"It feels a lot better. With a little ibuprofen I can probably put this sling away for good." He swiveled his chair to face her and his gaze settled on a spot about two inches below her nose.

"Jeff, what are you thinking? If Wes catches us he would harass—"

"Yeah. But we found a lawyer. Let's celebrate tonight. We can send Cliff for takeout. There's a great Thai place in Cave Junction. Then you and I can—"

"Jeff?"

"Yeah."

"A celebration sounds wonderful. But shouldn't we be a little, uh ..."

Allie was right. Everything about their relationship had moved too fast. And there was a discussion they needed to have, soon. One Jeff dreaded. "You're right. So why don't you and I just sample my Mom's record collection tonight. What kind of music do you like?"

"Let me think about that. I haven't heard all the pop music from the U.S., so I can only give you a generic description."

Jacobs, she's from another culture, one you know nothing about. You don't even know what kind of music she likes. You need to slow down, man.

* * *

"C'mon, Allie." Jeff nodded toward the living room.

Allie's mouth tingled from the spicy takeout Cliff brought for them. She stood and started to gather the dishes.

"Let's leave them for later." Jeff took her hand and led her to the long wall unit that spanned one side of the living room. He opened all the doors along the bottom. "Look, twelve hundred LPs and some 45s. Everything from Elvis Presley to Chuck Mangione."

"I recognize Elvis Presley, but I'm not sure about Chuck whatshisname."

"You don't need to know the artists. Like you said, just give me a generic description of your favorite music."

She closed her eyes and took a deep breath, imagining Jeff and her listening to romantic music. "Beautiful melodies, love ballads where the music swells and isn't too fast and has meaningful words. Not the fast junk with synthesized rhythm. Acoustic instruments are always better."

"Generic? That sounded pretty specific to me." Jeff knelt on the floor and tapped his finger on one end of the ten-foot shelf of vinyl records. "Let's see. It's coming to me. Something from the '60s. Intensely romantic. It should be about right … here." He pulled out a record.

"Is this from the hippy era? Folk music?"

He shook his head. "Hippies? They didn't dress like this." Jeff tapped the picture on the album cover, showing two men in white jeans and black shirts. "I think you'll really like this song. The title is *Unchained Melody* by the Righteous Brothers."

She followed Jeff to the turntable. "Melody that's completely free, unchained. The title sounds perfect. But, seriously, the Righteous Brothers? Is this religious music?"

"Yeah. Soul music. The religion of love." He loaded the platter and adjusted the stereo controls. "Wait until you hear it. You'll see."

Music rolled out of the stereo system. Incredible sounds for such small speakers. Piano, strings, and a voice expressive and longing. The words took her breath away. Somehow they captured the feelings she had for Jeff, feelings they seemed to share.

Allie wasn't a dancer, but the melody and the lyrics

pulled her in. How could she not dance to this song?

She pulled Jeff away from the wall unit onto the hardwood floor and wrapped her arms around his waist. "Hurry, before the music stops. Put your arms around me."

His arms circled her shoulders.

They held each other, but nothing else was happening. Could he really be that dense?

"Jeff, step out with your left—"

"You mean like this?"

He had her swaying gently to the music in a few seconds.

In this moment, Allie's troubles retreated into the distance. She soaked in the words. This sounded like a love letter, written while two people were apart. It expressed one person's need for the other's love.

It fit, except Jeff wasn't far away. She pressed her cheek into his chest and listened to the rhythm of his strong heartbeat. He was here, and she needed his love, needed his touch.

As the instruments and the vocalist's voice swelled in a slow crescendo, like the singer, Allie prayed for God to speed Jeff's love to her.

The singer's voice rose to a high note as the music crescendoed. And Jeff kissed her.

The song's meaning, its emotional intensity, and the love it conveyed—Jeff's kiss matched all of it ... and more.

Allie closed her eyes, laid her head on Jeff's shoulder, and savored the moment, a moment she became lost in.

When she found herself again, they were standing in the middle of the living room, still holding each other. But somewhere in the recent past the music had been replaced by a scratching sound, an irritating sound that kept repeating.

"I need to raise the arm before the needle wears out."

"Can we hear it again? Please, Jeff?"

The front door banged shut.

Cliff's voice rose. "How long ago?"

"Less than five minutes," Wes's voice came strained and tense, something she hadn't heard before.

Jeff led her to the wall unit and lifted a lever on the turntable.

"Jeff, something's wrong. I knew it was too good to last."

Wes stepped into the room. "I hate to break up the ball but, Jeff, you know that root cellar you showed me, the room on the side of your basement?"

"Yeah. What's up?"

"Take Allie down there, now. Hurry. And don't come out until we tell you to."

Chapter 22

Take Allie to the cellar? Why?

Jeff stared into Wes's eyes. "You're not helping anyone by keeping secrets, Wes."

"Let's go. I'll tell you on the way down to the cellar."

Jeff took Allie's hand and hurried to the basement door, then started down the narrow stairs.

"A trooper spotted a fifth wheel being pulled up a county road five miles to the east of here. It's not far from some camping areas, so he didn't stop the driver."

Jeff stopped at the cellar door.

Wes pointed at the door. "Don't stand out here, Jeff."

"There aren't any windows in the basement. We're safe. Finish your story."

"Take Allie inside, then I'll finish."

This wasn't making any sense. Were some goons trying to break into the house? He swept Allie through the cellar door with his good arm and followed her into the cellar.

Wes stopped in the doorway. "Later the trooper found the fifth wheel. It was one of those toyhaulers. They had abandoned it. The 'toy' compartment was empty, but there were ATV tracks on the dirt road. They went into the woods, heading to the west."

"So they're coming after us again." Jeff blew out a sharp breath. "How many were there?"

Wes shook his head. "We're not sure. We assume one driver and another guy on the ATV. Probably two men. Until we know we've got this situation under control, you two stay down here. I'll come and get you when we're sure it's safe. Understood?"

"Why the root cellar?" Allie peered around his shoulder at Wes.

"Because my instincts say you need to be down here. I need to help Cliff check out the area around the house before it gets any darker. I'll be back as soon as I can."

Jeff flipped on the cellar light.

Wes closed the door and left.

Allie's wide eyes stared up at him. "You'll never be safe as long as I'm around."

He put his hands on her shoulders. "How many of their men have seen me?"

Her shoulders dropped and her gaze went to the floor. "At least ten."

"How many of their men have I hurt or eliminated?"

"You've made your point. Jeff, I just wanted to do something to—"

213

"You can't take away the danger by some sacrificial act, Allie. So don't even think that way."

She stepped forward and pressed her head into his chest, crying softly. "I would do anything just to end it."

"I know you would, sweetheart." He curled his arms around her. "But it would kill me to lose you now. This could be the cartel's last-gasp effort to get even or keep us from testifying against them. So let's be careful. We stand to lose so much if ..." It wasn't a sentence Jeff wanted to finish.

"No matter what happens, Jeff, I've found more in the last three days than I ever dreamed possible."

"Me too. I lost my dreams, then my mother. But you've given me much more than I lost."

"Could you just hold me now until this part is over?"

He kissed her forehead. "Yeah. I can do that."

* * *

Allie stood against Jeff, wrapped up in his arms. She hadn't a clue how long. But Jeff was getting restless. Waiting for something to happen, hoping nothing would, frazzled her nerves, too. To push the worry away, she closed her eyes and focused on their time together in the living room and that song that captured so much of what she felt for Jeff.

When she opened her eyes, the dressing on his wounded left arm loomed only inches from her face. He hadn't complained about it in hours. Still, it could not feel good. She kissed the bulging muscles of Jeff's biceps below the wound, wishing she could remove the pain and

214

the injury.

He shifted his feet and gently lifted her chin. "I'm going upstairs to get an update from Wes or Cliff. They must know something by now. I'll be right back."

"Please don't go, Jeff. Wes said not to. And I don't want to be down here alone." She clamped her arms around him and held on tight. "If something happens to you, I—"

"Nothing's going to happen to me. I'll only be gone one or two minutes max. Maybe it'll be good news. Now, promise me you'll stay right here until I come back."

"I'll stay, but if you aren't back in two minutes, I'm coming up to find you."

"Be right back." Jeff twisted the knob and pushed the door open.

The pounding of running feet sounded through the ceiling.

A boom came like a blow to her head.

A bright flash blinded her.

Jeff's body crashed back into her knocking her down and slamming the door shut.

The room went black.

The concussion from the explosion left Allie's thoughts hazy and the physical world far away.

She fought the detached feeling and the fuzziness in her mind, then sat up and reached forward into the darkness. She jammed her fingers into a hard body. "Jeff, are you okay?"

"I'm okay."

"What happened?"

"I smell smoke. I need to look out." He pushed the door open.

Allie gasped.

The basement had filled with dust and smoke. The moon shined down on them, it's brightness dimmed by flames dancing on what little remained of the upper floor.

"It must have been an RPG. Like they used at Bolan Peak. Stay here, Allie. I need to see if Wes … if he survived."

She grabbed his arm with both hands. "You're not going anywhere without me, Jeff. Don't even try."

Jeff coughed when he tried to reply. Smoke was filling the basement as flames licked at the upstairs wall, visible through the gaping hole in the floor.

"They might have more grenades to shoot at us. You need to stay down here." He coughed again. "I'll close the door when I go out so you'll be sealed off from the fire, and you're surrounded by dirt. If the smoke gets too thick, you can get out through the trap door. It opens behind the garage, remember? But don't do that unless you have to. If you go outside, you won't be protected from another RPG." He paused to catch his breath. "If Wes survived, I need to get him away from the flames. I'll be back in a minute, Allie."

"Hurry, Jeff. Please be careful. I love you."

"Love you too."

She squeezed him and let him go.

Please, God, keep Jeff safe. Keep Wes and Cliff safe, too.

The door closed and Allie stood alone in a dark, smoky room.

Jeff's house had been destroyed. Wes and Cliff might be dead, and they—Allie gasped when a beam of light split the darkness of the cellar.

The trap door by the garage creaked open.

A shadowy figure behind the flashlight inched forward through the door.

The light beam moved around the cellar until it hit Allie's body.

And it stopped.

Chapter 23

Jeff's gaze swept the top of stairway. A fifteen-foot-wide hole in the ground-level floor stopped several feet from the stairs where flames burned near the top steps.

He sprinted the stairway. Halfway up, a step gave way. Jeff fell forward. His good arm caught his upper body inches before his face slammed into burning wood.

He stood and leaped past the flames.

Where had the running footsteps come from just before the RPG hit? It sounded like someone had sprinted toward the front door.

As Jeff skirted the hole in the ground-level floor, a siren sounded in the distance. Some kind of help was on the way. It may be too late.

He moved to the front door.

It had been blown off its hinges.

Jeff spotted the door out on the front lawn. About five feet from the doorway, a dark form lay sprawled across the sidewalk and onto the grass. It was a Wes-sized form.

Jeff rushed to him, knelt, and pressed his fingers against Wes's neck.

"Is that you, Cliff?"

The air in Jeff's lungs blasted out his relief. "No. It's Jeff. Where do you hurt, Wes?"

"It'd be quicker to tell you where I don't hurt. Got hit by the blast and some shrapnel. There's a small light in my coat pocket, right side. I can move, but I'd like an accounting of the damage on this side before I roll over."

Jeff fished out the light and locked it on. "You're bleeding some from your lower left leg, upper right leg too, and something creased your head. Wait a sec. Have you got a vest on?"

"Yeah."

"Good thing. You took a couple of hits that ripped the back of your shirt, but they must've glanced off your vest."

Wes rolled over. "Other side is okay. You don't have to check. I ran away from the rocket after Cliff yelled to warn me."

"Where is Cliff?"

"Don't know. Figured you were Cliff." Wes grunted as he sat up, then shoved a hand at Jeff. "Help me up. I have to find Cliff. I was trying to warn him about someone sprinting toward the house just before the rocket hit. "

Jeff pulled him to his feet. "You mean one of the cartel thugs might be here?"

More sirens sounded. They grew louder.

"That's what I thought I saw, a man running toward the house."

"Allie." Jeff turned toward the burning building. "She could be in danger."

* * *

There was no greeting, no voice at all coming from the external door to the cellar. When the light hit her and stopped, Allie rolled out of it and leaped toward the basement.

The light moved off her body. Something clattered onto the cellar floor, followed by a muted curse in Spanish.

When she heard the telltale double-click of an assault rifle's charging handle, Allie leaped to her right and into the basement. She had placed a wall between her and the intruder.

Gunfire sounded. It's staccato popping went from loud to muted. Glass shattered, spraying the cellar walls.

In the basement, with every breath she sucked in pure smoke. Air unfit to breathe. Allie coughed and choked on it. Her lungs burned.

I've got to hold my breath.

She tried, but her racing heart and burning lungs demanded air.

The room was too smoky to see anything except the left side of the basement. It glowed red with flames. The heat scorched her bare skin.

She turned from the heat. Her head swam. The room spun and she fell hard onto the floor. Allie struggled to breathe but only sucked in more of the choking mixture. Now, despite the brightness of the fire, everything faded to gray.

She would rather have faced the bullets than a fire. But now it was too late, too late to say goodbye to Jeff. Too late for anything ...

* * *

"You look for Cliff," Jeff called back to Wes as his leg muscles exploded into action.

He sprinted to the corner of the house, then cut between the house and garage. When he reached the back corner of the garage, the dim lights of O'Brien painted the silhouette of a man with his back toward Jeff.

Jeff slowed, trying to run more softly.

His arms reached toward the shadowy figure.

The double-click of a weapon jolted Jeff. Was the man loading or clearing a jam?

Now, it didn't matter.

Jeff's good arm clamped like a vise on the man's throat.

The gun fired a long burst, first down into the cellar, then the gun barrel rose into the sky.

Jeff arched his back, pulling the man off his feet. Jeff whipped his hips as if throwing a discus and slammed the man to the ground.

The air rushed from the gunman's lungs.

Jeff retained his one-hand chokehold on the neck and squeezed hard until the man's body went limp.

Someone ran toward Jeff from behind.

He grabbed the gun and whirled.

"No, Jeff!" Wes's voice.

Jeff grabbed the barrel and shoved the gun at Wes. "Here. I choked this one. But he could wake up any moment. Got to find Allie."

Jeff whirled and stuck his head inside the cellar door. A flashlight lay on the floor.

He picked an open spot on the floor lit by the light and jumped down.

Jeff hit the floor and went to his knees. A sharp sting came from one knee, then the sticky warmth of blood running down his leg.

Broken glass crunched under his shoes when he moved toward the flashlight.

Jeff grabbed the light and turned a complete circle. Allie wasn't there.

Crouching low to the floor, he stepped into the smoke-filled basement.

The heat from the burning stairs forced him to turn away.

The smoke had become dense. It filled his lungs, choking him.

He dropped to the floor to avoid the smoke and

bumped into a body. Allie.

He scooped her up and stumbled into the cellar, his tear-filled eyes stinging and his heart pounding out his panic.

She was right. He should never have left her alone.

Coughing, lungs on fire, Jeff staggered up the steps toward the external cellar door.

Hands reached out. Cliff's hands.

Jeff summoned the last of his strength to lift Allie up to Cliff, and collapsed on the steps gasping between hoarse barking coughs.

A hand found his. It pulled.

Jeff slid his feet under him and wobbled up the final two steps, alternately coughing and sucking deep breaths of fresher air.

Police cars now surrounded his house. The flashing red and blue lights tinted Allie's skin the frightening color of asphyxia.

She lay on the grass at Cliff's feet.

Jeff tilted her head back, took a deep breath, slid his mouth over hers, and blew.

Allie coughed. She wheezed, then coughed again. "Jeff... don't." She sucked in more air. "Your breath ... it's worse than the basement."

On his knees beside Allie, he took several wheezing breaths. "I thought you weren't breathing. That you were unconscious."

She sat up and put her arms around him.

Jeff picked her up in his arms, stood, and held her. "I thought I'd lost—"

"Shhh." Allie put her fingers over his lips. "Almost." She sucked in a raspy breath. "But not quite."

Firemen surrounded them.

"They both breathed a lot of smoke." Cliff's voice.

"You need to put her down." One of the firemen tried to take Allie from him.

"No!" Jeff yelled much louder than he intended.

The fireman jumped back at Jeff's outburst. "

"Sorry about that." He coughed. It lit a fire in his chest. "If you've got some oxygen, I think we could both use a little."

From a fire truck parked in front of his house, hoses streamed water onto the building. The firemen led Jeff to the truck and pushed a mask at him.

Allie coughed and pressed a hand to her chest.

Jeff took the mask and placed it over her face.

She breathed deeply for several seconds, then pulled the mask off and pushed it over his mouth and nose.

After they had shared the mask for a few minutes, Allie raised her head "You would recover faster if you put me down. Besides, I need to check your wound."

He set her on her feet and sucked more oxygen while

she rolled up his T-shirt sleeve.

"It's bleeding again. Jeff, you shouldn't have done so much with—"

"Is there anything you would've wanted me not to do?"

Allie responded with a smile, a genuine, beautiful smile.

Half his house had been blown up. Whatever was left of it was burning. He had nearly been shot, and he had sucked in who knows how many toxic chemicals, but the woman he loved was alive.

Beyond that—he hadn't a clue what they would do next.

* * *

Allie looked into Jeff's eyes, realizing he had saved her life again. If the man who'd found her running down that road had been any other man on the planet but Jeff Jacobs, she wouldn't be alive. God had protected her, yet again. And He'd used this incredible man to do it.

Wes tapped Jeff on the shoulder.

Allie pushed Wes's hand away. "Careful, Wes. Jeff's wound needs attention. It's bleeding again." She reached for his injured arm.

Wes glanced toward the garage, then looked back at Jeff. "I'll get the paramedic over here after he finishes the emergency trach on the dude you choked. He said he was a bit rusty. Doesn't have to do many tracheotomies. Jeff, where did you develop arm strength like that? With one arm you clamped so hard you crushed that guy's larynx."

Jeff glanced toward the paramedic hovering over a body lying on a stretcher. "Couldn't think of a better person for him to practice on. I was, uh, training for the decathlon. Takes a lot of arm strength."

Wes shook his head. "Arm strength, huh? You must've been pretty good."

Allie stuck her head between the two men. "How could anybody doubt that after all he's done?"

Wes frowned at her. "And you aren't biased, are you?"

Jeff looked down and shuffled his feet. He was obviously uncomfortable with this discussion.

She could help. "Wes, did you catch all the men responsible for this?" She swept her hand across the scene of destruction.

"We caught two."

"So there could be more RPG's or gunshots?" Jeff asked.

"No. We're still trolling for a few more fish. But they're all running for their lives. With a little luck, we'll catch our limit by tonight. If we come home with a full stringer, Intel says you two and Allie's family might actually be safe. In the past, the cartel leader hasn't gotten involved in the low-level stuff. We think he'll just write off this operation as a loss and tell his people to move on to other places and other drugs."

"That would be very good news for us and the people of O'Brien," Jeff said.

Allie cupped Jeff's cheek with her hand. "I'm so sorry

about your house."

"It's only a house, Allie. The most important thing in it is safe, standing right in front of me."

Events of the past hour and Jeff's words welled in Allie's heart and, now, tears welled in her eyes. They rolled down her cheeks and across her lips.

Intense emotions she had run far ahead of in her fight for life had finally caught up with her. Though she couldn't stop the salty tears, Allie smiled through them.

Jeff held her shoulders and studied her face. "Are you okay?"

"I'm certainly better than your house."

"The house can be rebuilt."

"But what about all your mother's things inside?"

"The pictures are divided between the bedroom and the study. Those rooms weren't damaged by the fire. Anything else can be replaced."

"Even her record collection?"

"It's at the end of the living room, down near the floor. It has a chance of surviving if the vinyl didn't get too hot. We'll check out the house tomorrow."

"What about tonight?"

"It's too dark to look tonight."

"No. I mean where are we going to stay tonight? And I'm back to only the clothes on my back."

Cliff approached them coming from his vehicle parked on the street. "The DOJ will put you two up for tonight. The inn at Cave Junction has a three-bedroom suite we can have for a few nights."

"We need to come back tomorrow to see what we can salvage, Allie's clothes, my computer, and some personal things."

"We can do that first thing in the morning." Cliff rubbed his chin and frowned. "Maybe we'll have those dudes all in custody and we can breathe a little easier."

"Yeah. Allie and I will be praying that happens."

"We will." Allie sighed heavily. "I'm suddenly feeling exhausted."

"Gee, I can't imagine why." Jeff gave her a hug.

"When can you take us to our room, Cliff?"

"You mean to your *rooms*." Wes's voice came from behind her. "Cliff, can you take them to the inn, then hold down the fort until I can spring free from here?"

Cliff motioned toward his car. "After you."

As they walked to Cliff's car, Allie listened to the two men speaking softly behind her.

"*You* are a lucky man, Jeff Jacobs."

"You really think so?"

"Yes, I do. Even if your house and everything in it is a total loss, you still have her."

"The way I see it that makes me a *rich* man. But, Cliff,

I almost lost her to the fire and the smoke."

"But you didn't. Let's get you two tucked in for the night. It's nearly 1:00 a.m."

Allie stopped beside Cliff's car. Tears flowed down her cheeks again, tears of joy.

Thank You for taking care of us this evening... all four of us.

Exhausted now, Allie leaned against Jeff's arm.

He curled it around her. His other hand brushed away her tears, while her head rested on his shoulder.

Allie's eyes closed. "I'm so tired, Jeff."

It seemed as if Jeff had picked her up.

As she surrendered to the gray fuzziness now claiming her consciousness, one thought lingered. The cartel hadn't feared the marshals protecting her and Jeff. Her family could also testify against the cartel. Would they try to breach ICE detention in Medford to kill her family?

Chapter 24

Allie rolled over, stretched, and opened her eyes. She gasped. Was she in a log cabin? Vaguely, she recalled the mention of an inn at Cave Junction.

She reached over her shoulder to scratch her back, then gasped again.

Bare skin.

Allie's hands traced the contours of her body under the covers.

"I'm in my underwear."

How she had gotten into this bed and who had removed what?

Three soft raps sounded on her door.

"Who is it?"

"It's Jeff. I need to talk to you. Are you decent?"

"That depends. Who, uh, tucked me in last night?"

"About that, I can explain, Allie."

"Jeff, you didn't—you wouldn't—"

"No. The maid helped you. When she heard who you were, she was glad to help."

Allie sighed and relaxed. "You can come in."

Jeff opened the door far enough to step in, closed it quietly behind him, and tiptoed to her bed.

She patted the bed and he sat. "I take it that Wes doesn't know where you are."

"Nor Cliff."

She gave him her best attempt at a smirk. "So what are you trying to do, sneaking into a defenseless woman's room when she's all alone?"

"I'm trying to tell you that Larry Wendell can see us this afternoon. His office is here in Cave Junction."

"Does that mean he's done his research?"

"Yeah. And it sounded like he has some good news."

"Oh, Jeff." Allie wrapped her arms around him.

"Allie, you're not wearing—"

"Oh! Jeff, what do you think you're doing?" She jerked the blankets around her, pulling them up to her neck.

"It wasn't me who wasn't thinking. Speaking of thinking, I think I should leave now. If Wes had walked in here while you were—well, he'd put me on a plane headed for Timbuktu."

"Just don't mention this to him. What time's our

appointment?"

"2:00 p.m. Oh, just a minute." He opened her door and picked up a plastic garment bag from the chair outside her room. "Here are your clothes, minus the smoke. The maid washed and dried them for you." He laid them on the bed.

"Let me hop into the shower and wash off the smoke. Then can we get something to eat? I'm starved."

He opened her guest guide on the nightstand and handed it to her. "Here's the room service menu." He laid it on her bed. "Pick out whatever you like, it's on the DOJ."

"That means on you, the taxpayer, Jeff."

"Yeah. Guess it does. Okay. Oatmeal and a slice of toast for you."

"I've paid taxes in the U.S. for three years now, Jeff Jacobs. Order me their big breakfast scramble in a pan. See you in a half hour. Then we can decide what to tell your lawyer friend."

* * *

At 1:55 p.m. Jeff led Allie up the sidewalk toward Larry Wendell's office. There had been so many setbacks over the past three days that Jeff refused to let his hopes get too high until Larry gave him some solid reasons for optimism.

The office door opened before he and Allie reached it. Larry's friendly face met them and his eyes studied them.

"Allie, this is Larry Wendell. Larry, meet Allie

Santiago."

After they exchanged greetings, Larry invited them into his small, tidy office and motioned toward two chairs in front of his desk. "Have a seat. I have a few questions for you, but this shouldn't take too long." Larry's gaze dropped to the stack of papers in front of him.

Jeff folded his hands on the edge of Larry's desk and waited until he looked up from the papers. "It looks like you've done your research."

"Part of it. I called the detention facility in Medford. It has a good record for getting people processed and back out again. They pride themselves in that and want the Santiago's out as soon as possible. But when I talked to your father about it, Allie, I don't think he trusted me, at least not over the phone. He wants to meet face to face and wants you two present."

"My father wants both Jeff and me?"

"Yes."

"See, Jeff. Papa trusts you."

Jeff drew Larry's gaze. "Does he know about ... the attack at my house?"

"No." Jeff slid a stack of papers to the side of his desk. "But everyone in O'Brien does. It's the most exciting thing that's happened here since, well ... probably since gold was discovered over a hundred years ago. But there are some gossips who aren't happy with your being in O'Brien, even though the police say it's safe now."

"I can understand that to a degree. But, Larry, the people in O'Brien have had problems with drug dealing in the area ever since the hippies moved in here in the late '60s. They had some grisly murders back then."

Larry nodded. "But that was all among the drug dealers, not the general population."

"Fine. If that's how people feel, I can move anywhere I choose. It doesn't affect my job. But I need to contact my insurance company about payment for my house and get approval for temporary housing. Maybe a rental closer to Cave Junction than O'Brien."

Allie eyed him suspiciously. "Jeff, what are you thinking?"

"You and your family can live with me as long as you need to, or want to, or ..." He smiled at Allie, trying to convey his desire to help the Santiago's.

Allie's beautiful face smiling back derailed his train of thought.

Larry glanced back and forth between the two of them. "I'm getting a picture here ... if you two are, uh, contemplating anything, it would help if you told me now."

Jeff grinned. "Oh, I'm contemplating a lot of things."

Allie's face turned pink. "Jeff Jacobs, if you don't behave, I'm going to tell Papa about—"

"About what? About how you shamelessly—"

"Please, spare me the details." Larry glanced at Allie, then Jeff. "But should you begin to contemplate anything like marriage, you need to let me know. It could have a bearing on the case."

"Yeah. We'll do that." Jeff paused. "So, what's our next

step?"

"I want to meet with Mr. Santiago as soon as possible, and both of you need to be present. It's the only way he'll open up to me. I need to get enough information to establish everyone's identity."

Larry picked up two papers and scanned them. "I believe you're covered, Allie, because of your student status." He clipped the papers together and slid them to the side of his desk. "I suggest we try to meet with the Santiago's tomorrow, in Medford."

"Call me on my cell when you've set up the meeting, Larry. I'll need to get the marshals on board with a trip to Medford."

Larry folded his hands and propped his elbows on his desk. "That brings us to the next item of business, one we have to move quickly on. A place for everyone to stay. We have to show that the Santiago's have somewhere to stay before they can be released."

Allie drew a sharp breath. "Do you mean they could be released soon?"

"If we get things lined up, and can pay their bond money, they might be released tomorrow."

Allie's eyes lit up and she looked at Jeff.

He needed some help here. A place for himself was one thing, but finding an available rental for five people wouldn't be as easy. "Larry, do you know anyone who has a big house for rent?"

Larry nodded slowly. "Do you know Mrs. Connerly at church?"

"Is she the short, gray-haired lady. A widow?"

"That's her. She recently moved to a retirement community and wants to rent out her house until she decides what to do with it. Last I heard she hadn't found a suitable renter."

"How big is her house?"

"Really big. It's a huge rambler with four or five bedrooms. It's also along Grayback Creek. A really nice property."

"I'll take it. But, before we sign any papers, I'll have to contact my insurance company. Mom has had the place insured with them for the past twenty-five years. It's a good company. They'll take care of me." Jeff paused and peered into Larry's eyes. "About paying you, Larry. I've got some money in—"

"Save it. This is immigration work. *Pro bono*. It's good for my business."

"I can pay. At least let me pay for your expenses."

"Jeff, the bond is going to be at least eight thousand dollars, four thousand each for Mr. and Mrs. Santiago. Allie's little brother won't require a separate bond. You do get the money back if they show up for all required hearings until their case is closed."

"Fine. I'll pay for your expenses, the bonds, and if you can contact someone about Mrs. Connerly's house—"

"No problem. My wife's a real estate agent, and she's managing the property."

"Then let's do this."

"I've got your cell number. I'll call you when I get the appointment set up so you can clear it with the marshals."

* * *

As they left Larry Wendell's office, Allie walked close by Jeff's side, curling her arm around Jeff's. "Are you sure you want to do all this for my family? What if you don't get along with them? What if you and I don't—"

"Allie?" He stopped her on the sidewalk and put his hands on her shoulders. "Are you having any doubts? I mean about us?"

"No. But how well can you really know me after four days, Jeff?"

"It's not the quantity of time. It's the quality."

"But the quality was awful. We were chased, shot at. We barely survived."

"That's my point." Jeff move closer to her. "Shared danger has a way of compressing time. Even if you were a guy, after what we've gone through, we would be bonded for life."

"But I'm not a guy."

"So I've noticed. And that opens up whole new vistas for bonding." He smiled and clasped his hands behind her neck.

Allie's heart raced. Jeff was on the verge of proposing to her. Not the marriage of desperation they had mentioned before, but the one born of a trust so deep, and a bond so strong, she couldn't escape it and had no desire to try.

She looked into Jeff's eyes trying to read them. What was coming next? Probably a kiss and then the words, but Jeff's face wore a frown.

"What's wrong, Jeff?" Her heart raced even faster.

His lips stretched into a thin smile. "I was thinking ... and I suppose worrying a little."

"Worrying?"

"Yeah. I've never done this before."

"It's alright, Jeff. You have nothing to worry about."

"Why don't you tell your father that. Rafael and I need to have a conversation tomorrow. I've got a question for him."

So Jeff was going to follow traditional protocol, get the father's permission first, then the woman's. Papa would like that, but Jeff should have her answer now. She wanted him to have it now.

Allie tilted her face up and looked into Jeff's eyes, their lips only inches apart.

"Allie, you should be ashamed of yourself, tempting me like this."

"Well, I'm not." She relaxed in his arms and waited as Jeff's lips loomed nearer to hers.

What was that noise?

Jeff sighed.

"Jeff?"

"It's either Larry or the marshals. I'd better answer this."

He flipped open his cell. "Hello... Hi, Larry. What's up? ... Nothing at all? ... Yeah. I'll ask Allie ..." He closed his cell and stared into the distance, his eyes clouded with confusion.

"What's happening? You need to tell me, Jeff. "

He sighed heavily. "Larry tried to find some identification for your father. The Mexican authorities said it isn't in the new identity database, the biometrics one. And it isn't in something called the CURP database. Officially, Rafael Santiago doesn't exist."

"But that's not possible." This could turn out badly. Allie's pulse pounded out her growing panic. There was only one explanation, and it brought a new kind of danger.

Chapter 25

Bumps, hurdles, then mountains. Every step of Jeff's journey with Allie had been a struggle. And now something unforeseen had been added to the list of obstacles.

"You need to tell me what it is that's not possible, Allie. I thought we were about to bring closure to the whole cartel mess."

She shook her head and her vision blurred from unshed tears. "Whenever the cartels are involved it is always a mess, a dangerous mess." Allie sighed and wiped her eyes. "Mexico began doing retina scans and taking fingerprints of all babies and children a few years ago in preparation for new biometrics-based ID cards. Papa and Mama were among the first of the older segment of the population to get the new card."

He brushed a stubborn tear from her cheek. "Shouldn't we be having this discussion with Larry?"

"I'm just giving you the nutshell version. Larry will probably have a lot more questions." She paused. "A lot of citizens opposed the new system because whoever controlled the database would have too much knowledge about the citizens. It could be used for evil purposes. The cartel must have bought someone in the federal government, someone who has access to the database. They deleted my family from it."

If they were in transition, surely this database had a predecessor that still existed. "What was used before the biometric system?"

"Mostly CURP, the system you mentioned during the phone call. Evidently, the cartel removed our family from the CURP database, too."

No ID. Illegal in the U.S., and illegal in Mexico for that matter. "It makes sense." He took her hand. "If they were going to use your family as slaves, it would be much safer if your family had no identity... no identity anywhere on the planet."

"I know. I'm guessing they erased my records too. But I established enough identity at OSU, and in the state of Oregon, that maybe I can get mine back."

"Oh, Larry said we leave for Medford at 8:00 a.m. tomorrow. Maybe we can brainstorm with him on the drive over. Medford's a little over an hour from Cave Junction."

She looked up at him, her dark brown eyes pools of sadness. "A few moments ago, I was so happy, Jeff. What is God doing to us?"

"Not God, Allie. More like His antithesis. Satan and the cartel are on the same side."

"For the rest of the afternoon, can we please do something fun, something to keep my mind off this? Let's go through your house and—."

"Fun? Looking at my destroyed house is fun?"

"No. But finding things that can be salvaged would be. Getting something good back when you think that it's lost, wouldn't that be enjoyable?"

"Yeah. I guess it would. You know, God is like that. He takes what's lost, then restores it or replaces it with something better. You'll see, Allie."

"I wish I had your faith."

"You do. Remember up on the mountain? You know, sometimes things happen that seem to cast a slur on God's name. They test our faith."

"Please ask Him to stop the tests and just give me the final exam. I'm so tired, Jeff." Her head leaned onto his shoulder Allie's arms circled his waist.

"His Word tells us that He can take everything that happens and use it for good. We need to wait, watch, and prepare to be amazed."

She looked up into his eyes with a weak smile on her lips, and tear tracks on her cheeks.

He cradled her head in his hands. "I'll do anything I can to help."

Before Jeff could react Allie kissed him, leaving behind the taste of salty tears.

She gasped and pulled her head back. "I'm sorry, Jeff. That wasn't something you do in ..."

"Generally, not in a public place. And definitely not in the middle of town."

She took his hand and squeezed it. "But you made me happy. Let's walk back to the inn and see if Wes will take us to your house."

* * *

Allie woke to soft praise and worship music on the clock radio in her room. Despite the potential impacts on her life that this critical day may bring, she was, for the most part, at peace. Jeff had given her what she most needed yesterday, hope and love. And they had rescued many records from his mom's collection, including *Unchained Melody*.

She quickly showered, dressed, and met Jeff in the living room of the suite where he sat talking to Wes.

Jeff stood when she walked in. "I ordered breakfast for us, Allie. It's on its way."

"Thanks. I'm starved." She glanced at Wes. "Who's driving us to Medford?"

"That would be me," Wes said. "The closer you are to your parents, the more we need to watch you. But there have been no more signs of the cartel since we ran them out of Dodge."

"You'll see signs of cartel activity today, signs of what they did a couple of weeks ago."

Wes nodded. "Jeff told me about the identity problems."

A knock sounded on the door.

Jeff headed for the door. "Let's eat. We've only got about twenty minutes. We can talk about this in the car with Larry."

Jeff's cell rang. He stopped and answered.

"What? You've got to be kidding ... So now what do we do?"

Jeff's clenched jaw and the tension in his voice sent an icy chill through her.

Jeff blew out a blast of air. "Okay. I'll tell them and let you know what they say when you get here." Jeff closed his cell and stared at the floor, avoiding her eyes.

Allie's heart revved. "Jeff, what is it?"

He slowly raised his face and met her gaze.

The fear in his eyes was contagious. It sent her heart into a wild rhythm.

"Allie ... ICE is sending your family to Portland. They just left Medford in a van."

"What? Why would they send my family to Portland?" Allie's world had moved again on the shifting sands of immigration policy. Breakfast might be on its way to their suite, but fear induced nausea had taken away what little remained of her appetite.

"Portland is the only place in Oregon where they have Immigration Court. Larry is on his way over, but he said ..." Jeff turned to Wes, "... we need to file a new flight plan. We're going to Portland, and we need to leave now. Would you please handle that, Wes?"

Wes gave him a palms-up shrug. "Why the hurry?"

Jeff looked at her, then back to Wes. "He's afraid ICE,

or an immigration judge, will send them to the regional detention facility in Tacoma. It's ... " Jeff cleared his throat, "... not a good place."

"Not good at all," Wes muttered. "But I'm on it."

Jeff's words hit her like a punch in the stomach. What more could go wrong? She and her family had helped stop a major marijuana operation, had nearly been killed in the process, and this was their reward? "Jeff, why is this happening?"

"I don't know. But we're going to have at least four hours in the car to discuss that with Larry."

Fifteen minutes later, Allie sat beside Jeff in the rear seat of the big sedan, her arm curled around his. "Mr. Wendell—"

"Just Larry, please."

"Larry, what happens if we can't find any documentation for my family?"

Larry turned in his seat and looked back at her. "If your parents ask for asylum, which I think is a good move on their part, the law says they don't have to produce documentation if it's not reasonable to do so or if it would endanger them. But few judges will grant asylum without some proof of identity. Where might we look for identity information besides the new database and CURP?"

"For me there's probably ample proof of who I am from all the documents on file at Oregon State University. My application for an international scholarship was pretty thorough in that regard." She shook her head. "It's not going to be nearly as easy for my parents."

245

"What other IDs do you carry in Mexico? A driver's license?"

"Yes. That would be worth checking, because each state maintains its own records. You could check with the State of Sonora. The cartel may have bought some employee in the federal government, but that doesn't mean they can remove my father's driver's license from a state-owned database in Sonora. But Mama didn't drive."

"If we can get your father's ID, and get him out on bond, your father's status will apply to your mother and brother. The judge will probably be lenient with your mother and brother. If you'll pardon me for a minute, I'll get my assistant on the driver's license search." Larry pulled out his cell and soon was engrossed in a conversation with his paralegal. "Allie, it's the state of Sonora right?"

"Yes, Sonora." She watched every expression on Larry Wendell's face.

He seemed pleased when he ended the call. "Now, for the next item of business. After we get them out on bond, we need to get a visa for them to stay in the United States?" He paused. "There are several approaches we could take, but what best fits your parents' case and puts them in a favorable position with the police is applying for a U visa with non-immigrant status."

The words, "non-immigrant status," sounded in her mind like a warning bell, more bad news. "Non-immigrant status sounds like it doesn't allow them to stay in the U.S."

"Not indefinitely. But what it does do is substantiate that they were victims of organized crime and that they're willing to testify against the cartel members we've taken into custody. That will allow your family to stay until the trials are over."

"How long might that be?"

"One to two years. But it also gives us time to petition for asylum based on all the evidence that will come out in the trials, including the attempts on their lives. I think it gives them an excellent chance at permanent residence and probably a path to citizenship, if they want it. And it buys us two years of time to make that happen."

"But so far, only Papa was targeted by the cartel."

"But the cartel enslaved all three of them, even you. But even if only your father had been endangered, all of the family except adult children could come with him." He paused. "Allie, I really believe this is the most honest way to go and the one most likely to give them the option of staying in the U.S. I prayed a lot about this last night and—"

"You prayed? Then let's do it." A lawyer that prayed. If she was in better spirits, there would probably be a good lawyer joke in there somewhere. But for now, she was just thankful Jeff had put her in touch with Larry. His ideas and knowledge gave her hope.

Larry bent over a writing pad and scribbled at a furious pace.

Allie rested her head on Jeff's shoulder, thankful they were making progress and that some good people had come to her rescue. She turned her head and scanned Jeff's face. Some very good people.

She gripped Jeff's arm, leaned on his shoulder again,

and prayed until, fatigued by the stress, she dozed off.

Wes glanced at the back seat. "Okay, everybody. This is our exit coming up,"

Allie brushed the cobwebs from her sleepy mind and sat up.

"Let's pray we can talk to an immigration judge before anyone here decides to send your family to Tacoma," Larry said.

This was the United States of America, supposedly the best legal system in the world. Allie stifled some harsh words before they reached her tongue. "Is this process really so out-of-control that nothing is predictable?"

"Unfortunately, yes, it is," Larry said. "There are groups that rate all the immigration judges in the U.S. One thing they rate is the asylum denial rate. The numbers vary from a judge who denies asylum to only 9% of the applicants to one who denies it for 97%. The high and the low number are both from judges in New York. Go figure."

In America? Surely Larry was wrong. "But how can that be?"

Larry shook his head. "Our immigration process is in a state of disarray. Every day people's lives dangle from the whims of a biased judge. Some judges throw out a lifeline, while others cut it. We need an unbiased, fair judge." He watched her reaction. Saw her shock and disbelief. "Don't get me wrong, Allie, the immigration judges aren't all bad, and they *have* been placed in an impossible situation."

"What do you mean?" Jeff leaned forward in the seat, frowning. "Many times they have the power of life and death over the people brought before them."

Larry blew out a blast of air. "For the immigration judges, it's like this. They hand down judicial orders. Let's say the orders are to deport a person, immediately. The guy is a murderer and a thief. Then the judge's orders are given to DHS, who executes them at their own discretion. So now we have non-judicial officials determining whether judicial orders will or will not be enforced. The judges have no further say in the matter. They can issue orders until they're blue in the face, but ..."

"That's crazy." Jeff shook his head. "The whole system is turned upside down. The immigration police pick out which laws they want to enforce on which people and the president, or attorney general, can determine what's enforced by issuing policies for the department."

Larry gave him a tight-lipped smile. "Welcome to the world of immigration law ... as practiced in the good ol' USA."

She started to pray that this crazy system wouldn't turn her life upside down, but realized it was too late for that.

God, don't let it destroy my family, please.

As Wes searched for a parking spot, Allie spotted an ICE van unloading. A dark-complected man stepped out with his back to her. He helped a woman, then a boy. "There's my family." She pointed to the van.

"You caught up with them. Way to go." Jeff slapped

Wes's shoulder.

Larry tapped Wes on his other shoulder. "Let us out here. I don't want to lose them." He twisted in his seat to face her and Jeff. "We'll walk single file. I want all of you to stay behind me, or we'll only cause trouble. We're going to follow them, because I think they're headed for the hearing rooms. But don't approach them until I tell you it's okay. Ready?"

Allie and Jeff nodded.

Shortly after they climbed out of the sedan, Wes pulled into a parking spot and ran to catch them as they headed toward the entrance to the building.

Two ICE employees, engaged in conversation, stood by the van that had brought her parents.

Allie listened as she passed by.

"Bill, you need to fill the tank while we're here. I heard we're headed for Tacoma late this afternoon or early this evening."

The other man nodded and climbed into the driver's seat.

Allie drew a sharp breath. "Larry, did you hear—"

"I heard, Allie. Try not to worry. We've got a solid case to present, a good one. I won't let anybody take them to Tacoma. Not without one heck of a fight."

"From what you told me, we also need a sympathetic judge." If anyone deserved asylum in the U.S., it was her father. He had led the group of businessmen that stood up to the cartel. It was more than many American authorities were willing to do against the powerful cartels.

After they had gone through a metal detector at the security checkpoint, a uniformed man escorted her parents to a room that didn't look like a court room. As they approached it, Allie could see it was a holding room, one with an armed guard at the door.

The door closed and her family disappeared inside.

Smiling, Larry strode up to the guard. "Sir, I'm Larry Wendell, attorney for the Santiago's, the folks who just entered this room."

"Wait a minute." The guard opened the door a crack, "You folks know of an attorney named Larry Wendell?"

She heard Papa's voice. "This is the man who called us, Mama. Yes, he is our attorney. May we see him?"

"If you made it this far, you may enter."

Allie followed Larry.

The guard grabbed her arm. "Not you, Ma'am."

Larry turned to face the guard. "Allie is assisting me today. I need her."

"But she's—"

"Hispanic. I may need a translator."

"Alright, you two may enter." The man turned to Jeff. "But who are you?"

"I'm a friend of the Santiago's."

"You might get to attend the hearing, but I can't let

you into this room while they're waiting for their hearing. It's our policy."

"I'll just wait out here for them."

Allie turned toward him. "I'll keep you posted, Jeff."

He nodded to her. "Good luck, Allie."

She followed Larry until the door closed. When it clicked shut, Allie ran to Papa's arms.

"Allie, how did you get here?" His arms wrapped around her.

Papa's arms were comforting, but for the first time in her life, Allie noticed there was something missing. Something she'd only felt when Jeff held her, the desire to be held that way for the rest of her life. She stepped back from her father.

"The lawyer that Jeff found for us, Larry Wendell, heard that you were being sent to Portland, to Oregon's Immigration Court. Papa, Mama, meet your attorney, Mr. Wendell."

Papa's smile faded. "Did you say Jeff found this lawyer?"

"Yes. He goes to Jeff's church. He is a good man. You can trust him."

"Then he will be the first trustworthy person we have met since they took us to the detention center in Medford." He studied Larry for a moment, then extended his hand. "Mr. Wendell, I am Rafael Santiago. If you are willing to help us, we will be truly grateful. I can pay you ... well, sometime soon I can pay you."

"Glad to meet you Rafael. Mrs. Santiago." He nodded to Mama. "And you must be Benjamin."

Benjamin nodded, his wide eyes filled with distrust.

"Don't worry about paying me," Larry said. "That's been taken care of."

Papa nodded slowly and remained silent.

"What we need to focus on now is first, getting you out of detention," Larry said. "And second, doing it in a way that enables you to stay here permanently, if you so desire."

"Mr. Wendell, if you can accomplish that, we will be eternally grateful."

"Please, call me Larry. Now here is what I propose. Let me tell you the entire plan, then you can let me know if you agree with it or not. There are other alternatives, but I believe this is the best for you and your family."

They all sat and Allie listened as Larry explained his option of getting the family released today on bond, seeking asylum through a U nonimmigrant visa, leading to application for permanent residency in the United States.

Papa nodded slowly. "I do not pretend to understand all the legalities you have presented. But I can follow your logic, Mr.—"

"Larry, please.

"I see the logic, Larry. Mama, I think we should do as he says."

Mama nodded and gave Larry a polite smile.

Good. It was settled. Allie prayed that by the end of the day Larry's plan would free her family from detention. But that outcome depended on several things coming together in the next few minutes. If anything failed, the outcome could be a death sentence for her family.

* * *

Jeff might not be able to go inside the holding room, but he would do whatever he could in the hallway outside. The only person around was the guard. There was only one way to find out if he could provide any helpful information.

Jeff walked up and down the hallway pretending to be antsy, nervous. He didn't have to try very hard. On his fourth pass, he stopped near the guard. "Did you hear about the family in there, the Santiago's?"

"No. I guess not."

"It's quite a story. They took out six of ten Sinaloa Cartel members who were holding them as slaves."

The big guard shook his head and grinned. "You're pulling my leg, right?"

"No. I know because I was there for part of it. Oh, we eventually got a little help. The FBI flew in a SWAT team to mop up. The father, Rafael, risked his life to save his family several times. Risked it to save mine once. And their daughter, Allie, she's a real tiger."

"You mean the little dark-eyed beauty that was with the lawyer?"

Oops. One slip-up. The price of opening his mouth. Allie went in as the lawyer's assistant. She would now come out as the Santiago's daughter, thanks to Jeff. "Yeah. She's in a Pharmacy doctorate program at Oregon State. The lawyer thought she could help both as a translator and a witness." Jeff paused and watched for any negative reactions from the guard. None. Maybe the big guy was on the slow side.

The guard rubbed his chin. "I heard about an FBI chopper that flew south. Someone said it was a drug raid."

"That it was. Three marijuana plantations were terminated. And, at this point, only one of the ten cartel members is still running loose. Say ... do you know which judge the Santiago's will be seeing today?"

"Unfortunately, I do. The only one that's working today, Judge Lynchesky. He's new here, but he's ... I really shouldn't be talking about him. Suffice it to say, life was much more pleasant here before he arrived."

"That bad, huh?"

"Yep." The guard's nod morphed to a shaking head. Then he launched into a character analysis of a very unpleasant human being. "Don't know how some of these people got to be judges."

"The Attorney General appoints them, usually with the president's approval." Jeff snorted. "Political favors, I believe it's called."

The guard responded with a derisive laugh. "Either that or getting your legislation passed from the bench."

Initially, big guy didn't look like the sharpest knife in the drawer, but Jeff's assessment of the man was rapidly changing.

"Sounds like a judge you don't want to have if you have problems producing ID papers."

"Exactly." The man's eyes focused on Jeff's face, studying him. "I don't mind people pumping me for information as long as it's for a good cause." He grinned. "Good luck. And I wish the Santiago's the same, including your girlfriend."

Was he that obvious about Allie? "Thanks."

The door by the guard creaked open and Larry led the Santiago's into the hallway.

It was time to see the judge. But before they did, Jeff needed to warn Larry about Judge Lynchesky.

Chapter 26

Jeff hurried down the hallway and fell in beside Larry. "I found out a little about the immigration judge we'll be seeing."

Larry's head snapped around toward Jeff. "Give me what you've got."

Allie moved to his side. There was no way to prevent her from hearing. It was better that she hear it from him than discover it during the hearing.

"Judge Lynchesky is a first-class jerk, according to the guard. He's not easy to deal with, has a bad temper, and he's vindictive."

Allie clutched his arm, her eyes pinched into a deep frown. "Great. He sounds like a good Sinaloan Cartel member. Isn't there any good news?"

"Looks like we'll have to make our own good news." Larry looked from Allie to Jeff. "Thanks for the warning."

Allie pulled Jeff close to her as they walked. "I'm so nervous I could, you know ..." She pursed her lips.

"Well don't do it here. We've got enough incontinence to deal with."

"Jeff, how could you—

"I mean Judge Lynchesky—emotional incontinence according to the guard. The guy's a time bomb dressed in a black robe."

"He really does sound like he'd fit right in with the Sinaloa Cartel. You're not making me feel any better, Jeff." She looked at him, her large brown eyes, pleading for something positive. "Will you sit beside me during the hearing?"

"Of course. But first I've got to take care of something, then I'll be right in."

"Hurry, Jeff. I need you in there."

They stopped while the guard opened the door.

"See you in a minute, Allie."

Allie's hand brushed his cheek, then she turned and walked into the court room.

Allie hadn't asked what he was going to do. She was probably too preoccupied. That was a good thing, because he hadn't a clue himself. Only a prompting from deep inside that he needed to do something.

Jeff paced the hallway outside the hearing room. Frustration over his inability to help Allie and her family ate at him like a beaker full of hydrochloric acid. And the rumor that they would soon move Allie's family to the Tacoma Detention Center drove him to near insanity.

Who did he know in Portland? Only one name came to

mind, and it was a very long shot. McCheney.

Jeff pulled his cell out of his pocket, opened the contacts list, and searched for the entry he'd added for McCheney.

Please. You've got to help me out here.

Jeff pressed the call icon.

The phone rang twice, then three times. His heart sank when he was transferred to an answering service. He left a message for McCheney, explaining the dire situation and the begging for any help the FBI agent could offer.

Jeff closed his cell. It felt like he was also closing the door on the last bit of hope he had for helping Allie. Maybe the guard had exaggerated the judge's shortcomings.

He sighed, dropped his phone into his pocket, and turned toward the hearing room.

His cell rang. He pulled it out and answered.

"Jeff, McCheney here."

Thank You, Lord.

"Sounds like Allie's folks got on the wrong side of ICE."

"That's putting it mildly."

"Do you know which immigration judge is hearing their case?"

"Yeah. Some fairly new guy here named Lynchesky."

"Lynchesky!" A stream of vulgar variations on idiot blasted from McCheney's mouth. "I can't believe he passed the bar. I can't believe someone actually appointed him to be a judge. That guy's got his head cross threaded."

"One of the people working here said he thought the plan was to send Allie's parents to the Tacoma detention facility. Is there any way we can stop that?"

"Allie's parents are good people. I know that from the dealings I had with them, and from the way they fought the cartel." McCheney's voice softened. "Rafael thought he was bringing his family here legally for a new life, and now this."

"Yeah. This."

"Jeff ... I've had some dealings with Lynchesky, some very unpleasant dealings. The man doesn't like me."

"Oh." So getting McCheney involved might make matters worse.

"Has the hearing started yet?"

"No. But the family's in the court room. It could start any minute."

"I've got a meeting now at a place about five minutes away from Immigration Court. See what you can do to stall things. Push it to the limits if you have to. Anything short of getting yourself arrested. I'll come over as soon as I can and try my hand at stirring the pot."

"Thanks, McCheney. I hope this isn't too much trouble."

"No trouble at all. But maybe I can stir up some of that commodity."

Jeff had no clue what McCheney had in mind. But he

would do his best to stall things until the FBI agent arrived.

He took a deep breath, opened the door, and strode into the hearing room.

Larry Wendell sat beside Rafael Santiago. Allie, her mother, and her brother sat in chairs directly behind them.

"All rise." The deep voice of a guard the size of an NFL offensive lineman resonated through the court room.

Everyone stood.

A tall thin man entered the room.

Jeff studied the man's face as the judge walked to his chair. Everything about his bearing exuded one thing, arrogance.

The judge sat and waited while everyone else took their seats.

Jeff hurried to a seat beside Allie.

"Obviously these four people are the Santiago's ..." Lynchesky's long, bony finger pointed at Larry, "...but who are you?"

"I'm Larry Wendell, attorney for the respondent."

"It is not required that you be here for this hearing, but I can't prevent it. Where's your EOIR 28? It's supposed to be in my files."

"Then why didn't you give advance notice of this hearing?"

"I don't have to—local rules. But if you don't have a completed EOIR 28—"

"It's right here, Your Honor." Larry held up a green form. "We also have an I-918."

"An I-918? Would you like to tell the court why—let me restate that—is the form certified?"

"It will be your honor."

"And I will consider it when it is, counselor."

The guard took the papers and handed them to the judge.

Jeff leaned toward Allie and whispered, "Like the guard said, this guy's a bona fide jerk."

"Shhh. He might hear you, Jeff. We've got enough trouble without making the judge mad."

"Allie, look at him. He looks like he was born mad then weaned on a dill pickle."

"Don't joke about it. It's not funny."

Judge Lynchesky scanned the forms then tossed them on the far corner of the desk as if they were only pieces of trash. He pulled out another form and read it. "Involved with a drug cartel. Sounds like they nearly killed you all. That's the price you pay for entering the country illegally and taking part in illegal activities like growing marijuana."

Larry stood. "But the Santiago's did not enter illegally."

"Then perhaps you would like to show me their IDs and visas."

"They don't have either. The cartel took their IDs, didn't give them their visas, and trafficked them, slave labor."

"So *they* say." The judge snorted. "What about Alejandra Santiago? The report says she's a student at OSU. At least you can show me *her* ID."

"No, Your Honor, we cannot. When the cartel captured her, her ID was left behind in her car."

"If Ms. Santiago's ID isn't provided to me during this hearing, she will be detained until I can hear her case. With the current backlog, that won't be soon. The other three Santiago's—perhaps all four— will be sent to the Tacoma Detention Center this afternoon, in preparation for deportation."

Was that a slip of the tongue, or was Lynchesky including Allie as a candidate for deportation? This was getting out of hand.

Where is McCheney?

Larry jumped to his feet. "Your Honor, that's completely uncalled for in this situation."

"Counsel, you can be held in contempt."

"The feeling is mutual," Jeff whispered to Allie then he stood.

Now the judge's bony finger pointed at him. "Sit down, young man, or you will be escorted from this room."

"But you need to hear these people's story. How they helped to stop drug operations by a Mexican drug cartel in Southern Oregon."

"I have the report from Medford. I've read their story. And I won't consider the I-918 for U Nonimmigrant Status until you file the supplement certifying it. So, I don't need to hear anything at all from you Mr.—"

"Jacobs." Jeff had the floor. Time to stall. "Jeff Jacobs. I worked closely with the FBI SWAT team to help rescue this family from the cartel that was using them for slave labor. The cartel had even worse plans for Allie ... Alejandra Santiago. I am willing to sponsor the Santiago's."

"A nice gesture, but it's irrelevant to the Santiago's status as illegal immigrants ... excuse me, as *undocumented* immigrants. No ID, no VISAs or papers of any kind. All they've got seems to be a potential sponsor who has no idea of the requirements for sponsorship."

"Sir, I can house them and my income can support them, indefinitely."

"Don't call me sir. I am not in the military and neither are—did you say your name was Jeff Jacobs?"

"Yes, your hon—"

The judge shoved his palm at Jeff. "The court will take a fifteen-minute recess."

Thank goodness. Maybe Jeff wouldn't have to do anything extreme to stall for McCheney.

Everyone stood as Judge Lynchesky left the room.

But the way the judge had said Jeff's name ... an uneasy feeling tingled up his spine.

Allie looked at him with a frown and welling eyes.

"What was that all about?" She wiped her eyes. "He's already decided to deport my family, hasn't he?"

Larry twisted in his chair and looked back at Allie. "I don't mean to alarm you, but I think he means to deport all of you. Based on what he said, that's the only conclusion that makes sense ... if any of this makes any sense."

"I'm a student. He can't deport me. The man's crazy. I'm—"

"I know, Allie." Larry said. "This man has no business sitting behind the bench and making judgments that impact people's lives. The Oregon Immigration Court has received bad marks for taking too long to resolve cases. Evidently, he doesn't want to add to his backlog and he doesn't care who he hurts to meet his goals."

Larry turned around and thumbed through his notes.

But nothing Larry found in his notes would change things in the court room. And whatever Judge Lynchesky was cooking up now would likely make matters worse. And the recess seemed to have been called after the judge repeated Jeff's name. That thought sent Jeff's heart thumping to a presto beat.

Please, God, don't let him go there.

Chapter 27

Where is McCheney?

Jeff glanced at the clock on the wall. It had been forty-five minutes since he talked to McCheney and twenty minutes since Lynchesky declared a recess. The FBI agent might be their last hope, provided he had something significant to contribute.

But this judge was a dictator and it appeared he could do whatever he chose with little or no consequences. And, if he had his way, Allie and her family would soon be stepping off a plane in Nogales. Minutes later, they would all be dead and the cartel would have its revenge.

Judge Lynchesky entered the court room and a guard gave the all-rise command. The judge carried some papers in his left hand and a smirk on his face. After he turned to sit, he locked gazes with Jeff for a moment, then glanced down at the papers.

Jeff looked down at Allie's intense eyes and read the desperation there. Her pulse throbbed through her hand and into his fingers wrapped around it.

"Mr. Jacobs ... "

Jeff's head snapped up when the judge called out his name.

"So you want to be the sponsor for the Santiago family?"

"Yes, Your Honor."

The judge shuffled the papers in front of him. "What do you believe are the requirements for becoming an immigrant sponsor?"

Where was this going. It sounded promising, but ... "Your Honor, I would have to provide for the needs of the family while they make the transition to American life. That takes an American citizen who has a sufficient income to provide their necessities."

"Is that all, Mr. Jacobs?" Lynchesky's wide eyes stared at Jeff like he was some kind of freak.

"Why are you asking—"

"Because you left out the most important characteristic of a sponsor. There's more to it than just signing an I-864. As a sponsor, you are introducing immigrants to the American way of life. Sponsors should be good American citizens, model citizens ... unlike Mr. Jeffrey Jacobs, a disgraced citizen, a man forbidden to represent his country." Lynchesky stopped.

Silence filled the court room.

Allie pulled her hand from his and squinted up at him, her brown eyes filled with uncertainty. "What's he talking about, Jeff?"

"I have the feeling he's about to make that pretty

clear."

In an ugly sort of way.

There was nothing Jeff could do to soften the blow for Allie if Lynchesky's revelation ran true to the man's character. But Allie knew Jeff. She would still trust him, wouldn't she?

The judge glanced down at a paper in his hand, then up at Jeff. "You were a gold medal contender, representing America in the Olympics. You even held the world record for the decathlon. But after the drug testing, you were exposed as a liar and a thief. You stole a spot on the American Olympic team that should have gone to another athlete, a clean athlete."

Lynchesky shuffled a page to the top of the papers in his hand. "You came on the Olympic scene out of nowhere, posting the best scores in the world along with some world records for decathlon events. That fact alone should have raised serious questions. Fortunately for the USA, the drug testing did. You are a doper."

The doping accusation and the smirk on the judge's face pulled Jeff out of his seat, ready to drive a fist through the arrogant man's nose. But when Jeff looked at Allie, his anger morphed to shame.

Allie leaned back in her chair, widening the gap between them. She stared up at Jeff, mouth open, but silent.

"Mr. Jeffrey Jacobs ..." The judge paused until Jeff looked his way. "You're a disgraced athlete who wasn't allowed to represent his country and you will not represent the USA to the Santiago's."

Just like all the times before—his college coach, the same coach again in Beijing, a professor from his *alma mater* during in his job search after he'd completed his master's program—there was always someone there to stab him in the back. But not Allie. She wouldn't.

Allie's head tilted downward.

How much of this was she buying?

Lynchesky continued. "Besides, after what they were involved in, the Santiago's need to be deported. So, as I have stated, I'm sending them to the Northwest Detention Center in Tacoma. All four of them. The van should be here in a few minutes."

All four of them? How could any judge be so unjust, so cruel, so wrong? Allie was the most innocent person in the room. She didn't deserve deportation.

He glanced her way again.

Her shoulders slumped. She stared at the floor with tear tracks on her cheeks.

This wasn't the Allie Santiago Jeff knew. Allie was a fighter. Why had she given up, surrendering to this judge's whim?

It had to be Jeff's fault. He had fallen from grace in her eyes and that must have broken her spirit ... and probably her heart.

Lynchesky's knife burned like white hot steel in Jeff's back. Stabbed again and he was about to lose a lot more than a spot on the Olympic team. He looked at Allie crying softly.

This time, I'm going to lose everything.

With the situation in the court room spiraling out of control, somebody needed to put on the brakes. Even if he lost Allie's trust and her love, he couldn't just let them take her away. Jeff looked at her family.

Benjamin's wide brown eyes stared back at him, pleading for help.

It couldn't have been worse even if the judge's accusations were true. Then again ... what was truth? It seemed that it was only what people in power wanted it to be? If they took Allie away now, Lynchesky's words might as well be true.

Had God deserted all of them? God may have reasons to desert Jeff, but not Allie and her family. Wasn't there help anywhere?

Jeff looked at Larry and opened his mouth to speak, but stopped when he noticed the change in Larry's eyes. They blazed with a fire Jeff hadn't seen before.

Please, God. Don't let it go down like this. You've got to give us something.

Larry stood and glared at Judge Lynchesky. "Your Honor, would you mind telling me where you plan to deport this family?"

"Mexico, of course."

"Look in Mexico's new ID database or in CURP. You won't find the Santiago's there. So I repeat my question. Where do you plan to deport Rafael Santiago and his family?"

The judge cleared his throat, but didn't' reply.

Larry continued. "You can't deport them. You know that. Because, at this point, they're stateless. You need to let them out on bond, have them report in until we can establish their identities. It's a very simple solution."

Jeff didn't fully understand Larry's legal point, but maybe the database snafu was a blessing in disguise.

Judge Lynchesky glared back at Larry. "I don't need an uninvited counselor telling me my job. But, if you wish to play that game ... guard, escort them to the holding room until the van arrives."

Larry turned toward Allie's father. "Rafael, he can't deport you. And he knows it. When he finds it, the same evidence that says you're from Mexico will give us the basis for asylum in the U.S."

Rafael returned Larry's gaze with laser-like intensity. "Will Allie and Benjamin be safe in this place called Tacoma?"

"Papa, we're not safe anywhere." Allie's voice grew angry and loud. "We never will be safe. Can't you see that?"

"There will be order in my court, Ms. Santiago. Guard, escort them out, now."

"Mr. Santiago, let's go." The big guard gestured toward the door leading to the hallway.

Jeff hooked Allie's arm as she tried to step by him. "Allie, I need to talk to you."

"It's too late, Jeff. Even if we—it's just too late." She

shook her head and wiped her eyes.

A guard opened the courtroom door. "Your Honor, the van just arrived."

Three more armed guards stood behind the man at the door.

"Very well. Put the Santiago's on it."

Allie turned to follow her father, then stopped and looked up at Jeff. "After what we heard, I don't know what to say. So I'll just say goodbye, Jeff." She turned away from him, not waiting for his reply.

"Allie..." Jeff turned to follow her.

"I'm sorry Mr. Jacobs." The guard shoved a big, meaty hand at him. "It's our policy. I can't let you go and possibly interfere with loading them on the van."

Jeff stopped and, with blurry vision, watched the only woman he'd ever loved leave the courtroom, leave his life. He hadn't said a word. Hadn't told her—no, he didn't have the right to tell her the things in his heart. To her, he was a failed protector and a failure as a man.

He watched, but she didn't even look back.

The door to the court room closed.

Allie was gone.

This time there was no deceptive note. The reality was clear. It was over between them and Allie would likely die in Mexico with her family after experiencing the horrors that threatened beautiful women in detention centers.

The room went silent except for the soft ruffling of

papers on the judge's desk and in Larry's hands.

But Jeff's mind was anything but silent. Crazy thoughts screamed for him to commit crazy actions, any of which would get him arrested or shot.

Larry closed his briefcase, then placed a hand on Jeff's shoulder. "I don't think he can deport them, Jeff. And Lynchesky is just a miserable excuse for a man who's trying to make everyone around him as miserable as he is. Don't worry, I'll get them out ... somehow."

"Get them out? Larry, we can't let them go in. Do you know how many immigrants in detention were sexually abused last year? Two-hundred and sixteen thousand. I read that when we researched the Santiago's situation. A woman like Allie will never be safe in a place like that."

The door of the court room clicked open then slammed shut.

Rapid footsteps echoed through the room.

Jeff's head snapped around toward the sounds.

McCheney.

Chapter 28

As McCheney walked down the center of the room toward the judge's bench, it seemed that someone had lit a fuse certain to end with an explosion. But would it be a firecracker or demolition charges? From the expression on McCheney's face, Jeff couldn't tell.

Jeff grabbed McCheney's arm as he drew near. "He's sending them to Tacoma for deportation."

The big FBI agent's bushy eyebrows rose. "Maybe, maybe not."

What was that supposed to mean?

McCheney walked on and stopped in front of the judge's bench.

"To what do I owe the displeasure of having you in my courtroom, Special Agent McCheney? And please note, you were not given permission to approach the bench."

"You're right about one thing, judge. It is at your displeasure. First, here's my certification of the Santiago's I-918. Check it out, judge. Then you and I need to have a little chat."

"You're out of order McCheney. I'll have you taken—"

"No, you won't. You'll meet with me in that little room behind you or I'm making a phone call right now. You know, about that little matter of ..." McCheney leaned forward and spoke softly to Lynchesky.

The judge winced at McCheney's words. "You need to leave my courtroom, now. Guard."

The guard took a step toward McCheney.

The big FBI agent stared the guard down.

The guard stopped.

McCheney pulled out his cell and started dialing.

"You cannot use a cell phone in my court room." The judge's voice turned to a raspy growl and he pointed a long, bony finger at McCheney.

McCheney paused, staring at the judge, with McCheney's own threatening finger hovering over the touchpad of his cell phone.

Lynchesky waved his hand. "All right. If it will get you off my back and out of my courtroom, you and I will meet in my chambers."

The judge had agreed but the expression on his face was anything by agreeable. Lynchesky had obviously made up his mind about the Santiago's before the hearing in the court room even began.

What could McCheney possibly do to change the cruel decision of such an arrogant, cruel man? Even if McCheney was successful, there was nothing Jeff could do to repair the damage done to his relationship with Allie.

The judge disappeared through the door at the front of the room. Before McCheney walked through it, he stopped and turned toward Jeff. "She's in the holding room, Jacobs."

So Allie hadn't left in the van? Even if she was in the holding room, Lynchesky's assassination of Jeff's character, and the role it played in getting her and her family sentenced to deportation, made it unlikely she would even listen to his side of the story. And trying to tell his side of the story might make matters worse.

No. The reality was matters couldn't get any worse. Allie had said her final goodbye to him and her eyes had confirmed the goodbye was just that ... final.

Was Lynchesky's knife one that Jeff could leave stuck in his back like all the others?

No. Not this time.

Jeff turned to Larry and blasted out a sharp sigh. "I'm going to the holding room."

* * *

A darkness she had never known settled over Allie when the guards pushed her up the steps into the big van. It seemed to obscure everything—hope, faith, even love. And when she landed in Mexico, the darkness would claim her life.

Allie slumped onto a hard, straight-backed seat in the van.

Papa and Mama sat across the center aisle from Allie, engaged in soft conversation.

From beside Allie, Benjamin's gaze kept seeking hers, seeking some kind of assurance.

The only assurance she could give him is that they would be promptly killed upon entering Mexico. With this cruel cartel, death may not be so prompt. Allie refused to dwell on that likelihood.

When she couldn't stand the haunted look of Benjamin's eyes for another second, the van door popped open and a guard stuck his head inside.

"You four are to come with me."

"Sir, if you do not tell me what you are doing with my family, perhaps we will not go." Papa's words came slow and controlled, but the tone of his voice said he was ready to take on the guard.

She couldn't let the situation turn violent. Allie sprang from her seat and grabbed Benjamin's hand. "Come on, Papa. Maybe the judge has reconsidered sending us to Tacoma."

"If he tries to send us to Nogales, I will—"

"Don't say it, Rafael." Mama put a hand on his shoulder. "Larry said he could not do that."

When they left the big, white van, two guards escorted them back into the building. Once inside, the guards turned toward the holding room.

Were they being held for another court appearance? Until she knew, Allie dared not raise her hopes. They would only be dashed again just like they had been with Jeff. People, even God, couldn't be trusted. Not with the important things in life. Once again, she had been let down by those she trusted the most.

Inside the holding room, Allie sought a place to be alone to nurse her wounds and to steel herself for what might be coming. She and Jeff had read about the horrors of large ICE detention facilities. The nearest thing to alone she could find was to take a seat part way across the room from her parents and Benjamin.

The muddle of depressing thoughts swirling through her mind froze when, across the room, the door clicked open and Jeff stepped in.

She stared at him across the room. But the man she saw wasn't the same Jeff. Had the judge's words changed him? What had happened to the confident, strong athlete who took on a drug cartel with his bare hands?

Regardless, his presence sent her defenses on high alert.

Don't trust anyone, Allie. They will always let you down.

As much as her heart wanted to, Allie couldn't squelch the annoying voice in her mind. The voice spoke the truth that she had pushed aside when she tried to believe Jeff's lies. No. It wasn't *his* lies; it had been Allie seducing herself into believing lies about Jeff. She should have known that the Jeff she had fallen for was too good to be true. No one could maintain such a façade forever. And it had finally been proven to be just that ... a false front on a flawed man.

Girl, if you'd never trusted him, you'd be dead.

Allie squelched the second voice in her mind and looked across the room at Jeff.

He stood with slumped shoulders, putting his hands in his pockets then pulling them out again. Now, he put them back in. Jeff was a man at the mercy of his past and of events he could no longer conceal or control.

Don't talk to him, Allie. You said goodbye. Stick to it.

But when their gazes locked, the tug on Allie's heart pulled her across the room to toward Jeff. As she approached him, her stomach grew queasy.

I can't do this.

"Allie, I need—"

"What you need, Jeff, is to get out of my life. I've made enough mistakes already, and I can't let what might be the last thing I do be the biggest mistake I've ever made."

Jeff opened his mouth, but closed it again. His gaze met hers. His eyes held the same look she'd seen in Benjamin's eyes on the van, the look of a little, lost boy.

Had she transformed the incredibly strong man, the leader and conqueror of international criminals, into this? That thought ripped through her heart like a dull knife. Tears blurred her vision.

Allie looked away so Jeff wouldn't see her cry. She left her questions unanswered and her eyes overflowing.

When Jeff turned toward her family, she glanced his way.

He wheeled and strode toward the door where he'd entered.

You're wrong, Allie.

Where had that thought come from. Or, was it a voice? It held her attention because the voice held authority.

As Jeff reached for the door to the room, Allie's voice spoke, though she wasn't sure she had willed it to. "Jeff, wait."

Jeff jerked to a stop and pulled his hand from the door handle. He turned to face her and studied her for a moment.

"Please ... come back. We need to—I need to—" Her voice broke. Allie fought hard for composure.

Slowly, Jeff walked her way. Hesitating with each step as if he might bolt and run away.

She needed to say something. Anything to restart their conversation. But she couldn't address the main issue between them. Not yet.

Hands in his pockets, Jeff closed the distance between them and stopped in front of her.

Maybe he knew why her family was taken off the van. It was a starting point for their discussion. "Do you know what's happening, Jeff? The guards put us on the van, then came and took us off."

Jeff's frown seemed to question her attempt to break the ice. He sighed and pulled his hands from his pockets. "Something changed when McCheney walked into the court room. But, Allie—"

"McCheney? What's he doing here?"

"I ... I called him. He's in Lynchesky's chambers having some sort of conversation with the judge."

"Why did you call McCheney?"

"Because I ... I'm not sure why. No. I called him because I was desperate. But when I called, he said to stall the hearing and he would get here as soon as possible. But, Allie, I need to talk to you. I need to explain—"

"Explain about Jeff Jacobs, Olympic gold medal contender? Why didn't this come up before now?" Questioning Jeff to his face sent her stomach churning, ready to give up its contents.

"Allie, I tried to talk to you at the hospital and again at my house."

She had cut Jeff off when he tried to tell her something about himself before the explosion.

"I need to explain, to tell you the whole truth."

"You mean Judge Lynchesky didn't?" Allie paused and tried to interpret the look in Jeff's eyes. The pain in them put her in a quandary.

Trust him, Allie.

She couldn't, could she?

But you can, if you want to.

Did she want to? That depended on Jeff, a man she'd already said she couldn't trust.

From somewhere deep inside of Allie, words came, words that expressed her deepest concern. "Are you about to break my heart, completely, Jeff Jacobs?"

"I hope not."

Jeff's answer did little to quell her queasy stomach. But maybe she should let him tell his story and hope, or pray, for the best.

Pray? How could she do that when she was this heartsick? And why had God deserted her and her family?

When her mind framed the question, God, Papa, and Jeff swirled together, first blending then separating in a confusing mixture of identities and characteristics.

"Let me tell you the story, Allie. You can ask questions anytime you want. I don't want to hide anything from you."

"Don't want to hide anything? If this was so important, why didn't you tell me before I—"

"Probably because it wasn't a matter of life and death."

"But it was a matter of life and love. We did talk about love."

"Yeah. While we were running for our lives."

"Is it a matter of love, Jeff?" She looked into his eyes, expecting to find reluctance or deceit. Gentleness, concern, and love were the only things in his eyes.

"Love? That's for you to decide, Allie. For you and you alone."

"You're scaring me again." She was in too deep to back out, now. "Just start your story."

He gestured toward a cheap, fake leather couch along a wall across the room from her parents.

They walked to it and sat.

Jeff sighed and looked across the room as if he was staring into space, or through time. "Since I was a kid I had the dream of making the U.S. Olympic team. The problem was, I couldn't find any one thing I was good enough in to be world class, except maybe the javelin throw. But I was pretty good at several track and field events."

Jeff started out portraying himself as a little boy. People often used children in stories to gain sympathy. Was he trying to play on her emotions to get her to—no. Jeff had never done that. She needed to let him talk. "It was a good dream for a boy to have. There are some who have much worse dreams, like Hector Suarez."

"Can we leave Hector out of this. Where was I? ... I tried all the decathlon events and found I was pretty good at all of them. We had this track coach at my high school who was really gifted at developing athletes. He trained me until I went off to college and the university track coach tried to stop him. The college coach didn't like my high school coach's methods. When I heard about that, I quit the university track team and resumed training under my former coach."

"How did your college coach react to that?"

"He was insulted and livid. I think he had a swollen head because he had been selected for a U.S. Olympic coaching position. Regardless, I found out he wasn't such a nice man. But back with my old coach my scores improved. I posted the second highest score in the nation early in my junior year." He paused. "The next year was an Olympic year. During the eight months leading up to the Olympic trials, I went from obscurity to an athlete posting the highest scores in the world."

"I've seen you do things I didn't think were possible. So that doesn't surprise me."

"Well it surprised me. It brought me some unpleasant scrutiny. But it also brought probes from several companies regarding advertising contracts." He wiggled his left hand and winced at the pain. "After being shot in the arm, I probably won't be world class anymore. Well ... a week before the U.S. Olympic trials my sore left elbow developed a raging inflammation. I couldn't throw, jump, vault, I couldn't even drive with my arms when I ran."

Allie could see where the story was headed. "That's awful, Jeff. When dreams are dashed, that hurts more than anything." Except maybe losing faith in someone. "What did you do?"

"There are drugs that athletes are only tested for just before competitions. Stimulants, prescription steroids, and some other drugs, like narcotics. If an athlete has a legitimate medical need to take a substance on the WADA prohibited list of—"

"Whatta list?"

"World Anti-Doping Agency list. With a legitimate need, athletes can apply for an exemption. The application requires a physician's explanation of the athlete's diagnosis and reasons why the medication is required."

"I went to a doctor I trusted, but it turned out that he wasn't up on all the Olympic requirements, at least not some of the fine print. He said the only thing that would give me a chance to compete was to shoot my elbow up with a steroid, one of the gluco-corticoids."

"A steroid? You mean something like prednisone?"

"Yeah. I knew there was a danger that it would show up in the drug tests. This *was* a legitimate use of the drug and, Allie, I just had to have a chance to compete."

She nodded.

"I told the doctor to shoot me up and give me a note telling what he had given me and why. But I didn't know I needed to file a TUE."

"A what?"

"A therapeutic-use exemption. He gave me the shot, and I was ready to go when the Olympic trials started. I finished first for the American team and then we flew off to Beijing. But there was a dispute about the drug test results. The tests were reviewed again and the TUE Committee accused me of using a steroid and said, regardless whether the use was legitimate, I didn't get the shot approved."

But that's just a mistake, Jeff. A bad mistake, but ..."

"It gets worse, Allie. My college coach was also one of our Olympic coaches. The man has held a grudge against me ever since I ditched him for my old coach. He leaked some misinformation to the media and they blew it all out of proportion. They said I'd used performance-enhancing drugs. Some sports writers said that was how I had posted such high scores over the past year. They were wrong, Allie. That was *me* performing at a level no decathlete has ever attained. But I had made a stupid mistake."

Could she believe Jeff? Really trust him? The past three days came storming back, painting a picture of Jeff that fit what she had seen and it fit Jeff's story. God, Papa, and Jeff seemed to settle into the places they belonged in her life. Different places, but each one filled with love. And that erased all of Allie's doubts. "Maybe it was a stupid mistake, Jeff."

Jeff raised his eyebrows. "Allie, you just ... I mean ... something about you changed."

"Finish your story, please. It was an honest mistake. It doesn't mean that you are a dishonest person."

"It didn't' feel that way. I went from being a potential gold medal winner to a disgraced athlete. I was banned from the Olympics for eight years. Some people who knew me disputed the ruling. But the ruling stood, and now I'll probably never compete in the Olympics again."

He shook his head. "Every time I read those press reports, I almost believe them myself. The media loves a good scandal and they can create them even when they don't exist."

His gaze dropped to the floor. "The only good thing was that I didn't have to give up an Olympic gold medal like some have had to do. Only my spot on the U.S. team."

He looked up and into her eyes. "It all happened less than two years ago. If you associate with me, you'll probably have your integrity questioned at some point. Maybe in twenty years it will mostly be forgotten, but the erroneous charges will remain a part of recorded history. My history."

Allie looked into Jeff's intense eyes and saw the man who saved her life more times than she could count. "Jeff, you were treated so badly. What they did wasn't fair."

"Allie, you haven't read the articles in the newspapers and sports periodicals. You've only heard my side."

"I think Lynchesky gave us the other side."

"Before you draw any conclusions about me, you need to read—"

"No, I don't. Without any drugs, you performed incredible things to save my life. When I sat on your couch and heard you casually refer to how you carried me home, I knew you had great athletic abilities. That's how you found me in the camp, wasn't it? You never told me, but you ran down their ATVs, didn't you?"

"That's not quite what happened."

The deep longing to be in this man's arms, to share his life, returned, intense and consuming. "Jeff, to me you *are* a gold medal winner." Allie stepped close to Jeff and pressed her cheek into his chest.

Powerful arms closed around her and pulled her snugly to him.

"Allie … remember, McCheney is still in the judge's chambers and I don't have a clue what their talking about. For you and I to have a chance, we need something good to come out of that conversation."

Allie looked up into Jeff's eyes, still reeling from the pendulum-like swings of her most deeply felt emotions. "Yes, we do. But this has turned out to be a nightmare. I'm not sure that anything can—"

A loud click sounded as the door to the holding room opened.

A guard stuck his head in. "The Santiago's are to return to the court room."

As Allie entered the court room at Jeff's side, voices coming through the wall behind the judge's bench crescendoed, turning to loud shouts. McCheney's voice drowned out the other voice, but the words were not distinguishable.

The voices in the other room stopped.

A few seconds later, McCheney opened the door behind the judge's bench, stepped into the court room, and walked down the aisle to leave. But he winked at Jeff and Allie as he walked by.

Allie tracked McCheney noting that he stopped at the rear of the room, by the entryway door, and turned around.

"All rise."

Judge Lynchesky entered. His face wore a different sort of scowl than she'd seen before. He focused on Larry. "Mr. Wendell, if you have justification for Mr. Santiago being set free on bond, I am prepared to hear it now."

Jeff leaned toward her, "If he's prepared, I'm guessing McCheney prepared him."

Allie drew a sharp breath. If Papa would be set free, then surely the whole family would be, too.

The judge folded his hands on his desk. "And you will report to this court once a month until you have a valid ID, then we'll review your case."

"And Ms. Santiago?" Larry looked questioningly at the judge.

"She needs to keep her visa and ID with her at all

288

times. See that you do, Ms. Santiago."

Allie nodded. Finally, the nightmare had ended.

The courtroom door closed with a metallic click. McCheney had left.

Judge Lynchesky cleared his throat.

Allie looked up at his face, a face wearing an arrogant smirk.

"But, Mr. Jacobs and Mr. Santiago, this is all predicated on a certain condition."

* * *

After Jeff saw the frown deepening on Allie's brow, the meaning of the judge's words sank in. With McCheney gone, no more Mr. Nice Guy. And now the judge's menacing gaze had locked on Jeff.

"Mr. Jacobs, perhaps I was too harsh in my judgment about your disqualification at the Beijing Olympics two years ago. If you were to be reinstated, proving you are worthy of the responsibilities of sponsorship, perhaps I would reconsider your request to sponsor the Santiago's."

Where was the judge's bait luring him? Reinstatement would take time. "Your Honor, if I agree to seek reinstatement, will you allow the Santiago's to stay in with U.S. under my sponsorship?"

"That's not exactly what I said. If you sign as their sponsor, your responsibilities will not allow you time to train for the Olympics. I could not allow you to be their sponsor under those conditions. However, if you were to be reinstated, Mr. Jacobs, it would prove to The Court that you are a worthy sponsor. And I would, at a later date, consider your request to sponsor the Santiago's."

Allie's hand took his.

Jeff looked down into her warm, brown eyes. "Jeff, this can work out for the best. You don't have to give up your dreams."

Allie wasn't getting it. She understood, in part, how deeply he wanted to fulfill his Olympic dream. But she didn't know about ...

Jeffrey, get re-instated. Go back and win gold. Do it for your father.

The empty spot in our trophy case isn't for my medals. It's for you, son. For Olympic gold. You were born for this, not me.

He had made promises to his mother but, given the circumstances, wouldn't she understand?

Dude, you can win gold in two years. But you wait six years or more, not gonna happen.

Judge Lynchesky's sadistic little game was forcing Jeff to make a painful choice. "And what happens to the Santiago's while I wait for a reinstatement ruling, Your Honor?"

The judge folded his hands on his desk and smiled at Jeff. "ICE must hold them in detention, of course."

"For how long, sir?"

"By law, not more than six months, but—"

"But the Santiago's are seeking asylum. How long for

asylum seekers?"

The judge gave Jeff a crooked smile. "Asylum. That's quite another matter. The time period is indefinite, but they could also be deported at any time."

Deported at any time. That was probably the judge's plan all along.

"Mr. Jacobs ..." The judge resorted to his voice of authority. "I've had the van held for the Santiago's, pending your decision."

"Jeff ..." Allie's eyes looked up at him full of concern. "Larry can find us another sponsor."

"Mr. Jacobs ..."

Jeff ignored the judge. "You don't understand, Allie. For you, immigration detention wouldn't be any safer than sending you back to Nogales. And I think this judge means to give you both."

"Guard, have the Santiago's escorted to the van."

Jeff couldn't ignore these words from the judge. He whirled toward the bench. "No! Give me the blasted I-864. I'll sign it."

Larry grabbed his arm. "Settle down, Jeff."

"I could hold you in contempt." Lynchesky's voice boomed out from the front of the court room.

A Freudian slip? The judge already held Jeffrey Jacobs in contempt. "Your Honor, I just want to sponsor the Santiago's. They're good people. The kind America needs. They helped to take down a drug operation along the California border."

"Guard, you know where the forms are. Bring Mr. Jacobs an I-864."

Larry pulled some papers from his briefcase. "May they fill it out online, Your Honor?"

"No, Mr. Wendell. I don't want this case added to my backlog. The form is about twelve pages."

"I know, Your Honor. I have the form." Larry held up the papers.

"Very well, then. You may go to the holding room to fill it out. Give it to the guard, then you are free to go."

The guard gave the all-rise order and the judge left whistling the Olympic fanfare.

Larry and Rafael huddled at the far end of their row of seats.

Allie looked up at Jeff, eyes brimming with unshed tears. "Are you sure about this, Jeff? All you get instead of the medal you deserve is me. No advertising contracts, no—"

"Allie, stop." He placed a hand on her shoulder. "For you, I would give up all eighteen gold medals that U.S. swimmer won."

"You mean nineteen. You earned another one when you ran down those ATVs and saved me." She smiled for the first time in hours.

Her smile drew Jeff closer to her. "I'd give up all the gold in Fort Knox. Allie, I know I've failed in too many ways to count. But you can count on this. If I ever hurt you or break your heart, you can trust me to fix it or die trying."

She laid her head on Jeff's shoulder. "Can we—how do you say it here in the U.S.—close the book on this issue? Please? And can you forgive me for doubting you?"

"Yeah. I can do that and the book's closed."

Allie circled Jeff's neck with her arms and pulled him so close their lips nearly touched.

Jeff cast a sideways glance at Rafael.

He had pulled out of the huddle with Larry and was definitely watching.

Jeff returned Allie's hug, then whispered in her ear. "Before we do that in front of them, I need to have a talk with your father."

"If you're sure, absolutely sure, Jeff Jacobs, then I think you should have that talk right now."

"I will. Right after Larry explains the ramifications of what just transpired. If I understand correctly, with me as your sponsor, we're good to go with only minor restrictions."

"That's about the size of it." Larry's voice. He had been listening to them. "Aren't you glad you signed that employment contract last month? Otherwise, this would have been a much harder sell."

"Yeah. And thanks for reviewing it for me." Jeff looked down into Allie's searching eyes.

"You said you were going to teach some college classes online. Is that your only work?"

"It's my only paying work. I'm an assistant coach at the middle school. A volunteer."

Rafael's watching eyes were still focused on Jeff.

Larry's voice rose. "To sum it all up, Jeff, you've got Mrs. Connerly's house to rent for as long as you need it. I'll provide any advice you need when the cartel trials start. The only unanswered question is who's going to rent a car so we can take you all back to Cave Junction? And we need to check with the marshals about protection. My guess is that it won't be needed much longer."

"There is another issue, Larry."

"Did I overlook something?"

"A couple of things. First, we need to send Special Agent McCheney a really nice gift for sticking his neck out and his nose in. Maybe Mariner's or Seahawks' tickets. I think you all recognize what he did for us. And second ... Larry, would you take this group to the holding room and start on the form. I need to have a private talk with Mr. Santiago."

Allie smiled at Jeff.

Rafael did not.

Chapter 29

Jeff stood waiting until Larry followed Allie, her mother, and Benjamin out of the court room and closed the door. Alone with Rafael now, Jeff's pulse revved. "Mr. Santiago?"

"To you I am Rafael. Also, I am very indebted."

"But I believe this is a Mr. Santiago kind of question."

"I see. Does this concern Allie?"

"Yes, sir. And me." He took a breath, then blew it out to release the tension. "May I have your permission to court Allie, if she is willing?"

Rafael sighed heavily. "Every father who has a daughter knows such a time is coming from the moment she becomes his baby girl. The question you ask fills a father with dread, especially when they have only known the suitor for a short time. But Jeff, you have proven yourself to me. Yes, you have my permission to pursue marriage with my daughter. That is what you mean by courtship, is it not?"

Jeff nodded.

Rafael placed a hand on Jeff's shoulder. "And you have my blessing when she accepts your proposal."

Jeff released the air in his lungs in a single blast, not realizing how long he had been holding it. "Thank you, Rafael." He reached out his hand.

Rafael gave him a firm handshake.

"I have one more thing to ask of you, sir."

Rafael gave him a thin-lipped smile. "Isn't Allie enough? You can't have any more of my family."

He returned Rafael's smile. "Actually, I want all of your family. As your sponsor, I would like you to make your home with me for now, and for as long as you wish, while you are adjusting to life in the United States. I have plenty of room and a place for a large garden, actually for a small farm. Well ... I will have when my house is rebuilt."

"So your house needs to be rebuilt, but you are asking us to live with you? I do not understand."

"Yeah. I guess you wouldn't. You see, the Marshall, Wes, saved Allie's life and mine by sending us to the cellar just before a cartel thug sent an RPG into my house. It took out the—"

"Ai yai yai." Rafael shook his head. "They wanted badly to kill you. Would my family be safe staying with you?"

"Would you be safe if you didn't stay with me? I'm still under protection by U.S. marshals. That U visa that Larry Wendell mentioned is granted to foreigners testifying against those who have committed crimes in the United States. I believe it comes with protection, if that is deemed necessary. What better arrangement for protection than having us all in one place?"

"You do have a point." Rafael rubbed his chin. "But do you have a place to live?"

"My insurance company will pay for temporary housing until my place is rebuilt. The house Larry mentioned, Mrs. Connerly's place, is a nice five-bedroom house along a mountain stream. Plenty of room for all five of us until my place is rebuilt, which may take until next spring"

"You are a generous man, Jeff. But what about the next few days?"

"The rental should be available by tonight. Allie and I scavenged enough beds, blankets, and other necessities from my house that we can all stay in the rental tonight."

"Thank you again for your offer. I will need to talk to Mama before we decide. I'll let you know later today."

"My big old house has been a lonely place since my mother died. I really would like for you to stay with me."

"Don't you have any other relatives?"

"Only aunts, uncles and cousins. My parents couldn't have any more children."

"It is not good to live without family. But let me talk to Mama first."

* * *

Allie hooked Jeff's arm when they exited the building. Two cars rolled to a stop down on the street. Wes sat in the driver's seat of one, Cliff drove the second car.

She pulled Jeff toward Cliff's car. "Come on. Let's ride with Cliff. It will be quieter there."

"Since when did quiet become important?"

"Since things ... quieted down. We haven't had any quality, relaxing time together. Wes talks a lot."

"Allie?"

A tug on her arm pulled her gaze down to her little brother's eyes. "What is it, Bennie?"

"Can I ride with you and Jeff? Papa says it's okay with him."

Benjamin idolized Jeff. She couldn't say no to his pleading eyes. "Sure. You can ride with us. But Jeff and I get the back seat, okay?"

"I know why, Allie. You and—"

"Enough, or I'll change my mind."

His eyes widened until he saw her smile.

"Cliff is a U.S. Marshal. Maybe he can tell me some marshal stories."

"Cliff's a little quiet." Jeff mussed Benjamin's hair. "But if you pester him enough, he'll talk to you. Ask him to tell you about the RPG."

"What's an RPG?" Benjamin's furled brow turned toward Jeff.

"It's a rocket propelled grenade. Designed to take out tanks."

"Holy smoke! That is a story I want to hear."

Allie's eyes scolded Jeff. "You shouldn't have suggested that." Her voice dropped to a whisper. "It might scare Bennie."

"Not as much as it scared you and me."

"It's not funny, Jeff."

"Then I'll tell him about how you and I rolled that boulder and squashed that loud-mouthed—"

She clamped her hand over his mouth.

Bennie glanced toward the back seat. "Can I hear that story, too?"

* * *

Bennie's large brown eyes stared up into Jeff's.

Jeff gasped when he saw eyes that so closely resembled Allie's. This bright-eyed boy would soon be his brother. That's what he needed to be discussing with Allie.

"Can I hear the story about the rock that squashed the bad hombres?"

"Sure, Bennie. Sometime I'll tell you. But right now you'd better take advantage of Cliff. Have him tell you his marshal stories. And while you do, I have another story that I need to tell Allie."

Allie stood silently reading him until she seemed satisfied, then stepped close. She circled him with her arms and gave him a quick hug. "Come on, Jeff, Bennie. Cliff is waiting ... and, Jeff, I'm waiting, too."

Allie held his gaze and waited.

The new look Allie's eyes held seemed open, nothing held back. She was inviting him into her life, intimately, completely, and was waiting for his words to give her that same invitation.

In that moment, he caught a small glimpse of being the recipient of Allie's love, of being the recipient of Allie herself. The words he meant to say were lost in the presence of Allie as she looked up into his eyes.

"Jeff?" She whispered the question.

"You two need to get in the car." Cliff's voice. But cliff would have to wait.

"Alejandra San—"

Her fingers stopped his lips. "Allie ... just Allie." She smiled as she corrected him.

"Your father said I had his blessing to—"

"I knew he would see what I saw in you. Well, part of what I saw." Her lips found his, softly, sweetly, and far too briefly.

Cliff's hand found the horn. "Hurry up, you two. You're making me nervous. Save that for when you're safe inside the car."

"Come on, Jeff." She pulled him toward the big sedan. "We have a lot to talk about on the way home."

Home? Yes. Even without a house, he had a home. Anywhere with Allie was home. And the courtship—a mere formality. They both knew where it would lead. So why not let it take them there now. All that remained was popping a certain question. But Allie had said there was more to talk about.

He followed Allie into the back of the sedan, wondering what else she had on her mind.

Wes's car led the way out of the parking area.

Cliff drove behind Wes out onto city streets and into freedom. Freedom for Allie's family.

"I've got some news for you all." Cliff's gaze met Jeff's via the rear-view mirror. "About ten minutes ago they caught the last cartel member in the Southern Oregon gang. Looks like he was the big kahuna in that area, which means you and the Santiago's are probably safe unless the trials in a few months draw some more cartel attention."

"Cliff, does that mean we might lose you and Wes?" Jeff hoped not.

"Not exactly. Depending on the housing arrangements, you'll probably be graced with either my face or Wes's ugly mug."

"Haven't you got that backwards?"

"No. Wes is ugly and he knows it," Cliff said.

"I asked Rafael if the entire family would stay with me."

"For how long?" Cliff asked.

"Indefinitely."

Allie's head snapped around toward him. "What did Papa say?"

"That he has to talk to your mother first. But they'll come. It makes good sense."

"Makes it easier for us, too. Wes and I alone can watch all of you if you're in one place. That's a good thing because the marshals are getting spread a little thin these days."

Allie nudged him. "Look. Bennie's zonked. He was probably exhausted after all we've been through."

Jeff slipped an arm around her shoulders. "How are you holding up?"

"I'm good for another discussion."

Where was she preparing to take him? "Okay. Shoot."

"Can we eliminate the shooting, please?" She folded her hands around his." The main reason I entered the Pharm D program was to help support my family. The cartel's extortion made it impossible for Papa to do that alone. But now, they just need a little help getting started in the U.S. Papa is a good businessman. He just needs some capital to get started."

"Allie, you're not thinking about dropping out of school and giving up your scholarship are you?"

"Jeff, the best way I can help them is to work for a while, starting very soon. If I take the Pharm Tech exam—I know I can pass it because we've covered everything on it during my first three years of pharmacy school. I can make forty to fifty thousand a year."

"Would you finish the Pharm D program later?"

"No. It might be difficult to get readmitted at OSU.

Besides, I want to home school my kids."

"You'll have kids eventually, depending on—

"Depending on you. Jeff, I'm talking about getting married, now. Beginning our life together as soon as possible. We've seen that you can't take life for granted. It can end in an instant."

"Did you just propose to me?"

"No, you already proposed to me.

That's not how I remember it. You said you were going to marry me and that you knew how to convince me to do it."

"Would you please forget all that and just do it, Jeff?

"Just like your dad. You get right to the point. But shouldn't we court for a while first?"

"Why? Two days, two weeks, two months—regardless, it's going to turn out the same way."

He sucked in a deep breath, then peered into Allie's eyes until he was lost in their depths. "Allie Santiago, will you do me the honor of marrying me?"

"Of course I'll marry you." Her coy smile appeared. "On two conditions."

"Am I going to like these conditions?"

"Wrong question, Jeff. How much do you like me? Are two measly little conditions even worth—"

"Okay. I'll marry you regardless of your conditions. Uh … what are they?"

She loosened her seatbelt and swiveled to face him. "First, you must marry me within a month. I don't want to wait any longer than that."

He circled her neck with his arms. "No objection. We can make that happen."

She smiled warmly. "This is the best part. We must spend the first part of our honeymoon in the Bolan Peak lookout tower."

"Allie ... there's no running water and only an outhouse forty yards down the trail. What if the place is booked for the rest of the summer?"

"Jeff, we were just attacked by a drug cartel up there. People died. It was a war zone. That's been in all the newspapers and on TV. Do you really think anyone is going to rent it this summer?"

"You're probably right. We're the only two who'd still want the place."

"And there are lots of reasons for me to want it. It's spectacularly beautiful and so much happened up there. My life was changed forever. I fell in love. We stayed there once and survived." She lowered her voice to a whisper. "I can guarantee you this time will be much, much nicer."

All of the sweetness, the goodness, and the beauty of Allie she had offered to him. "You know, you are pretty convincing."

Jeff pulled her gently toward him. "*Mi amor,* we need to seal this deal."

"Alright." Allie pressed her lips against his.

"Hey, you two." Cliff's voice.

He ignored it for the moment.

"*Mi amor.*" Allie whispered.

"Cliff, you and Wes are both fired as chaperones. We don't need you anymore."

"You two need three or four chaperones the way you carry on."

"Not anymore." Allie cut in. "We're getting married in two weeks."

Chapter 30

Allie Jacobs studied the lookout above them as Jeff braked his truck to a stop on the small dirt road. "Jeff, something is different. I don't remember—"

"Allie, *everything* is different. You're my bride and I—"

"Don't say it again." She was nervous enough on her wedding night without Jeff's remarks. He enjoyed watching her blush.

"Yeah. Something is different, alright." Jeff studied the tower from the driver's side window.

Allie opened her door and stood on the door frame looking over the top of the cab. "The lookout looks like a rainbow."

"Oh, man," Jeff moaned. "We've been had. I told Wes and Cliff we were spending three nights up here so they could watch the road. Come on. Let's see what kind of damage they've done."

She followed Jeff from the truck to the trail and began the short, steep walk to the pinnacle of Bolan Peak where the lookout tower sat like a crown on the mountain. "They wouldn't ruin our wedding night, would they?"

"Ruin it? No. Just make it a little inconvenient." He stepped in front of her after they rounded a large rock. Jeff glanced toward the tower then back at her. "You didn't happen to bring a hat pin, did you?"

"What are you talking about, Jeff Jacobs?" She stepped past him and gasped. "The whole thing is filled with balloons."

"Like I said. You didn't happen to bring a hat pin, did you?"

A surge of anger brought heat to her cheeks. "I'll kill Wes when I see him."

"Allie..."

She looked up at Jeff.

"You're so beautiful. Even when you're angry."

Her anger evaporated like water on the Sahara. She smiled and shook her head. "So what are you planning to do about this?"

His lips inched closer to hers. "Maybe I should really make you mad so you could look even more—"

She poked his ribs. "Teasing and torment. Is that what I have to look forward to for the next sixty years?"

He took her hand and pulled her toward the lookout. "Sixty years? We can't worry about the next sixty years when we've got sixty minutes of hard work to do or we won't even have tonight to —"

"You're doing it again, Jeff."

"Sorry. Wait here. I've got an idea."

Jeff ran back to the truck then returned with one of their packs in his hand. He opened it, rummaged through it, and pulled out a paring knife. He shoved the handle toward her. "Take it. I'll use my pocket knife." Jeff opened the door to the lookout. Balloons of various sizes and nearly every color of the rainbow flowed out the door.

"Clear to the ceiling." He shook his head, opened his pocket knife, and stabbed several of the bright colored intruders. "When I clear an opening, you take the right and I'll take the left side. Race you around the room."

The staccato popping of balloons sounded similar to the assault rifles the cartel gunmen shot at them on this mountain. Allie buried that thought, stepped into the room, and buried the paring knife to the hilt into a big blue balloon.

The balloon popped and died. The race was on.

Twenty minutes later, she was drenched in sweat from her stabbing spree in the late afternoon heat trapped inside a glass-enclosed room. She stopped jabbing when her blows came uncomfortably close to Jeff.

"Careful, Allie. Let's clean out the center of the room now."

She turned and raised her arm high to kill a large gray balloon in the middle of the room.

Jeff's hand clamped like a vice around her wrist. "Hold it. Let me move some of these balloons." His arm swept away a cluster of bouncing balloons.

She drew a sharp breath. "I almost killed a bed....our

bed?"

"Yeah. Underneath a year's worth of Goodyear's production, Wes and Cliff actually left us something nice. Beats sleeping on that old bed frame."

Allie's cheeks felt warm. Her arms circled Jeff's waist while she avoided his gaze. "Very nice. A queen-size inflatable bed."

Jeff kissed her forehead and bent over the bed. "I'm going to inspect this seemingly nice bed for booby-traps."

"They wouldn't?" she huffed, hands on her hips.

"I wouldn't bet on that." He finished poring over the bed, then sat on it. "Comfy. Care to try it out, Allie?" His deep blue eyes peered into hers.

"How could you suggest... Jeff, I'm all hot and—"

"Really?"

"I meant that I'm sweaty and gross."

He stood and clasped his hands behind her neck. "Sweaty, yes. But you're never gross. Not to me. Let's drive down to the lake, take a dip, and come back to watch the sunset."

She pressed her cheek into his chest. "That sounds nice, very nice."

An hour later, the sun sat on the Western horizon painting the coastal mountains orange, while the peaks around them turned a golden yellow.

Allie spread a folded blanket across a flat rock and sat on it. It made a comfortable seat on top of the world. She pulled Jeff down beside her.

He curled his arms around her. "There it goes, Allie. It's down. Now watch the colors change."

She looked up at the indigo sky above them, sprinkled with bright sparkles of light. The twilight deepened the blue in Jeff's eyes. The sun, now over the horizon, turned the moon into a golden disk hanging over the eastern mountains. "It's so peaceful here tonight. Not like when we first met."

"When we met, you were being chased."

She leaned her head onto his shoulder. "Chased right into your arms. Chased by thugs. But I think God was chasing me all the time."

"There's a song about thousands of years of chasing. It's by a guy named Andrew Peterson. I think you'd like it." He smiled at her. "But, you know, at some point, you turned and started chasing the truth."

"I caught the Truth, and He set me free. My family came here chasing freedom." She looked into his eyes. "When you first saw me, I was running, chasing freedom, too. And look what I found."

He looked down into her eyes. "I caught what I've been chasing, too. You."

She kissed him softly for the first time giving in to all the feelings pent up inside. "It's time to finish watching the sunset fade. The stars feel so close from up here, and the moon is twice his normal size. Let's watch together, and then we can see what happens after the chase."

"After the Chase, that's a Christian acoustic group. I know you'd really like them because—"

She pressed her fingers over Jeff's lips. "Hush, Jeff. We can make our own music." Allie looked up at the stars then let her gaze slide down to the brilliant western horizon. "It's incredible what a person finds when they're truly chasing freedom."

EPILOGUE

Allie steered her big SUV into a parking spot at The Old Mill in Redmond. "And that's how Jeff and I met and married. Then, about a year later, after Mama and Papa had settled in, Jeff and I moved here."

Itzy popped her seatbelt off and leaned against the back of Allie's seat. "And Uncle Jeff was the best decaf wheat in the world, huh, Aunt Allie?"

"He was, Itzy. In fact, after they sent him home, his old coach made him go through all ten decathlon events just like he was in competition. His coach scored Jeff. He would have easily won the gold."

A vaguely familiar sounding melody came from behind her. Allie twisted in her seat and looked back at KC.

Julia pointed toward KC's cell. "A Beethoven sonata for your ring tone? Seriously?"

Now, an unmistakable male voice accompanied the instruments. "Beethoven and Billy Joel," KC said. "It's Brock calling ... it's a long story. But the men have only been on the course for an hour. They can't be done yet."

She pressed the touch screen on her cell. "Hello, sweetheart."

Obviously, she had turned on the speakerphone. What was that about?

"Kace, I've got some news to tell you, but first … you know what just happened to me?"

"Now how would I know that? Suppose you tell me." An impish grin twisted KC's lips and she turned up the volume on the speakerphone.

"We're on number five," Brock said.

"An hour out. On number five. You're right on pace, Brock. But what happened? You didn't you try to drive across that big old canyon, did you?"

"Of course. Kace, I crossed the canyon and the ball dropped right onto the green. But those Juniper trees block your view from the tee. I could have sworn the ball landed right at the pin."

"Did you end up in that nasty sand trap?" KC's voice dripped with melodramatic sympathy.

"No. Well, I don't know. My golf ball disappeared."

"Sweetheart, you weren't swearing were you?"

"Come on, Kace. I don't talk like that. But this was my first chance to par this hole—maybe get a birdie or even an eagle."

KC grinned and winked at Allie. "Brock, I hope you're not accusing me of throwing your ball into the canyon."

"It's that kid." Jeff's voice. "There he goes, Brock."

"Yeah. A scrawny little redheaded kid." Steve's voice, now.

"And he's got my golf ball. Stop him, Jeff."

"Why me, Brock?"

"You're the Olympian. Run that kid down and make him put my ball back on the green. Hold it, Jeff. The kid's coming back with my golf ball. Wait a minute, kid! No, kid! Don't do that! Please!" A blast of static came through KC's cell. "He did it." Brock's voice trailed off in a pitiful whimper.

"Don't tell me he threw it into Crooked River Canyon, sweetheart." KC paused. "Brock ... Brock ... What are you doing? Don't hurt him."

"Mister, it wasn't your ball. It wasn't your ball." The distant, pleading voice of a young boy came through the speakerphone. "See, here's your golf ball ... the Noodle 3 you were playing."

"If that's my ball, suppose you tell me where my drive ended up? I might have eagled that hole, but now it'll never be considered legitimate."

"But, Mr. Daniels, I marked your ball. See the orange marker?"

"A foot from the hole? Kid are you—"

"He's telling the truth, Brock," KC said. "What goes around comes around." KC giggled. "I made Jimmy promise to mark your ball if you hit the green. And you'd better not hurt him. He's the course marshal's grandson."

"You really did set me up. I'm going to kill you, Kace."

"Can't you take a joke, sweetheart?"

Julia broke out in hysterical laughter.

Allie joined her.

Itzy sat wide-eyed with her mouth open.

"Now you know what it feels like to be on the receiving end of your childhood pranks."

"But they were all your idea, KC. Evidently, they still are," Brock growled.

How angry was Brock? Maybe Allie should try to defuse things. "Brock, didn't you tell KC you had some news for her?"

"Yeah." A heavy sigh, accompanied by static, whistled from the speakerphone. "But now I'm not sure KC deserves to watch me pitch in Seattle tomorrow night."

KC sat up in her seat. "They called you up from Tacoma, really?"

"Yep. Langford pulled a groin muscle in the All-Star game last night, so I'm their closer when we start up after the break. If I do well, this could last a while."

"Do well? You've closed ten times for the Rainiers and your ERA is zero ... nada. Only gave up a broken-bat single."

"But this is a different level, Kace. Not Triple-A ball. And you know who's going to be there tomorrow night?"

"All of us, I hope."

"Yeah. I got six tickets. But someone else will be there,

too. Somebody who just got transferred to JBLM."

"Captain Craig? Craig's really going to be there?"

"Yeah. Except it's Major Craig, now. And, get this, he's bringing his redheaded girlfriend with him. Kace, he—"

"Don't say it, Brock. I knew what he was really asking that night in the RV Park. But I was already taken. You just finish your round. We'll shorten up our shopping so we can all get back to Julia's and pack for our trip to Seattle. Who are the Mariners playing?"

"The Rangers. We're right behind them in the standings. One game out of first place."

"Brock, how much are they paying you for this?"

"Minimum wage, Kace. These days that's about $3,000 a game. But if I can just—"

"You will, sweetheart. You were born to do this. We'll be praying for a close game so the Mariners will need a closer. And major league baseball is about to see something it's never seen before."

"What's that, KC?" Julia opened the door and slid out with Itzy right behind her.

Itzy ran around to the passenger side of the SUV.

"A one-hundred-ten mile-per-hour fastball." KC opened the passenger-side front door, still holding her cell.

Allie slid out of the driver's seat. "We're going to see baseball history in my first ever major league game." She looked down the walkway in front of her SUV.

Three twenty-something guys walked their way, eyes

roving all over Allie and Julia.

They were only looking at this point, but Allie couldn't let it go further or this might become a very unpleasant shopping experience. She opened her mouth to address the leader of the three men, but closed it when KC spoke.

"Brock, three guys are walking our way and they seem overly interested in Allie and Julia."

"Evidently, they can't see *you*, Kace."

"I'm on the other side of the car."

The tall leader of the group spoke. "You ladies look like you need some company. How about joining us for the concert at the amphitheater?"

Julia looked at Allie, frowned, and shook her head.

Brock's voice squawked through the speakerphone. "Kace, just walk around and stop beside Allie."

"What is this? Payback for the golf ball prank?"

"Just do it."

The leader of the three men took a step toward Allie. "Well, how about it, ladies?"

KC strode around the SUV, cell phone by her ear, and planted herself between the man and Allie.

As KC's red curls blazed in the sun, one of the two men in back whistled.

The other man grabbed the whistler's shoulder. "Do you know who she is?" He nodded toward KC.

"Oh, man. It's KC Banning."

"You mean KC Daniels. And I'll bet it's Brock Daniels she has on that cell phone. These three women and their men wiped two detachments of special forces, maybe more."

The leader took a step backward. "Sorry to have bothered you ladies. Have a nice day." They strode away pointing accusing fingers at one another.

Allie laughed. "You know something, we're probably the best-protected women in the U.S. Steve can kill you in at least four dozen different ways. Brock can stone a person to death with one rock, and Jeff can run a person down, jump on them or spear the bad guys with a javelin."

Julia giggled. "Then there's KC's reputation."

Allie rubbed her stomach which had gone queasy again. "I could puke on them."

"Ebola puke," Itzy said. "It's real dangerous."

"You got that right." KC mussed Itzy's hair and looked at Julia. "And you've got two notches on your gun."

Allie scanned the faces of her two friends, friends who had grown as close as sisters. "After all we've been through together, and considering the men God brought into our lives, whether we're being chased by a rogue president or we're chasing freedom, I'd say we are safe against all enemies."

AUTHOR'S NOTES

While reading *Chasing Freedom*, you may have noticed differences (from books 1 and 2) in my writing and the story structure. If so, it's probably because *Chasing Freedom* was my NaNoWriMo (National Novel Writing Month) story written four years ago—55,000 words penned in less than four weeks.

I've learned a lot about the craft of fiction since that time, but could only bend the story a certain amount without breaking it. Of my seven novels published so far, *Chasing Freedom* is my wife, Babe's, favorite. However, I still see a slightly flawed story when I read it. But such stories can still be enjoyable and I hope you found it so.

I love writing, but sometimes I'm a bit lazy and often impatient. So, when I started writing *Voice in the Wilderness* and needed to caste a couple in a supporting role, I chose a couple I knew well, Jeff and Allie Jacobs. I hope you have enjoyed reading about their whirlwind romance incited by a Mexican drug cartel.

For book 2, *Voice of Freedom*, I borrowed part of the setting of *Chasing Freedom*—told you I was lazy. Jeff's house, Bolan Peak, the lookout tower, and the surrounding mountains, known as the Siskiyous, were all pilfered. There's a reason for that.

The Siskiyou Mountains in Southern Oregon and Northern California were a wonderland for boys who loved adventure, fishing, swimming and hiking in the '50s and '60s. Some of the stories of me growing up there made it into my childhood adventure stories, *Colby and Me: Growing Up in the '50s*. It's still available on Amazon, if you're interested. I love this area and wanted to set an adventure story where I had experienced so many wonderful adventures.

The Bolan Peak lookout is still rented during the summer. So, if you would like a half-star resort for your honeymoon, as Allie requested, just Google "rent Bolan Mountain Lookout" and you should get all the information you need. If you'd like to see the place first, someone posted a very nice slideshow on YouTube. The Google query I mentioned should return a link to the slideshow.

Chasing Freedom looks at the U.S. immigration system from the point of view of a family being abused by it. Our immigration system is fraught with problems. Corruption is widespread within Customs and Border Protection (CBP). That should not be surprising because CBP has absolutely no investigative oversight other than a hundred different congressional committees. Of course, such diluted oversight is ineffective.

But I want to be clear here—not many immigration judges are villains as depicted in my story. Every day these judges make what is tantamount to life and death decisions for people, and they do so having very little information to make such determinations. And a judge's backlog of cases is usually horrendous due to our porous borders and an administration that prefers to do nothing to alleviate the situation. Furthermore, a judge's orders are carried out at the whims of enforcement agencies which are, in turn, impacted by the policies of the current administration. This is equivalent to someone being tried and found guilty of murder, but then having the police decide when, or if, the criminal will ever be put in prison. It's insanity, pure and *simple*, as Jeff and the lawyer, Larry Wendell, point out in the story.

Now, if you're still reading my author's notes, here's a

gift for not bailing on me. On the next page, you'll see the final scene from the *Against All Enemies* series. Originally, I used this scene to end the epilogue for *Chasing Freedom*, but Babe said to take it out. I did, but I put it here as an added bonus that you can read, if you wish.

The scene chronologically follows immediately after the epilogue to *Chasing Freedom*, continuing the story for a bit longer. It's shown through Allie's eyes, but it focuses on Brock Daniels' dream and, to a lesser extent, Jeff's dreams of Olympic Gold.

Hope you enjoy it!

Final Ending to the Against All Enemies Series

Allie Jacobs sat between her husband, Jeff, and KC Daniels in the coveted seats directly behind home plate at Safeco Field. Steve, Julia, and Itzy sat behind them and Major Craig sat in front of Allie with a beautiful redhead named Kate at his side.

KC had gotten what she'd asked for, a close game. The score stood 3 to 2, Mariners leading the Rangers in the top of the ninth, and the manager had signaled for Brock to come in from the bullpen to close.

Everyone stood and cheered as Brock trotted across the green turf to make his major-league debut.

Allie leaned toward Jeff. "See, Jeff. It might have seemed like it while Hannan was chasing us, but Brock's dream wasn't out of reach. So when are you going to call your old coach? The Olympic Trials are less than two years away."

Jeff heaved a sigh and kissed her forehead. "If you'll stop bugging me about it, I'll call him next week. Now, can we just enjoy the ninth inning?"

Allie grinned. "You mean enjoy this foreshadowing of your—"

Jeff stopped her words with a finger over her lips.

Allie turned her head, pulling her lips from Jeff's annoying finger, and studied KC's face.

KC's gaze was locked on Brock as he stepped up to the rubber and threw his first warm-up pitch. The radar gun reading, displayed on the big screen, read 93 miles-per-hour.

Brock slowly cranked up the speed with each pitch. His last warm-up throw was a fastball clocked at 105 miles-per-hour. It looked effortless.

The crowd roared its approval.

The extraordinary abilities of this rookie closer from Tacoma had preceded Brock, and Safeco Field was abuzz with chatter and electric with excitement by the time the catcher caught Brock's last warmup and threw a frozen rope to second base.

The top of the Ranger's lineup was coming to bat in the ninth. A best-case scenario for the team from Texas.

Their lead-off hitter strode from the on-deck circle to the plate and the stadium went silent as every fan in the place waited for Brock to throw a blazing fastball.

Allie drew a breath when Brock stepped high. He whipped his arm toward the plate.

The ball flew inside, at the batter's hands. He jerked them back to protect his fingers.

The baseball leap sideways, catching the inside corner of the plate.

The umpire captured the drama with an enthusiastic, "Strike one!"

When the big screen registered the pitch at ninety-eight miles-per-hour, the noise in the stadium grew until Allie started to plug her ears. Then, as quickly as it started, Safeco Field grew quiet.

Steve tapped Jeff's shoulder. "That was the fastest slider in baseball history. The batter thought it was gonna break his hands, so he bailed on it."

"You got that right, bro," Jeff said. "Who would have thought a ball thrown that hard could jump like that?"

Allie swiveled in her seat and looked at Julia.

Her open mouth and raised eyebrows displayed a horrified expression, then a smile grew on her lips. "Brock scared the living bejeebers out of that guy. He's too intimidated to hit the ball, now."

Steve curled an arm around her shoulders. "For somebody who doesn't know much about baseball, you're catching on fast."

Two 100 mile-per-hour fastballs above the knees on the outside corner and the leadoff hitter went down looking.

The second man up looked at a 105 mile-per-hour fastball, then leaned away from a slider called a strike. He chased a 106 mile-per-hour fastball up around the letters. After the embarrassing strikeout, he pounded his bat on the ground and headed for the dugout.

The Safe was rocking after watching the big man on the mound overpower two excellent hitters.

The Rangers number three man was no slouch, but their cleanup man was the consensus best batter in all of baseball. What a matchup that would have been.

Allie leaned toward KC. "Too bad we won't get to see Brock pitch to Martinez."

KC took Allie's hand. KC was trembling.

"Are you nervous, KC?"

"Almost as much as when ... well, we don't want to get into that right now. And we don't want the tying run on base, either." KC cupped her hands around her mouth. "Strike him out, Brock!"

Brock leaned forward, ready to deliver his first pitch. He started his motion then stepped in back of the pitching rubber with his left foot.

"That's a balk!" the umpire yelled. He pointed at Brock and waved the batter down the baseline toward first.

Was Brock smiling? Yes, but it looked like he was trying to hide the smile with his glove.

The crowd booed as the runner trotted down to first base. Then the booing quickly faded to near silence.

Allie looked up at her husband's frozen face. "Jeff, what just happened?"

Steve slapped Jeff on the back. "Brock wants to pitch to the cleanup man and he didn't want to throw four balls to make it happen. That balk was intentional."

It may have been intentional, but it brought the manager out to talk to Brock.

As the crowd caught on, the noise in the stadium grew from a drone to a roar.

After Brock and the manager finished their chat, Martinez stepped into the box.

The stadium erupted with noise.

Allie had heard how loud the Clink could get during a Seahawks game. But the Clink couldn't have been any louder than Safeco Field was right now.

Allie plugged her ears and waited eagerly for the showdown—a new, potentially phenomenal closer against the consensus best batter in all of baseball.

Safeco Field went dead silent when Brock planted the ball on his right hip. He massaged it with his fingers as he shook his head several times at the catcher.

From the stretch, Brock pulled his throwing hand to his mitt, extended his arm, and let the ball fly.

The audience appeared to be mesmerized, and the stadium remained silent.

Something was different about this pitch. Allie heard the ball sizzling as it raced toward the plate. But Brock had thrown the ball behind the batter. What was he doing?

Allie cringed as the ball raced toward Martinez's body.

The batter leaned in toward the plate to let the ball pass behind him.

The ball jumped hard left in front of the plate.

Martinez dropped to his knees to avoid being hit.

Brock's pitch narrowly missed the squatting man's head as it clipped the inside corner of the plate.

"Steerike!" The umpire's call drew an explosion of noise from the stands.

Martinez threw his bat down and charged the mound.

Brock turned his back on home plate and calmly adjusted his cap.

The umpire yelled a warning and Martinez stopped. He turned, slowly made his way back to the box, and picked up his bat.

Safeco Field grew quiet again.

Brock seemed in no hurry to deliver the next pitch. Was he letting the drama build or ... was it that strange sound that made him pause?

The sound was a chant that had started in the stands on the third-base side.

More voices joined the chant. As it grew in volume, the words became distinguishable. "*We will, we will, Brock you!*"

The chant spread through the stands at the speed of sound. When the fans' feet stomped, after *Brock you,* the stadium trembled.

"Feels just like the Nisqually quake," a fan near Allie said.

Steve and Jeff joined the chant, hand clapping, foot stomping included. They looked like a couple of idiots.

Allie plugged her ears.

Brock threw his second pitch, a fastball, low on the outside corner.

"Steerike!"

Martinez's face contorted into an ugly caricature of the man. He gritted his teeth, pawed at the dirt with his spikes, and readied his bat.

It didn't seem possible, but the chant grew louder. "*We*

will, we will, Brock you!"

Brock's windup was exaggerated. His kick high. His arm whipped faster than Allie's eyes could follow.

The man on first took off toward second.

Martinez chased the pitch up around his letters, but was far behind it.

The radar gun blinked the speed in red on the scoreboard ... 110 miles-per-hour. The fastest pitch ever recorded in baseball by over four miles-per-hour.

The end of the game brought pandemonium to the Safe.

Brock's first save was historic. Allie suspected it was the first of many.

The team mobbed Brock.

KC hugged Allie, squeezing so hard that KC might have gotten an unpleasant surprise. But Allie's nausea had faded over the past hour. She was ravenous.

For the second time, Brock Daniels' name was written into the book of American history. He saved his country and broke a long-standing record in saving a baseball game. And, at 24 years of age, how many more times might his name be written in the history books?

Only God could answer that question. And Allie would leave that question with Him, because what she really wanted to celebrate Brock's save was a peanut butter sandwich with a thick layer of sliced dill pickles on it.

And, right now, I could eat the whole thing.

Made in the USA
San Bernardino, CA
28 January 2020